Waltzing the Cat

Pam Houston

A *Virago* Book

Published by Virago Press 1999

First published by W.W. Norton and Company, Inc.,
New York 1998

Copyright © Pam Houston 1998

The moral right of the author has been asserted

A CIP catalogue record for this book is
available from the British Library

ISBN 1 86049 638 5

Printed and bound in Great Britain by
Clays Ltd, St Ives plc

Virago Press
A Division of
Little, Brown and Company (UK)
Brettenham House
Lancaster Place
London WC2E 7EN

This book is for
David Hicks

and

Dr. Andrew Loizeaux

Contents

Acknowledgments

The following stories have appeared in these journals:

"Then You Get Up and Have Breakfast," *Elle* and *Fish Stories*.
"Waltzing the Cat," *The Mississippi Review, Redbook,* and *These Are the Stories We Tell* (an anthology).
"Three Lessons in Amazonian Biology," *Ploughshares.*

This book owes a tremendous debt to the people who believed in it when no one else did, especially Shelton Adams, Roy Parvin, Terry Tempest Williams, Judith Freeman, Marie Howe, Louis Owens, and Fenton Johnson. I would also like to thank Carol Houck Smith for her vigorous editing, Liz Darhansoff for her honesty, Tal Gregory for his work on my behalf, Charlotte Gullick for her ear and her ideas, and Leo Geter, whose creative spirit is a constant source of inspiration. Most of all I would like to thank my workshop students, all across the country, because it is their talent and enthusiasm—more than anything else— that sends me back to my computer again and again.

July 23, 1869: On starting, we come at once to difficult rapids and falls, that in many places are more abrupt than in any of the canyons through which we have passed, and we decide to name this Cataract Canyon.

—From the diary of John Wesley Powell, *The Exploration of the Colorado River and Its Canyons*

Waltzing the Cat

The Best Girlfriend You Never Had

A PERFECT DAY IN THE CITY always starts like this: my friend Leo picks me up and we go to a breakfast place called Rick and Ann's where they make red flannel hash out of beets and bacon, and then we cross the Bay Bridge to the gardens of the Palace of the Fine Arts to sit in the wet grass and read poems out loud and talk about love.

The fountains are thick with black swans imported from Siberia, and if it is a fine day and a weekend there will be wedding parties, almost entirely Asian. The grooms wear smart gray pinstripe suits and the women are in beaded gowns so beautiful they make your teeth hurt just to look at them.

The Roman towers of the Palace facade rise above us, more yellow than orange in the strengthening midday light. Leo

15

has told me how the towers were built for the 1939 San Francisco World's Fair out of plaster and papier-mâché, and even though times were hard the city raised the money to keep them, to cast them in concrete so they would never go away.

Leo is an architect, and his relationship to all the most beautiful buildings in this city is astonishing given his age, only five years older than me. I make my living as a photographer; since art school I've been doing magazine work and living from grant to grant.

The house Leo built for himself is like a fairy tale, all towers and angles, and the last wild peacock in Berkeley lives on his street. I live in the Oakland Hills in a tiny house on a street so windy you can't drive more than ten miles per hour. I rented it because the ad said this: "Small house in the trees with a garden and a fireplace. Dogs welcome, of course." I am dogless for the moment but it's not my natural condition. You never know when I might get overwhelmed by a desire to go to the pound.

It's a warm blue Saturday in November, and there are five Asian weddings underway at the Palace of the Fine Arts. The wedding parties' outfits do not match but are complementary, as if they have been ordered especially, one for each arch of the golden facade.

Leo reads me a poem about a salt marsh at dawn while I set up my old Leica. I always get the best stuff when nobody's paying me to shoot. Like the time I caught a bride waltzing with one of the caterers behind the hedgerow, his chef's cap bent to touch the top of her veil.

16

Then I read Leo a poem about longing in Syracuse. This is how we have always spoken to each other, Leo and I, and it would be the most romantic thing this century except that Leo is in love with Guinevere.

Guinevere is a Buddhist weaver who lives in a clapboard house on Belvedere Island. She makes cloth on a loom she brought back from Tibet. Although her tapestries and wall hangings have made her a small fortune, she refuses to use the air conditioner in her Audi, even when she's driving across the Sacramento Valley. Air conditioning, she says, is just one of the things she does not allow herself.

That Guinevere seems not to know Leo is alive causes him no particular disappointment, and that she forgets—each time she meets him—that she has met him several times before only adds to what he calls her charming basket of imperfections. The only Buddha I could love, he says, is one who is capable of forgetfulness and sin.

Guinevere is in love with a man in New York City who told her in a letter that the only thing better than three thousand miles between him and the object of his desire would be if she had a terminal illness.

"I could really get behind a relationship with a woman who had only six months to live," was what he wrote. She showed me the words as if to make sure they existed, though something in her tone made me think she was proud.

The only person I know of who's in love with Leo (besides me, a little) is a gay man named Raphael who falls in love with one straight man after another and then buys each one a whole new collection of CDs. They come, Leo says, as if from the

Columbia House Record Club, once a month like clockwork, in a plain cardboard wrapper, no return address and no name. They are by terrific musicians most people have never heard of, like The Nields and Boris Grebeshnikov; there are Andean folk songs and hip-hop and beat.

Across the swan-bearing lake a wedding has just reached its completion. The groom is managing to look utterly solemn and completely delirious with joy at the same time. Leo and I watch the kiss, and I snap the shutter just as the kiss ends and the wedding party bursts into applause.

"Sucker," Leo says.

"Oh, right," I say. "Like you wouldn't trade your life for his right this minute."

"I don't know anything about his life," Leo says.

"You know he remembered to do all the things you forgot."

"I think I prefer it," Leo says, "when you reserve that particular lecture for yourself." He points back across the lake where the bride has just leaped into her maid of honor's arms, and I snap the shutter again. "Or for one of your commitment-phobic boyfriends," Leo adds.

"I guess the truth is, I can't blame them," I say. "I mean if I saw me coming down the street with all my stuff hanging out I'm not so sure I'd pick myself up and go trailing after."

"Of course you would," Leo says. "And it's because you would, and because the chance of that happening is so slim, and because you hold out hope anyway that it might . . . that's what makes you a great photographer."

"Greatness is nice," I tell him. "I want contact. I want someone's warm breath on my face." I say it as if it's a dare, which we both know it isn't. The flower girl across the lake is throwing handfuls of rose petals straight up in the air.

I came to this city near the ocean over a year ago because I had recently spent a long time under the dark naked water of the Colorado River and I took it as a sign that the river wanted me away. I had taken so many pictures by then of the chaos of heaved-up rock and petrified sand and endless sky that I'd lost my balance and fallen into them. I couldn't keep separate anymore what was the land and what was me.

There was a man there named Josh who didn't want nearly enough from me, and a woman called Thea who wanted way too much, and I was sandwiched between them, one of those weaker rock layers like limestone that disappears under pressure or turns into something shapeless like oil.

I thought there might be an order to the city: straight lines, shiny surfaces and right angles that would give myself back to me, take my work somewhere different, maybe to a safer place. Solitude was a straight line too, and I believed it was what I wanted, so I packed whatever I could get into my pickup, left behind everything I couldn't carry including two pairs of skis, a whole darkroom full of photo equipment, and the mountains I'd sworn again and again I couldn't live without.

I pointed myself west down the endless two lanes of Highway 50—*The Loneliest Road in America* say the signs that rise out of the desert on either side of it—all the way across Utah and Nevada to this white shining city on the Bay.

I got drunk on the city at first the way some people do on vodka, the way it lays itself out as if in a nest of madronas and eucalyptus, the way it sparkles brighter even than the sparkling water that surrounds it, the way the Golden Gate reaches out of it, like fingers, toward the wild wide ocean that lies beyond.

I loved the smell of fresh blueberry muffins at the Oakland Grill down on Third and Franklin, the train whistle sounding right outside the front door, and tattooed men of all colors unloading crates of cauliflower, broccoli, and peas.

Those first weeks I'd walk the streets for hours, shooting more film in a day than I could afford in a week, all those lives in such dangerous and unnatural proximity, all those stories my camera could tell.

I'd walk even the nastiest part, the blood pumping through my veins as hard as when I first saw the Rocky Mountains so many years ago. One night in the Mission I rounded a corner and met a guy in a wheelchair head on who aimed himself at me and covered me with urine. Baptized, I said to my horrified friends the next day, anointed with the nectar of the city gods.

I met a man right off the bat named Gordon, and we'd drive down to the Oakland docks in the evening and look out at the twenty-story hydraulic boatlifts which I said looked like a battalion of Doberman pinchers protecting the harbor from anyone who might invade. Gordon's real name was Salvador and he came from poor people, strawberry pickers in the Central Valley, two of his brothers stillborn from malathion poisoning. He was handsome even as a boy, with jet black hair, dark skin, and his mother's gene for blue eyes. He left the valley and moved to the city when he was too young by law to drive the truck he stole from his father's field boss.

He left it double-parked in front of the Castro Theatre, talked a family in the Mission into trading work for floor space, changed his name to Gordon, changed his age from fifteen to twenty, and applied for a grant to study South American literature at San Francisco State.

He had his Ph.D. before he turned twenty, a tenure-track teaching job at Berkeley by twenty-one. When he won his first teaching award his mother was in the audience; when their blue eyes met she nodded her approval, but when he looked for her afterwards, she was nowhere to be found.

"Can you believe it?" he said when he told the story, his voice such a mixture of pride and disappointment that I didn't know which was more unbelievable, that she had come or that she had gone.

"If one more woman I used to date turns into a lesbian," Leo says, "I'm moving to Minneapolis."

The wedding receptions are well under way and laughter bubbles toward us across the lagoon.

"It's possible to take that as a compliment," I say, "if you want to bend your mind that way."

"I don't," he says.

"Maybe it's just a choice a woman makes," I say, "when she feels she has exhausted all her other options."

"Oh, yeah, like you start out being a person," Leo says, "and then you decide to become a car."

"Sometimes I think it's either that or Alaska," I say. "The odds there, better than ten to one."

I remember a bumper sticker I saw once in Haines, Alaska,

near the place where the ferries depart for the lower forty-eight: *Baby*, it said, *when you leave here you'll be ugly again.*

"In Alaska," I say, "I've actually had men fall at my feet."

"I bet a few men have fallen at your feet down here," he says, and I try to look him in the eye to see how he means it, but he keeps them fixed on the poetry book.

He says, "Aren't I the best girlfriend you never had?"

The last woman Leo called the love of his life only let him see her twice a week for three years. She was a cardiologist who lived in the Marina who said she spent all day with broken hearts and she had no intention of filling her time off with her own. At the start of the fourth year, Leo asked her to raise the number of dates to three times a week, and she immediately broke things off.

Leo went up on the Bridge after that. This was before they put the phones in, the ones that go straight to the counselors. It was a sunny day and the tide was going out, making whitecaps as far as he could see into the Pacific. After a while he came down, not because he felt better but because of the way the numbers fell out. There had been 250 so far that year. Had the number been 4 or 199 or even 274 he says he might have done it, but he wasn't willing to go down officially with a number as meaningless as 251.

A woman sitting on the grass near us starts telling Leo how much he looks like her business partner, but there's an edge to her voice I can't identify, an insistence that means she's in love with the guy, or she's crazy, or she's just murdered him this morning and she has come to the Palace of the Fine Arts to await her impending arrest.

"The great thing about Californians," Leo says when the woman has finally gotten up to leave, "is that they think it's perfectly okay to exhibit all their neuroses in public as long as they apologize for them first."

Leo grew up like I did on the East Coast, eating Birds Eye frozen vegetables and Swanson's deep-dish meat pies on TV trays next to our parents and their third martinis, watching *What's My Line* and *To Tell the Truth* on television and talking about anything on earth except what was wrong.

"Is there anyone you could fall in love with besides Guinevere?" I ask Leo, after he's read a poem about tarantulas and digger wasps.

"There's a pretty woman at work," he says. "She calls herself The Diva."

"Leo," I say, "write this down. I think it's a good policy to avoid any woman who uses an article in her name."

There are policemen at the Palace grounds today handing out information about how we can protect ourselves from an epidemic of car-jackings that has been taking place in the city for the last five months. The crime begins, the flyer tells us, with the criminal bumping the victim's car from behind. When the victim gets out of the car to exchange information, the criminal hits her—and it's generally a woman—over the head with a heavy object, leaves her on the sidewalk, steals her car, and drives away.

The flyer says we are supposed to keep our windows rolled up when the other driver approaches, keep the doors locked, and say through the glass, *"I'm afraid. I'm not getting out. Please follow me to the nearest convenience store."* It says under no circumstances should we ever let the criminal drive us to crime scene number two.

"You couldn't do it, could you," Leo says, and slaps my arm like a wise guy.

"What do you think they mean," I say, "by crime scene number two?"

"You're evading the question because you know the answer too well," he says. "You're the only person I know who'd get your throat slit sooner than admit you're afraid."

"You know," I say to Leo, to change the subject, "you don't act much like a person who wants kids more than anything."

"Yeah, and you don't act like a person who wants to be married with swans."

"I'd do it," I say. "Right now. Step into that wedding dress, no questions asked."

"Lucy," Leo says, "seriously, do you have any idea how many steps there are between you and that wedding dress?"

"No," I say. "Tell me."

"Fifty-five," he says. "At least fifty-five."

Before Gordon I had always dated the strong silent types, I think so I could invent anything I wanted to go on in their heads. Gordon and I talked about words, and the kind of pictures you could make so that you didn't need them, and I thought what I always thought in the first ten minutes: that after years and years of wild pitches I'd for once in my life thrown a strike.

It took me less than half a baseball season to discover my oversight: Gordon had a jealous streak as vicious as a heat-seeking missile and he could make a problem out of a paper bag. We were asked to leave two restaurants in one week alone, and it got to the point fast where if the waitperson wasn't female, I'd ask if we could go somewhere else or have another table.

Car mechanics, piano tuners, dry cleaners, toll takers: in Gordon's mind they were all out to bed me and I was out to make them want to, a tenderloin, he'd called me once, and he said he and all other men in the Bay Area were a love-crazed pack of wolves.

When I told Guinevere how I'd fallen for Gordon she said, "You only get a few chances to feel your life all the way through. Before—you know—you become unwilling."

I told her the things I was afraid to tell Leo, how the look on Gordon's face turned from passion to anger, how he yelled at me in a store so hard one time that the manager slipped me a note that said he would pray for me, how each night I would stand in the street while he revved up his engine and scream *please Gordon, please Gordon, don't drive away.*

"At one time in my life I had breast implants just to please a man," she said. "Now I won't even take off my bracelets before bed."

Guinevere keeps a bowl of cards on her breakfast table between the sugar and the coffee. They are called Angel Cards and she bought them at the New Age store. Each card has a word printed on it, *sisterhood* or *creativity* or *romance*, and there's a tiny angel with her body in a position that is supposed to illustrate the word.

That morning I picked *balance*, with a little angel perched in the center of a teeter-totter, and when Guinevere reached in for her own word she sighed in disgust. Without looking at the word again, without showing it to me, she put the card in the trash can and reached to pick another.

I went to the trash can and found it. The word was *surrender*, and the angel was looking upwards with her arms outstretched.

"I hate that," she said, her mouth slightly twisted. "Last week I had to throw away *submit*."

Guinevere brought me a cookie and a big box of Kleenex. She said that choices can't be good or bad. There is only the event and the lessons learned from it. She corrected my pronunciation gently and constantly: the *Bu* in Buddha she said is like the *pu* in pudding and not like the *boo* in ghost.

When I was twenty-five years old I brought home to my parents a boy named Jeffrey I thought I wanted to marry. He was everything I believed my father wanted: He had an MBA from Harvard. He had patches on the elbows of his sportcoats. He played golf on a course that only allowed men.

We spent the weekend drinking the wine and eating the pâté Jeffrey's mother had sent him from her *fermette* in the southwest of France. Jeffrey let my father show him decades' worth of tennis trophies. He played the piano while my mother sang her old torch songs.

I waited until I had a minute alone with my father. "Papa," I said—it was what I always called him—"how do you like Jeffrey?"

"Lucille," he said, "I haven't ever liked any of your

boyfriends, and I don't expect I ever will. So why don't you save us both the embarrassment, and not ask again."

After that I went back to dating mechanics and river guides. My mother kept Jeffrey's picture on the mantel till she died.

The first time I was mugged in the city I'd been to the late show all alone at the Castro Theatre. It's one of those magnificent old movie houses with a huge marquee that lights up the sky like a carnival, a ceiling that looks like it belongs in a Spanish cathedral, heavy red velvet curtains laced with threads that sparkle gold, and a real live piano player who disappears into the floor when the previews begin.

I liked to linger there after the movie finished, watch the credits and the artificial stars in the ceiling. That Tuesday I was the last person to step out of the theater into a chilly and deserted night.

I had one foot off the curb when the man approached me, a little too close for comfort even then.

"Do you have any change you can spare?" he said.

The truth was I didn't. I had scraped the bottom of my purse to put together enough quarters, nickels, and dimes to get into the movie, and the guy behind the glass had let me in thirty cents short.

I said I was sorry and headed for the parking lot. I knew he was behind me, but I didn't turn around. I should have gotten my keys out before I left the theater, I thought. Shouldn't have stayed to see every credit roll.

About ten steps from my car I felt a firm jab in the middle of my rib cage.

"I bet you'd feel differently," the man said, "if I had a gun in my hand."

"I might feel differently," I said, whirling around with more force than I intended, "but I still wouldn't have any money."

He flinched, changed the angle of his body, just slightly back and away. And when he did, when his eyes dropped from mine to his hand holding whatever it was in his jacket pocket, I was reminded of a time I almost walked into a female grizz with a nearly grown cub. How we had stood there posturing, how she had glanced down at her cub just that way, giving me the opportunity to let her know she didn't need to kill me. We could both go on our way.

"Look," I said. "I've had a really emotional day, okay?" As I talked I dug into my purse and grabbed my set of keys, a kind of weapon in their own right. "And I think you ought to just let me get in the car and go home."

While he considered this I took the last steps to my car and got in. I didn't look in the rearview mirror until I was on the freeway.

By midafternoon Leo and I have seen one too many happy couples get married and we drive over the Golden Gate and to Tiburon to a restaurant called Guaymas where we drink margaritas made with Patrón tequila and eat seviche appetizers and look out on Angel Island and the city—whitest of all from this perspective, rising like a mirage out of the blue-green bay.

We watch the ferry dock and unload the suburbanites, then load them up again for the twice-hourly trip to the city. We are jealous of their starched shirts and brown loafers, how their clothes seem a testament to the balance in their lives.

The fog rolls over and down the lanyard side of Mount Tamalpais, and the city moves in and out of it, glistening like Galilee one moment, then gray and dreamy like a ghost of itself the next, and then gone, like a thought bubble, like somebody's good idea.

"Last night," I say, "I was walking alone down Telegraph Avenue. I was in a mood, you know, Gordon and I had a fight about John Lennon."

"Was he for or against?" Leo says.

"Against," I say, "but it doesn't matter. Anyway, I was scowling, maybe crying a little, moving along pretty fast, and I step over this homeless guy with his crutches and his little can and he says, 'I don't even *want* any money from you, I'd just like *you* to smile.'"

"So did you?" Leo says.

"I did," I say. "I not only smiled, but I laughed too, and then I went back and gave him all the money in my wallet, which was only eighteen dollars, but still. I told him to be sure and use that line again."

"I love you," Leo says, and takes both of my hands in his. "I mean, in the good way."

I am told that when I was four years old and with my parents in Palm Beach, Florida, I pulled a seven-hundred-pound cement urn off its pedestal and onto my legs, crushing both femurs. All the other urns on Worth Avenue had shrubs in them trimmed into the shapes of animals, and this one, from

29

my three-foot point of view, appeared to be empty. When they asked me why I had tried to pull myself up and into the urn I said I thought it had fish inside it and I wanted to see them, though whether I had imagined actual fish, or just tiny shrubs carved into the shape of fish, I can't any longer say.

The urn was empty, the story goes, and waiting to be repaired, which is why it toppled over onto me. My father rolled it off with some of that superhuman strength you always hear about and picked me up—I was screaming bloody murder—and held me until the ambulance came.

The next six weeks were the best of my childhood. I was hospitalized the entire time, surrounded by doctors who brought me presents, nurses who read me stories, candy stripers who came to my room and played games.

My parents, when they came to visit, were always happy to see me and usually sober.

I spent the remaining years of my childhood fantasizing about illnesses and accidents that I hoped would send me to the hospital again.

One day last month Gordon asked me to go backpacking at Point Reyes National Seashore, to prove to me, he said, that he could take an interest in my life. I hadn't slept outside one single night since I came to the city, he said, and I must miss the feel of hard ground underneath me, must miss the smell of my tent in the rain.

Gordon borrowed a backpack, got the permit, freed the weekend, studied the maps. I was teaching a darkroom workshop in Corte Madera on Saturday. Gordon would pick me up at four when the workshop ended; we'd have just enough time to drive up the coast to Point Reyes Station and walk for an hour into the first camp. A long second day would take us to the beach, the point with the lighthouse, and back to the car with no time again to spare before dark.

I had learned by then how to spot trouble coming and that morning I waited in the car with Gordon while first one man way too young for me and then another way too old entered the warehouse where my workshop was going to be held.

I got out of the car without seeing the surfer, tall and blond and a little breathtaking, portfolio under the arm that usually held the board. I kept my eyes away from his but his handshake found me anyway. When he held the big door open I went on through. I could hear the screech of tires behind me through what felt like a ton of metal.

That Gordon was there when the workshop ended at 4:02 surprised me a little. Then I got in the Pathfinder and saw only one backpack. He drove up the coast to Point Reyes without speaking. Stinson, Bolinas, Dogtown, and Olema. The white herons in Tomales Bay had their heads tucked under their arms.

He stopped at the trailhead, got out, threw my pack into the dune grass, opened my door, and tried with his eyes to pry me from my seat.

"I guess this means you're not coming with me," I said, imagining how we could do it with one pack, tenacious in my hope that the day could be saved.

What you're thinking, right now, is why didn't I do it, get out of that car without making eye contact, swing my pack on

31

my back and head off down the trail. And when I tell you what I *did* do, which was to crawl all the way to the back of the Pathfinder, holding on to the cargo net like a tornado was coming, and let go with one earsplitting head-pounding scream after another till Gordon got back in the car, till we got back down the coast, back on the 580, back over the Bridge, and back to Gordon's apartment, till he told me if I was quiet, he'd let me stay, you would wonder how a person, even if she had done it, could ever in a million years admit to such a thing.

Then I could tell you about the sixteen totaled cars in my first fifteen winters. The Christmas Eve my father and I rolled a Plymouth Fury from meridian to guardrail and back four full times with nine complete revolutions, how they had to cut us out with chainsaws, how my father, limber from the Seagram's, got away unhurt. I could tell you about the neighbor girl who stole me away one time at the sound of my parents shouting, how she refused to give me back to them even when the police came with a warrant, how her ten-year-old hand must have looked holding my three-year-old one, how in the end it became a funny story that both sets of parents loved to tell. I could duplicate for you the hollow sound an empty bottle makes when it hits Formica and the stove is left on and the pan's started smoking and there's a button that says off but no way to reach.

I could tell you the lie I told myself with Gordon. That anybody is better than nobody. And you will know exactly why I stayed in the back of that Pathfinder, unless you are lucky, and then you will not.

"Did I ever tell you about the time I got mugged?" Leo asks me, and we both know he has but it's his favorite story.

"I'd like it," I say, "if you'd tell it again."

Before Leo built his house on the street with the peacocks he lived in the city between North Beach and the piers. He got mugged one night, stepping out of his car fumbling for his house keys; the man had a gun and snuck up from behind.

What Leo had in his wallet was thirteen dollars, and when he offered the money he thought the man would kill him on the spot.

"You got a cash card," the man said. "Let's find a machine."

"Hey," I say when he gets to this part, "that means you went to crime scene number two."

The part I hate most is how he took Leo's glasses. He said he would drive, but as it turned out he didn't know stick shifts, and the clutch burned and smoked all the way up Nob Hill.

"My name's Bill," the man said, and Leo thought since they were getting so friendly, he'd offer to work the clutch and the gearshift to save what was left of his car. It wasn't until Leo got close to him, straddling the gearbox and balanced against Bill's shoulder, that he smelled the blood under Bill's jacket and knew that he'd been shot.

They drove like that to the Marina Safeway, Bill's eyes on the road and his hands on the steering wheel, Leo working the clutch and the shifter according to feel.

At the cash machine Leo looked for help but couldn't get anyone's eyes to meet his, with Bill and his gun pressed so close to his side.

They all think we're a couple, he thought and laughter bubbled up inside him. He told Bill a lie about a hundred-dollar ATM limit, pushed the buttons, handed over the money.

They drove back to Leo's that same Siamese way, and when they got there Bill thanked Leo, shook his hand, asked one more favor before he took off.

"I'm going to give you a phone number," Bill said. "My girlfriend in Sacramento. I want you to call her and tell her I made it all right."

"Sure," Leo said, folding the paper.

"I want you to swear to God."

"Sure," Leo said, "I'll call her."

Bill put the end of the gun around Leo's belly button. "Say it, motherfucker, say, I swear to God."

"I swear to God," Leo said, and Bill walked away.

Back in his apartment Leo turned on Letterman. When the shaking had stopped he called the police.

"Not much we can do about it," the woman at the end of the line told him. "We could come dust your car for fingerprints, but it would make a hell of a mess."

Two hours later Leo looked in a phone book and called a Catholic priest.

"No," the priest said, "you don't have to call her. You swore to God under extreme circumstances, brought down upon you by a godless man."

"I don't think that's the right answer," I had said when I first heard the story and I say it again, on cue, today. The first time we had talked about the nature of godlessness, and how if a situation requires swearing to God it is—by definition—extreme.

But today I am thinking not of Bill or even of Leo's dilemma, but of the girlfriend in Sacramento, her lover shot, bleeding and hijacking architects, and still remembering to think of her.

And I wonder what it was about her that made her stay with a man who ran from the law for a living, and if he had made it home to her that night, if she stood near him in the kitchen dressing his wounds. I wonder how she saw herself, as what part of the story, and how much she had invested in how it would end.

"I'm so deeply afraid," Gordon had said on the docks our first night together, "that I am nothing but weak and worthless. So I take the people close to me and try to break them, so they become as weak and worthless as me."

I want to know the reason I could hear and didn't hear what he was saying, the reason why I thought the story could end differently for me.

Things ended between Gordon and me in a bar in Jack London Square one night when we were watching the 49ers play the Broncos. It was Joe Montana's last year in San Francisco; rumors of the Kansas City acquisition had already begun.

It was a close game late in the season; the Broncos had done what they were famous for in those days, jumped out to a twenty-point lead, and then lost it incrementally as the quarters went past.

The game came right down to the two-minute warning, Elway and Montana trading scoring drives so elegant it was like they shook hands on it before the game. A minute twenty-seven left, ball on the Niners' twenty-two: Joe Montana had plenty of time and one last chance to shine.

"Don't tell me you're a Bronco fan," a guy on the other side of me, a late arrival, said.

"It's a tough job," I said, not taking my eyes off the TV set. For about the hundredth time that evening the camera was off the action and on a tearful, worried, or ecstatic Jennifer Montana, a lovely and protective hand around each of her two beautiful blond little girls.

"Geez," I said, when the camera came back to the action several seconds too late, "you'd think Joe Montana was the only football player in America who had a wife."

The guy next to me laughed a short choppy laugh. Joe took his team seventy-eight yards in seven plays for the win.

On the way to his Pathfinder, Gordon said, "That's what I hate about you sports fans. You create a hero like Joe Montana just so you have somebody to knock down."

"I don't have anything against Joe Montana," I said. "I think he throws the ball like an angel. I simply prefer watching him to watching his wife."

"I saw who you preferred watching," Gordon said as we arrived at the car and he slammed inside.

"Gordon," I said, "I don't even know what that man looked like."

The moon was fat and full over the parts of Oakland no one dares to go to late at night and I knew as I looked for a face in it that it didn't matter a bit what I said.

Gordon liked to drive the meanest streets when he was feeling meanest, and he was ranting about me shaking my tail-feathers and keeping my pants zipped, and all I could think to do was remind him I was wearing a skirt.

He squealed the brakes at the end of my driveway and I got out and moved toward the dark entryway.

"Aren't you going to invite me in?" he asked. And I thought about the months full of nights just like this one when I asked his forgiveness, when I begged him to stay.

"I want you to make your own decision," I said over my shoulder, and he threw the car in gear, gunned the engine, and screeched away.

First came the messages taped to my door, the words cut out from ten different typefaces, held down with so many layers of tape it had the texture of decoupage. Then came the footprints in my garden, the Karo syrup in my gas tank, my scarves tied like nooses in the branches of my trees. One day I opened an envelope from a magazine I'd shot for to find my paycheck ripped into a hundred pieces and then put back in the envelope, back in the box.

Leo and I trade margaritas for late-afternoon lattes, and still the fog won't lift all the way.

"What I imagine," I say, "is coming home one night and Gordon emerging from between the sidewalk and the shadows, a Magnum .357 in his hand, and my last thought being, 'Well, you should have figured that this was the next logical thing.'"

"I don't know why you need to be so tough about it," Leo says. "Can't you let the police or somebody know?"

I say, "This is not a good city to be dogless in."

37

Leo puts his arm around me; I can tell by the way he does it he thinks he has to.

"Do you wish sometimes," I say, "that you could just disappear like that city?"

"I can," Leo says. "I do. What I wish more is that when I wanted to I could stay."

The ferry docks again in front of us and we sit quietly until the whistles are finished and the boat has once again taken off.

"Are you ever afraid," I say to Leo, "that there are so many things you need swirling around inside you that they will just overtake you, smother you, suffocate you till you die?"

"I don't think so," Leo says.

"I don't mean sex," I say, "or even love exactly, just all that *want* that won't let go of you, that even if you changed everything right now it's too late already to ever be full?"

Leo keeps his eyes fixed on the city, which is back out again, the Coit Tower reaching and leaning slightly like a stack of pepperoni pizza pies.

"Until only a few years ago, I used to break into a stranger's house every six months like clockwork," he says. "Is that something like what you mean?"

"Exactly," I say. A band of fog sweeps down, faster than the others, and takes away the city, even the site of Leo's mugging, even the apartment where Gordon now stays.

When I was eighteen years old I met my parents in Phoenix, Arizona, to watch Penn State play USC in the Fiesta Bowl. I'd driven from Ohio, they'd flown from Pennsylvania, and the three of us—for the first time ever—shared my car.

My father wanted me to drive them through the wealthy suburbs, places with names like Carefree and Cave Creek. He'd been drinking earlier in the day than usual, they both had, and he got it into his head that he wanted to see the world's highest fountain shoot three hundred gallons of water per minute into the parched and evaporative desert air.

We were halfway through Cave Creek, almost to the fountain, when the cop pulled me over.

"I'm sorry to bother you," he said, "but I've been tailing you for four or five minutes, and I have to tell you, I really don't know where to start."

The cop's nameplate said Martin "Mad Dog" Jenkins. My father let out a sigh that hung in the car like a fog.

"Well, first," Officer Jenkins said, "I clocked you going forty-three in a twenty-five. Then you rolled through not one but two stop signs without coming to a safe and complete stop, and you made a right-hand turn into the center lane."

"Jesus Christ," my father said.

"You've got one taillight out," Officer Jenkins said, "and either your turn signals are burned out too, or you are electing not to use them."

"Are you hearing this?" my father said to the air.

"May I see your license and registration?"

"I left my license in Ohio," I said.

The car was silent.

"Give me a minute, then," Officer Jenkins said, "and I'll call it in."

"What I don't know," my father said, "is how a person with

39

so little sense of responsibility gets a driver's license in this country to begin with."

He flicked the air vent open and closed, open and closed. "I mean you gotta wonder if she should even be let out of the house in the morning."

"Why don't you just say it, Robert," my mother said. "Say what you mean. Say *daughter, I hate you*." Her voice started shaking. "Everybody sees it. Everybody knows it. Why don't you say it out loud."

"Ms. O'Rourke?" Officer Jenkins was back at the window.

"Let's hear it," my mother went on. "*Officer, I hate my daughter*."

The cop's eyes flicked for a moment into the backseat.

"According to the information I received, Ms. O'Rourke," Officer Jenkins said, "you are required to wear corrective lenses."

"That's right," I said.

"And you are wearing contacts now?" There was something like hope in his voice.

"No sir."

"She can't even lie?" my father said. "About one little thing?"

"*Okay now, on three,*" my mother said. "*Daughter, I wish you had never been born.*"

"Ms. O'Rourke," Officer Jenkins said, "I'm just going to give you a warning today." My father bit off the end of a laugh.

"Thank you very much," I said.

"I hate to say this, Ms. O'Rourke," the cop said, "but there's nothing I could do to you that's going to feel like punishment."

40

He held out his hand for me to shake. "You drive safely now," he said, and he was gone.

When the Fiesta Bowl was over, my parents and I drove back up to Carefree to attend a New Year's Eve party given by a gay man my mother knew who belonged to a wine club called the Royal Order of the Grape. My father wasn't happy about it, but he was silent. I just wanted to watch the ball come down on TV like I had every year of my childhood with the baby-sitter, but the men at the party were showing home movie after home movie of the club's indoctrination ceremony, while every so often two or three partygoers would get taken to the cellar to look at the bottles and taste.

When my father tried to light a cigarette he got whisked outside faster than I had ever seen him move. I was too young to be taken to the cellar, too old to be doted on, so after another half hour of being ignored I went outside to join my father.

The lights of Phoenix sparkled every color below us in the dark.

"Lucille," he said, "when you get to be my age, don't ever spend New Year's Eve in a house where they won't let you smoke."

"Okay," I said.

"Your mother," he said, as he always did.

"I know," I said, even though I didn't.

"We just don't get love right, this family, but . . ." He paused, and the sky above Phoenix exploded into color, umbrellas of red and green and yellow. I'd never seen fireworks before, from the top.

"Come in, come in, for the New Year's toast!" Our host was

calling us from the door. I wanted more than anything for my father to finish his sentence, but he stabbed out his cigarette, got up, and walked inside. I've finished it for him a hundred times since then, but never to my satisfaction.

We pay the bill and Leo informs me that he has the temporary use of a twenty-seven-foot sailboat in Sausalito that belongs to a man he hardly knows. The fog has lifted enough for us to see the place where the sun should be, and it's brighter yet out by the Golden Gate and we take the little boat out and aim for the brightness, the way a real couple might on a Saturday afternoon.

It's a squirrelly boat, designed to make fast moves in a light wind, and Leo gives me the tiller two hundred yards before we pass under the dark shadow of the bridge. I am just getting the feel of it when Leo looks over his shoulder and says, "It appears we are in a race," and I look too and there is a boat bearing down on us, twice our size, ten times, Leo tells me, our boat's value.

"Maybe you should take it, then," I say.

"You're doing fine," he says. "Just set your mind on what's out there and run for it."

At first all I can think about is Leo sitting up on top of the bridge running numbers in his head, and a story Gordon told me where two guys meet up there on the walkway and find out they are both survivors of a previous jump.

Then I let my mind roll out past the cliffs and the breakers, past the Marin headlands and all the navigation buoys, out to some place where the swells swallow up the coastline and

Hawaii is the only thing between me and forever, and what are the odds of hitting it, if I just head for the horizon and never change my course?

I can hear the big boat's bow breaking right behind us, and I set my mind even harder on a universe with nothing in it except deep blue water.

"You scared him," Leo says. "He's coming about."

The big boat turns away from us, back toward the harbor, just as the giant shadow of the bridge crosses our bow. Leo jumps up and gives me an America's Cup hug. Above us the great orange span of the thing is trembling, just slightly, in the wind.

We sail on out to the edge of the headlands where the swells get big enough to make us both a little sick and it's finally Leo who takes the tiller from my hand and turns the boat around. It's sunny as Bermuda out here, and I'm still so high from the boat race that I can tell myself there's really nothing to be afraid of. Like sometimes when you go to a movie and you get so lost in the story that when you're walking out of the theater you can't remember anything at all about your own life.

You might forget, for example, that you live in a city where people have so many choices they throw words away, or so few they will bleed in your car for a hundred dollars. You might forget eleven or maybe twelve of the sixteen-in-a-row totaled cars. You might forget that you never expected to be alone at thirty-one or that a crazy man might be waiting for you with a gun when you get home tonight or that all the people you know—without exception—have their hearts all wrapped around someone who won't ever love them back.

"I'm scared," I say to Leo and this time his eyes come to meet mine. The fog is sitting in the center of the Bay like it's over a big pot of soup and we're about to enter it.

"I can't help you," Leo says, and squints his eyes against the mist in the air.

When I was two years old my father took me down to the beach in New Jersey, carried me into the surf until the waves were crashing onto his chest and then threw me in like a dog to see, I suppose, whether I would sink or float.

My mother, who was from high in the Rocky Mountains where all the water was too cold for swimming and who had been told since birth never to get her face wet (she took only baths, never showers), got so hysterical by the water's edge that lifeguards from two different stands leapt to my rescue.

There was no need, however. By the time they arrived at my father's side I had passed the flotation test, had swum as hard and fast as my untried limbs would carry me, and my father had me up on his shoulders, smiling and smug and a little surprised.

I make Leo drive back by the Palace of the Fine Arts on the way home, though the Richmond Bridge is faster. The fog has moved in there too, and the last of the brides are worrying their hairdos while the grooms help them into big dark cars that will whisk them away to the Honeymoon Suite at the Four Seasons, or to the airport to board planes bound for Tokyo or Rio.

Leo stays in the car while I walk back to the pond. The sidewalk is littered with rose petals and that artificial rice that dissolves in the rain. Even the swans have paired off and are swimming that way, the feathers of their inside wings barely touching, their long necks bent slightly toward each other, the tips of their beaks almost closing the M.

I take the swans' picture, and a picture of the rose petals bleeding onto the sidewalk. I step up under the tallest of the arches and bow to my imaginary husband. He takes my hand and we turn to the minister, who bows to us and we bow again.

"I'm scared," I say again, but this time it comes out stronger, almost like singing, as though it might be the first step—in fifty-five or a thousand—toward something like a real life, the very first step toward something that will last.

Cataract

I GUESS I SHOULD have known the trip was doomed from the start:

When Josh forgot the Coleman stove *and* the five-gallon water thermos but only remembered to tell me about the stove on the truck-stop phone, and Henry's plane, four hours late into Salt Lake City from Chicago, he and Thea fighting over the Wagoneer's front seat, baiting each other like teenagers before we even got on the I-15 headed south.

I put in a Leonard Cohen tape, which Thea exchanged for something grungy and indecipherable, which Henry exchanged for Jimmy Buffett's *Living and Dying in 3/4 Time*.

Thea said, "Henry's not happy unless the music he listens to exploits at least three cultures simultaneously."

It had been three years since Josh had come into my life wanting to know how to run rivers, two years since I taught him to row, six months since he decided he knew more about the river than I did, two weeks since he stopped speaking, since he started forgetting indispensable pieces of gear.

By the time we got to Hite's Crossing, ready to leave the truck at the takeout, we couldn't find the pilot who was supposed to fly us back upriver.

The little Beechcraft 270 sat on the runway, wings flexing against the wire tiedowns, and I knew that meant we were paying for ground time while we all walked around separate coves and inlets trying to find the pilot, hands over our eyes, over our sunglasses, trying to fend off the glare and the hot wind and the waves of dizzying afternoon heat.

By the time we did find him the wind was up further, and he said it was too rough to fly, and would we mind keeping him posted while he ran down to the trailers where he had a little girlfriend, and it wouldn't—he winked at Henry—take him but a minute to go down there and see about her.

Thea and I sat on the short runway in the shade of the plane's left wing and looked out across the surface of Lake Powell, almost turquoise in the late-in-the-day sun, and the white-and-rust-colored mesa tops that receded into forever beyond it.

"Not a bird, not a tree, not even a blade of grass," Thea said. "What precise level of hell is this?"

I looked at the scaly bathtub ring that circled the canyon walls thirty feet above the reservoir's present surface, at the log and silt jam that floated in the dead space where what used to be the Colorado River once came roaring through.

"Somebody's bright idea," I said. "Land of Many Uses."

The wind howled across the surface of the water making a hundred thousand rows of diamonds moving toward us fast.

"And there's really a river up there?" Thea said, pointing with her chin to the north, to the other side of the logjam, a hundred miles beyond that to the put-in where Russell and Josh and the boats had been ready for hours, to the place the plane would take us if the wind would ever stop.

"Thirty miles up-canyon," I said, "is the wildest whitest water in America. The wind can howl up that canyon all day sometimes, and once you get through the rapids, once you hit lake level, you can row as hard as you want to—you won't be going anywhere but upstream in a blow even half this strong."

"Lucy," she said, "you're always going upstream."

"I know," I said, "but not as bad as that."

I looked along the shore to where the pilot had disappeared and tried not to think about the river level, 61,000 cubic feet of water per second and rising. Everybody who ran Cataract Canyon knew the sixty thousands were the most difficult level to negotiate, not counting, of course, the hundred-year flood.

I'd been running rivers a lot of years by then but I didn't overwhelm anybody with my level of confidence, hadn't ever acquired what I would call an athlete's natural grace.

It all went back to my father, I guess, as most things did, how he'd wanted me to be Chris Evert—not to be *like* her, understand, but *be* her. And *being her* always meant *to the exclusion of me*.

I got decent on the tennis court when I was seven and twelve and fourteen but could never move my feet fast enough across the hard clay surface to win a first-place prize.

I'm strong for a girl, and stubborn enough not to give up without a dogfight. I took to the river because I believed it talked to me.

I believed that I could read the river, that I could understand its language, that I could let it tell me, sometimes even mid-rapid, exactly where it wanted me to be.

Thea said, "So how *are* things between Josh and you anyway."

"Stagnant," I said, "is the word that comes to mind."

"You invited Josh to go to sleep," Henry said, startling us from behind. "He accepted."

"Easy thing to do, sleep," I said, "when you keep your eyes closed all the time."

"You're getting smarter," Henry said, "slowly."

"That's quite the blessing," Thea said, "coming from you." She turned back to me. "I, by the way, have ended things with Charlie."

"Charlie," I said. "Did I know about Charlie?"

"He was in love with me," Thea said. "I was in love with the Universe."

"You can't be fussy," Henry said, "if you're gonna fuck 'em all."

"When are you gonna bring one of these guys down the river?" I asked her.

"With us?" she said, "With you? Never in a hundred billion years."

49

Henry and Thea had come into my life in the same year and both because of photography. Thea was my student at a semester-long seminar I taught in Denver, and Henry had bought one of my prints out of a gallery in Chicago and liked it so well he'd hunted me down. They had taken an instantaneous dislike to each other at a party I'd had the summer before to celebrate the summer solstice. I was running four or five rivers a year in those days and Thea hardly ever missed a launch date. Cataract was Henry's first trip.

I had been down Cataract Canyon three times before, but always in the drought years, thumping along through the Big Drops in the slow motion of six or eleven or fifteen thousand cfs while the Park Service waited for the one big snow that was going to come down from the high country as meltwater and fill the reservoir to the top again.

Now the river had come back with a vengeance, filling the lake and threatening daily to burn up the dam's sluggish turbines. The spillways were carrying too much water, and the sandstone was being eaten away on either side of the dam. Thirty miles upriver, five people were dead at the bottom of Satan's Gut already, the season barely three weeks old.

"Tell me about the people who died," Thea said, and I blinked at her, my eyes dry as sockets in the wind. She read my mind like that a couple of times daily. It still unsettled me.

"Well," I said, "two of 'em were that father and son that came down the Green in their powerboat, got to the confluence, and turned the wrong way."

50

Thea nodded and I knew she'd have studied the maps before she came.

She didn't have a lot of experience but she wanted it bad, was the best student of the river I'd ever trained. When we were in the boat all I'd have to do was think of something I needed—a throw line or a spare oar blade, even a drink of water—and I'd open my mouth to ask her for it and there she'd be already putting it into my hand.

"And another one," I said, "was that crazy who tried to swim the whole series at highwater each year."

"Twenty-six rapids?" Thea said.

"In the drought years the water is warmer," I said, "and there's ages of time between falls. They say he wore three life jackets, one right on top of the other. I know it sounds impossible, but there were witnesses, five years in a row."

"Not this year," Henry said.

"No," I said, "he was dead before he even got to the Big Drops."

"And the other two?" Henry said.

"The other two were experienced boaters," I said, "out to have a little fun."

"Just like us," Thea said.

"Yep," I said. "Just like us."

The wind died right at seven like an alarm clock, and the pilot flew along the tops of the canyon walls, our flight path winding like a snake no more than two thousand feet above the surface of the water.

To the east we could see the heaved-up blocks of the Devil's

Kitchen, the white humped back of Elephant Hill, the red and yellow spires of the Needles District, lit up like big bouquets of roses by the setting sun.

To the west was Ernie's Country, the Fins, and the Maze, multicolored canyon walls repeating and repeating themselves like God gone mad with the Play-Doh.

After thirty miles the long finger of lake turned into a moving river again, the canyon walls squeezed even tighter, and in two more bends we could see the falls that were known as the Big Drops.

The rapids in Cataract Canyon are not named but numbered, 1 through 26, a decision that said to me *for serious practitioners only.* The rapids come after three whole days of hot and silent floating without so much as an eddy, a riffle, a pool.

Numbers 20, 21, and 22 are bigger and badder by far than the others, deserve to be named a second time and are: Big Drop 1, Big Drop 2, Big Drop 3. Big Drop 2 is famous for being the third-highest runable falls in America. Big Drop 3 is famous for the wave in the dead center of it: an unavoidable twenty-foot curler by the name of Satan's Gut.

Even from that far above them, I could feel the rapids roar, and my stomach did flip-flops while the pilot dipped first one wing and then the other so that Henry and Thea and I could see.

I could see the rock in Big Drop 2, dangerously close to the only safe run and bigger than a locomotive, saw the havoc it created in the river on every side.

Below it, in 3, the Gut surged and receded, built to its full height and toppled in on itself. Bits of broken metal and brightly painted river gear winked up at us from the rock gardens on either side.

People said I was good at running rivers and I'd come to believe that they liked me because of it. I never gave much thought to what would happen if I stopped. I just kept taking each river on, like I took on every other thing my life served up to me: not an *if*, but a *how*.

The nineteen rapids above the Big Drops sailed under us like an old-time movie in reverse, and before we knew it we were over Spanish Bottom.

The pilot circled the confluence, the place where the waters of the Green and the Colorado come together. The waters don't mix right away, but flow along side by side for almost a mile before mingling, the greenish Colorado, the browner Green finally becoming indistinguishable in the bend that leads to rapid #1.

The pilot dipped his wing one more time before turning for the airstrip, and pointed toward the severed brown and green edges of the formation called Upheaval Dome.

"They used to think the dome was made of salt," he said, "squeezed out of the ground hundreds of thousands of years ago, built up and up like a pillar before time collapsed it, before weather turned it into the crater you see. But now they think it's the site not of a rise but of an impact, the place where a meteorite one third of a mile in diameter crashed into the side of the earth."

I talked the pilot into driving us to the City Market so we could replace the cookstove, talked him further into taking us the eighteen miles to the put-in, out of town and back down-river, near the mostly defunct Potash Mine.

By the time we got there it was almost nine o'clock, near dark with a full moon on the rise right above the canyon, the mosquitoes so thick I was worried for the grocery bags of food.

Josh and Russell had the boats in the water and were trying to keep the bugs off by drinking beer and smoking fat cigars. Russell was a sports photographer from San Diego who had been a conference buddy of mine until the day he met Josh and our friendship instantly receded.

"Took you long enough," was the first thing Josh said, and then when he saw me put the new stove into my boat he said, "Oh yeah, I forgot the water thermos too."

We studied each other in the moonlight for a minute.

"It's not like it's any big deal," he said. "We can manage without it."

And technically speaking he was right. But it was July 15th, the quick-baked middle of the hottest month on the river, and we had four full days to get ourselves good and dehydrated under the Utah summer sun in the bottom of a canyon that didn't know the meaning of the word shade.

The drinking water would heat up to ninety degrees in no time, would taste like the hot insides of a melting plastic jug. A thermos would keep ice through the first day, maybe into the second. We could steal a half a block a day from the food cooler after that.

The mosquitoes weren't going to let anyone sleep, that was clear, and I was too mad at Josh to lie next to him, so I set out walking for the City Market, which I knew was open twenty-four hours a day.

"Where the hell do you think you're going?" Josh called after me, and I didn't turn around, even though I had set out without a water bottle, and I could already feel my throat start to close, even in the first half mile, even in the dark of the night.

The summer triangle hung bright in the sky above me, and the tamarisk, still in their spring blossoms, scraped the canyon walls in a wind that had all of a sudden rekindled itself. A couple of tiny stones skittered down the wall and onto the road in front of me and I strained my eyes upward in the twilight looking for whatever it was, wild sheep or coyote, that might have knocked them off.

My throat got drier still and I was almost ready to give up and turn back when I saw headlights behind me, moving slow and from a long ways off.

I thought briefly about the part of the world I was in, a place so far away from the city that the danger curve had bottomed out and started to rise again, a place where raping a woman and cutting her up into little pieces could be seen either as violence or religion, depending upon your point of view.

Then I thought about how mad I was at Josh, how dry my throat was, how dry it would be in five days without a water cooler, and I smiled into the oncoming lights and stuck out my thumb.

He worked the late shift, just off duty from the Potash plant. He was born again, recently, had sworn off liquor and cocaine. He was a big fan of Red Skelton, was picking up part-time work as an extra in a movie they were making in Lavender Canyon. He played a cowboy, he said, and the funny thing was he'd never gotten near a horse in his life.

The more he talked the slower he drove. But every time he got to saying how lonely he was, how in need of female company, I just sat up straight like one of the boys and said I knew that if he stayed sober one day soon something good would come his way.

When he stopped the car in front of the market I was out the door and running before his hand was off the gearshift and I didn't stop until I felt the whoosh behind me of the automatic doors.

I bought the thermos, filled it with ice cubes, and started the long walk back to Potash. The town was deserted, except for the trucks that lined the roadway, their decorator lights glowing, their radios murmuring softly in the dark.

"Where do you think that little girl's going with a great big water jug at this time of night?" a husky voice crackled loud across the citizens band.

I hunched my shoulders over and didn't lift my eyes. Eighteen miles was a long way, but I had water now, and by first light I'd have more than half the distance behind me and there would be friendlier cars on the road by that time, mountain bikers and climbers, and everything would look different than it did in this eerie two a.m.

I walked through the portal, the big sandstone gate that says soon the Colorado River will start to plunge again. Above me lay the Land Behind the Rocks: a wilderness of knobs and chutes and pinnacles, a playground for mountain lions and coyotes, for lizards, tarantulas, and snakes.

I considered climbing the broken rock wall a couple thousand feet up and into it. Taking my thermos and getting lost back there for as long as I could make the water last. Staying up there till the level of the river ran itself back down into the fifty thousands. Till Josh and Russell and Henry had floated on down deep into the heart of the canyon. Then Thea and I would make our run, barely speaking, never shouting, the boat moving through the rapids as easily as if it had wings.

Russell was pretty impressed that I came up with the water cooler before he'd even gotten out of his sleeping bag, and Henry was impressed generally. Being from the city, even the put-in felt like a million miles from anywhere to him. Thea just smiled as if doing a thirty-six-mile turnaround in the middle of the night without a vehicle was the most logical thing in the world.

Henry said, "I think that girl's in awe of you."

And Josh said, "I'm afraid it's even worse than that."

We launched early, before the sun crawled over the canyon wall, Russell and Henry in Josh's sixteen-foot Riken, Thea and I in my Achilles, a foot shorter than Josh's boat, and the tubes less than half as big around.

"Damned if it isn't hot already," Henry said.

We hooked the boats together with a carabiner and let them float down the river, all the way to Dead Horse Point with only a few words between us, the sun climbing higher in the sky, the canyon walls slick with desert varnish, the heat pressing down on us, not a breath of breeze, too hot it seemed even to lift the water jug to our lips.

Then it got hotter still and we lay stretched out across the tubes like sea lions, hands and feet dangling in the water. We could have all slept like that till nightfall, till three days later when we'd hit the rapids, till the late-summer rains came at last to cool us down.

"Well, what I think," Henry said, breaking at least an hour's silence, "is that things will never get right in the world until women are willing to give up some of their rights and privileges."

That's how it was with Henry, always had been, when the silence got too much.

"Say that again . . ." Thea said, and then they were off and into it: custody rights and fetal tissue, maternity leaves and female sportscasters in locker rooms, job quotas and income tax breaks.

I picked up the oars for a minute and gave the boats a nudge away from the bank, back toward the center of the river.

"Okay," Henry said, "if we're all so equal, then tell me this. Why is everybody so goddamn accepting of hetero girls falling in love with each other?" He looked from Josh to Russell and then back to Thea. "Why's there no similar deal between heterosexual men?"

I watched both Russell and Josh startle, watched them arc their bodies slightly away from Henry as if in a dance.

"Maybe in your fantasies, Henry," Thea said, not quite under her breath.

"LUGS," I said, louder than I meant to, trying to remember, and all four heads turned my way. "Lesbians Until Graduation," I said. "In college we called them LUGS."

"It's not that it's unacceptable," Russell said, his voice rising. "Men just aren't attracted in that way to other men."

"I hope that isn't true," Thea said, "for all your sakes."

"But it is," Henry said. "Women are trained to appreciate each other's bodies. Men aren't. Josh, for instance, would never tell Russell that he had a nice ass."

"Even if he did," I said, and winked at Russell.

My mind was running three days ahead to the rapids, and how our lives might depend on resolving our sociological differences if we all found ourselves in the water, needing to work together just to survive.

"It's just not something I'm interested in," Russell said, "and don't tell me I'm in denial."

"When a woman meets someone," Thea said, "she decides whether or not she is attracted to them prior to noticing if it's a man or a woman."

"*Prior to?*" said Henry.

"Separate from, if you like," said Thea, "but I really do mean prior to."

"Let me put it this way," Russell said. "I've never gotten a hard-on for a man. That's the bottom line, isn't it?"

"How lucky for you," Thea said, "to have such an infallible bottom line."

Thea unhooked the carabiner that held the two rafts together and gave their boat a push. We floated to the other side of the river and began my favorite girls' boat conversation, naming in order all the men we'd made love to in our lives.

My total always came out somewhere between twenty-three and twenty-seven, depending on how sharp my memory was that day, and also what we'd all agreed would count. Thea had had only half as many, but she was five years younger and, because of her stepfather, a whole world angrier at men than me.

We camped that night on a fin of Navajo sandstone and listened to the thunder rumble, watched far-off lightning flash a warning in the darkening sky. I made Josh and Russell cool their beer in the river, which made Josh even madder, though he was the one who had told me aluminum eats up cooler ice fastest of all.

After dinner we ran out of talk so Thea started us singing songs we could all agree on: "Pancho and Lefty" and old Janis Joplin, "Moon River," "You Don't Know Me," and "Light As a Breeze."

"So Thea," Henry said before we'd been floating five minutes the next morning, "who's the better river runner, Lucy or Josh?"

"Please let's talk about something else," I said.

"Josh has a lot of strength," Thea said. "Lucy has a lot of patience."

"Patience?" Russell said. "Like for what?"

In the days when I called Josh and me the perfect couple, I said it was because his carelessness tempered my exactitude; I had too many fears, he had none.

Josh was strong enough to get himself out of tight corners where the river tossed him, and brave enough to go for the odds-against run. He had no fear of the river, which only I saw as a problem. Everything he knew about reading water would fit on the blade of an oar. I still led us into all the major rapids, but I knew those days were numbered, maybe even gone.

"Lucy waits on the river," Thea said, "waits for it to help her. Like her goal—once in the rapid—is not to have to use the oars."

"That's lovely, Thea," I said.

"I've seen her use her oars a few times," Josh said.

"Okay," I said, "can we please talk about something else?"

"I don't know why she wouldn't use them," Russell said, kicking Josh's oar with his foot. "They don't weigh a third of what these do. Have you felt Lucy's oars, Henry? They're like toothpicks, like feathers, compared to these."

"But generally speaking, Thea," Henry said, "you have to admit that the average man is better equipped to run rivers than the average woman."

"Not," Thea said, "unless it's one of those special trips where the only thing you're allowed to use is your dick."

"Is everybody drinking enough water?" I said. "Has everybody peed at least once today?"

"Yes, your majesty," Josh said, "Oh Great Protectress of the Block Ice."

I sent Thea and Russell hiking up and over a big sandstone fin that the river took six miles to circle, folding back on itself and winding up, as the crow flies, less than a hundred yards from where I dropped them off. Then I made Henry row my boat the six miles.

The only good thing about how hot it was, was that it might stop the river rising, that with heat so severe and no rain, evaporation and usage would start to surpass runoff; not too long after that, the river would fall.

In the afternoon, thunder rumbled again in some far-off corner of the sky, and by the time we entered Meander Canyon a few clouds were sailing in the wind that must have been whipping somewhere high above the canyon, and a rainbow stretched above us, reaching from rim to rim.

On the third day we came to the confluence and Russell dove into the place where the rivers ran alongside each other and tried to mix the two strips of colored water together with his hands. We stopped at the huge salmon-colored danger sign to take pictures, and I wondered how the men in the power-boat could have missed it, wondered how any boatman could be mistaken about whether he was moving upstream or down.

We camped that night in Spanish Bottom, two miles upriver from the start of the rapids, knew we'd hear them roaring all night long. Thea and Russell and I climbed up the canyon rim to the Doll's House, its candy-striped spires like a tollbooth, taking tickets for Cataract's wild ride. We goofed around at the base of the towers, took pictures of each other and laughed a lot, and I thought how different the trip might have been without Henry, who caused trouble everywhere he went, and Josh, who could get so far inside himself that the sound of his laughter would make everybody feel hollow and afraid.

To the north Junction Butte rose like the Hall of Justice on the horizon, and behind it the big flat mesa top called Island in the Sky. Russell went off to explore on his own and left Thea and me sitting on a big slab of orange rock.

"If the Doll's House were my doll's house," I said, "I wouldn't have wanted to play ball with the boys."

"Lucy," Thea said, "have you ever made love to a woman?"

"I've been in love with a woman," I said. "More than one."

"That's not what I asked you," she said. "It's not the same thing."

"No it isn't," I said. "No I haven't."

"And *no* to the next question," Thea said. "And *no,* and *no,* and *no* again."

During dinner we watched a thunderstorm roll down the canyon, turning the clouds behind the mesa tops black and lifting the sand into Tasmanian devils all around us. The sun broke low out of the clouds just before setting and lit the buttes bright orange against the black.

Then we heard a rumble above our heads, a noise I first associated with an earthquake in a city, highway overpasses tumbling into each other, apartment buildings buckling and collapsing in on themselves.

We jumped out of the low folding chairs and ran to the top of a dune and looked back toward the Doll's House.

"There," Thea said, pointing. We followed her finger to a large wash that plummeted into Spanish Bottom just north of the Doll's House. A thick ribbon of what looked like molten chocolate had just crested the rim and was thundering down the vertical face of the wash. It took something like ten seconds for the front of it to reach the bottom, where it exploded into a giant fan, covering half the floor of Spanish Bottom.

As it got closer we could see the cargo it carried: tree trunks, car parts, something that looked like the desiccated carcass of a sheep.

"You think the tents are all right?" I said to Josh.

"Yeah," he said. "The ground is a little higher here, and anyway, this thing won't last."

As if in response to his voice the fan closed itself down by a third in that instant, and the thunder coming down the face of the wash changed into a much duller roar.

A rumble began out of sight down-canyon, and then another beyond it, even farther down.

"I guess we don't have to worry about the river falling to below sixty thousand now," Josh said.

The next day, we all hit the rapids smiling.

Thea and I strapped everything down twice, threw our shoulders into it and hauled on the straps, fastened each other's life jackets and pulled the buckles tight. The water was thick after last night's thunderstorms, roiling, still the color of hot milk chocolate.

I led us out among the tree limbs and tires that the flood had brought down, wondered if the debris would give us any trouble, but forgot my worry instantly as I felt the tug of the V-slick in rapid #1.

We rambled through the first several rapids in short order, me pulling hard on the oars, Thea watching for holes and bailing. We got knocked around pretty good in 9, and we filled the boat in the upper reaches of 15, and in 19 I had to spin around backwards to make the final cut.

I was feeling a little outmuscled by the river, feeling like maybe it was trying to tell me something I ought to hear, but as we pulled over to scout Big Drop 1 we were still smiling and, thanks to the sun, almost dry.

In the sixty thousands Big Drop 1 is huge, but not technical, and Thea and I eased through it with so much finesse it was a little scary, the water pounding all around us, my hands strong on the oars. Thea was ready to bail at any second, but we were so well lined up, so precise in our timing, and the river so good to us we hardly took on enough water to make it worthwhile.

We pulled to the side and watched Josh bring his big boat through the rapid. Then we walked downriver to look at Big Drops 2 and 3. There was no way to stop between them. If you flipped in 2 you swam Satan's Gut, sacrificed yourself to it like a kamikaze.

I looked hard at the boat carnage that littered the sides of the canyon: broken oars, cracked water bottles, even rafts damaged so badly they were unsalvageable, their tubes split open on the toothy rocks, their frames twisted beyond repair.

I knew the river was telling me not to run it. *Not in that little boat*, it said, *not with only the two of you*, *not during the highest water in a decade,* not when it was roaring past me, pounding in my ears, telling me *no*.

I watched Josh's jaw twitch just slightly as he stared at the rapid and I knew we wouldn't have to portage. He was going to go for it. And if he didn't die taking his big boat through, he'd like nothing better than a second chance at it in mine.

"I don't want to run it," I said, for the very first time in my boating career. "It's too big for me."

65

Henry and Russell lowered their eyes, as if I'd just taken off my shirt.

"It's a piece of cake," Josh said. "No problem. Why don't you follow me this time, if you're nervous. Then you don't have to worry about where to be."

I looked at the big rock I'd seen from the airplane, the size of a seven-story apartment building, and at the torrent of water going over its top.

"I don't know," Henry said, "it doesn't look all that bad to me."

"You take my boat through then, Henry," I said, and he smacked me on the butt with his life jacket and turned to Josh, who shrugged.

"It's not a piece of cake," Thea said. "It's a son of a bitch, but I believe you can do it."

"Okay," I said, tugging the straps on her life jacket down and tight, "then let's just the hell go."

We agreed that we were going to try to enter the rapid just right of a medium-sized rock that was showing midstream, then we'd turn our noses to the right and keep pulling left and away from the seven-story rock, which we'd leave to our right as we entered the heart of the rapid. Once through the biggest waves we'd have to row like hell to get far enough back to the right again to be in position for Big Drop 3.

I was worried about a funny little wave at the top of 2 on the right-hand side, a little curler that wouldn't be big enough to flood my boat but might turn it sideways, and I needed to hit every wave that came after it head on.

Josh said that wave was no problem, and it wasn't for his boat and his big tubes, but I decided I was going to try to miss it by staying slightly to the right of wherever he went in.

We pulled away from the bank, my heart beating so fast I could feel it there between my palms and the oar handles. I watched Josh tie his hat to his boat frame, take a last-minute drink of water.

"Watch the goddamn rapid," I muttered, and finally he looked up.

"Does he seem too far right to you?" Thea said, fear edging into her voice.

"There's no way to tell with him right in front of us," I said. "We'll just have to take him at his word."

It was right about then that I saw the funny little wave I had wanted to miss more than thirty yards to the left of us and then I saw Josh's boat disappear, vertically, as if it had fallen over a cliff, and I realized in that moment we *were* too far right, *way* too far right, and we were about to go straight down over the seven-story rock. We would fall through the air off the face of that rock, land at the bottom of a seven-story waterfall, where there would be nothing but rocks and tree limbs and sixty-some thousand feet per second of pounding white water which would shake us and crush us and hold us under until we drowned.

I don't know what I said to Thea in that moment, as I made one last desperate effort, one hard long pull to the left. I don't know if it was *Oh shit* or *Did you see that* or just my usual *Hang on* or if there was, in that moment between us, only a silent stony awe.

And as we went over the edge of the seven-story boulder, down, down, into the snarling white hole, not only wide and deep and boat-stopping but corkscrew-shaped besides, time slowed to another version of itself, started moving like rough-cut slow motion, one frame at a time in measured stops and starts. And of all the stops and starts I remember, all the frozen frames I will see in my head for as long as I live, as the boat fell through space, as it hit the corkscrew wave, as its nose began to rise again, the one I remember most clearly is this:

My hands are still on the oars and the water that has been so brown for days is suddenly as white as lightning. It is white, and it is alive and it is moving toward me from both sides, coming at me like two jagged white walls with only me in between them, and Thea is airborne, is sailing backwards, is flying over my head, like a prayer.

Then everything went dark, and there was nothing around me but water and I was breathing it in, helpless to fight it as it wrapped itself around me and tossed me so hard I thought I would break before I drowned. Every third moment my foot or arm would catch a piece of Thea below me, or was it above me, somewhere beside me doing her own watery dance.

Then we popped up, both of us almost together, out of the back wave and moving by some miracle downstream. The boat popped up next to us, upside down and partly deflated, but I grabbed onto it, and so did Thea and that's when the truth about where we were got ahold of me and I screamed, though it was more of a yowl than a scream, an animal sound, the sound maybe of the river itself inside me. And though there were words involved, words that later we decided were

Heeeeeeelllllllppppppp uuuuuussss! it was some part of me I didn't recognize that made that noise in the rapid, a part just scared enough and mad enough to turn into the face of the river and start fighting like hell for its life.

Thea's eyes got big. "It's okay," she said. "Come here."

I smiled, a little embarrassed and human again, as if to say I was only kidding about the scream and Thea laughed with me for a moment, though we both knew it had been the other voice that was the truest thing.

The waves were getting smaller, only pulling us under every now and again, and I knew we were in the calmer water between 2 and 3. I got a glimpse of Josh's boat, somehow still topside, Russell and Henry bailing like crazy, Josh's face wild with fear and red.

"Help us!" I screamed again, like a human being this time, and Josh's eyes widened like his face was slapped and I knew that his boat was full of water, way too heavy to move, and that he was as out of control as we were, and that Thea and I were going to have to face Satan's Gut in our life jackets after all.

"Leave the boat and swim to the right!" Josh screamed, and it took me a minute to realize he was right, to picture the way the rapids lined up when we scouted, to realize that the raft was headed straight into another rock fall, one that would snap our bodies like matchsticks before we had time to say casualties number six and seven, and that our only chance of surviving was to get hard and fast to the right.

I took off swimming, hoping to God Thea was behind me, but I only got about ten strokes in when I saw Josh's boat disappear sideways into the heart of the Gut, which meant that I was too far to the left of him, and Thea farther left still, maybe already in the rock garden, maybe dead on impact, maybe drowning in her own blood.

This is the one that gets me, I thought, as I rode the V-slick right into the heart of Satan's Gut and all twenty feet of back-wave crashed over my head. The white water grabbed me for a minute and shook me hard, like an angry airport mother, and then just as roughly it spat me out, it let me go.

Wave after wave crashed over my head, but I knew I was past the Gut so I just kept breathing every time I got near the surface, choking down water as often as air. My knee banged into a rock during one of the poundings and I braced for the next rock, the bigger one that would smash my back or my spine, but it never came.

Finally the waves started getting smaller, so small that I could ride on top of them, and that's when, in between them, I got a glimpse of Josh's boat, still topside, and Thea inside it, safe.

"Throw the rope!" Josh said to Russell, and he did throw it, but behind me, and too far to the left. He pulled it in fast to throw it again but by that time I was well past him, not very far from exhaustion, and headed for the entrance to rapid #23.

That's when the water jug popped up beside me, and I grabbed for it, got it, and stuffed it between my legs. Rapid #23 isn't big, unless it's high water and you are sitting not in a boat but on a five-gallon thermos. I gripped the thermos between my thighs like it was the wildest horse I'd ever been on and rode the series of rollers down the middle, my head above water, my feet ready to fend off the rocks.

Then the rapid was over, and Josh was rowing toward me, and Russell had the throw rope again in his hands. This time he threw it well and I caught it, wrapped my hands around it tight. Henry hauled me to the boat and then into it, and I found myself for a moment back under the water that filled it, clawing my way up Russell's leg, trying just to get my head high enough to breathe.

"Grab that oar," Josh shouted to Henry, and he did, and I saw that it was one of mine, floating near to us, and for the first time I wondered how the wreck of my boat would look.

Josh got us to shore and the three men went back to look for the boat while Thea and I coughed and sputtered and hugged and cried together there on the sand.

The boys came back lining my boat down the side of the river, one tube punctured and deflating badly, the spare oar gone to the bottom of the river, but other than that, not too much the worse for wear. I looked for a minute toward the remaining rapids, zipped up my life jacket, and jumped into the boat.

"Come on," I said to Thea. "Let's get through the rest of these mothers before we run out of air."

All we had left before us was a long pull out of the canyon. We'd lose the current gradually over the next twenty miles, and eventually—ten miles from the takeout—we'd hit the backwash of Lake Powell and lose it altogether.

We agreed to float until our progress slowed to less than three miles an hour, then we'd row in half-hour shifts, all night if it was required, to miss the winds that would start early in the morning and could keep us from getting across that last long arm of the lake.

For the first time we all sat together on Josh's boat and I made sandwiches. Thea and I couldn't stop burping up river water, and every now and then one or the other of us would erupt into a fit of the chills.

Henry and I sang "A Pirate Looks at Forty," and Thea and I sang "Angel from Montgomery" and then Thea sang "Duncan" all by herself. My boat, half deflated, limped along in tow.

"Well," Henry said, raising his sandwich, "now that we're all safe and sound and feeding our faces, I'd like to tell you that *I,* for one, have had the perfect day."

"Hear, hear," Russell said. "Here's to Josh, river guide extraordinaire." He raised the bilge pump to his forehead in salute. "I would go anywhere with this man."

I could feel Thea's eyes on me but I kept my head down.

"It was good fun," Josh said, waving away the bilge pump, "nothing more or less than that."

"You girls should have seen it," Henry said. "You should have heard the way Josh shouted those commands."

I handed Thea her sandwich and the back of her hand rested, for a moment, on mine.

"I'm telling you guys," Henry said, "the day couldn't have been any better."

"Good fun," Josh said again, like it was an expression he was learning.

"Henry," Thea said, "weren't you ever just a little concerned that one of us might not make it?"

"I know what you're saying," Henry said, "I do. But Josh had it under control right from the beginning. And what a rush it was." He grabbed my elbow. "I wish I had a photo of your face when I pulled you in."

"I would go anywhere with this man," Russell said again, dozing now, his words little more than a murmur.

"What I always wish," Josh said, "is that we could go back up there and do it again."

I studied his profile in the rose-colored light of a sun long gone behind the canyon wall.

"I saw your face while I was in the water," I said. "I know you were scared."

"What do you mean?" he said.

"Your face," I said. "It was red. You were worried about me, I know."

A light snore came from Russell's lips. Henry jiggled his shoulder.

"What color do you think my face should have been?" Josh said. "I was trying to move two hundred gallons of water."

Night fell on the canyon softly just as we decided we'd crossed the three-mile-an-hour line, but the sky in the east was already bright with the moon, the canyon walls so well defined that rowing all night would be no problem.

Russell took the first shift, then Henry, then Thea, then me. Josh slept in a hammock he'd rigged up between his frame and the oarlocks on my boat.

"You know, Lucy," Henry said, "I know you were only kidding when you said I should have taken the boat through the

Big Drops, but looking back now . . . I really think I could have done it."

Thea snorted, didn't speak.

"Josh's turn," I said, when my watch beeped.

"Let him sleep," Henry said. "I'll cover him. He's done enough for one day."

I turned the oars over to Henry, watched the moon rise into fullness on the rim of the canyon, saw in its reflection everything wrong with how I'd come to the river, everything wrong with why I stayed.

"They'll never get it," Thea said. "You can't expect them to."

But I was thinking, in fact, about my father, who wasn't now and never would be on that river, how even if I made a hundred runs through the Big Drops, I'd never be Chris Evert, not in a hundred billion years.

Thea and I moved to the back of the raft and sang every song we could think of with Continental Divide in the lyrics until it was our turn to row again.

"What I wanted just one of them to say," Thea said, "is that they were glad we made it."

"What I wanted one of them to say," I said, "is *tell me what it felt like under there.*"

Eventually, Russell and Henry faded, and Thea and I took fifteen-minute shifts till we crossed under the bridge that meant the reservoir, the parking lot, civilization, and a world once again bigger than just us five.

The moon was high in the sky by then, and lighting the canyon walls like daylight. We'd rowed ourselves right into the logjam and I couldn't see the edges of it, so I said we should try to sleep until first light, which I knew couldn't be far.

I could see the lights in the trailer court and tried to imagine which one belonged to the pilot's girlfriend. The marina would be a ghost town, they said, before the end of the century, completely silted in and useless, a graveyard for cows and cottonwoods and car parts, every dead thing the river brought down.

We were cold by then, sick from the river water, and shaken from the ten-minute swim, the long night of rowing, and all that remained unspoken between us, though I didn't know whether it was terror, or love.

"Lucy," Thea said, "if you were to kill yourself ever, what would it be over?"

"A man," I said, though I didn't have a face for him. "It would only be over a man. And you?"

"I don't think so," she said. "Maybe something, not that."

"What then?" I said. But she didn't answer.

"If you are ever about to kill yourself over a man," she said, "get yourself to my house. Knock on my door."

"You do the same," I said. "For any reason."

"We'll talk about what it was like being under the water," she said, "what it was like when we popped out free."

"Maybe we should talk about that now," I said.

"I don't think so," she said. "Not quite yet."

On the long drive home from Cataract, Thea and I slept in the back of the Wagoneer curled around each other like puppies while the boys told and retold the story, trying to keep Josh and each other awake.

I dreamed of the place where the scream lived inside me. I dreamed I was a meteor returned again to crash into the top of Upheaval Dome. I dreamed of riding the V-slick again and again into the dark heart of a rapid. I dreamed of a life alone inside the Land Behind the Rocks.

"Christ almighty," I heard Henry say, "did you see the way Josh passed that semi?"

The sun beat down through the windows and the sweat poured out of me and I couldn't tell Thea's breathing from my own. In my dream everything around us was soft and bright, like water.

Waltzing the Cat

FOR AS LONG AS I can remember, my parents have eaten vicariously through the cat. Roast chicken, amaretto cheese spread, rum raisin ice cream: there is no end to the delicacies my parents bestow on Suzette. And Suzette, as a result, has developed in her declining years a shape that is at first glance a little horrifying. It isn't simply that she is big—and she *is* big, weighing in at twenty-nine pounds on the veterinarian's scale—but she is alarmingly out of proportion. Her tiny head, skinny tail, and dainty feet jut out from her grossly inflated torso like a circus clown's balloon creation, a nightmarish cartoon cat.

I remember choosing Suzette from a litter of mewing Pennsylvania barn cats, each one no bigger than the palm of my hand. I was sixteen then, and I zipped Suzette inside my ski jacket and drove back to the city with my brand-new license in the only car I ever really loved, my mother's blue Mustang convertible—the old kind—passed on to me and then sold, without my permission, when I went away to college.

At first Suzette was tiny and adorable, mostly white with black and brown spots more suited to a dog than to a cat, and a muddy-colored smudge on her cheek that my mother always called her coffee stain. But too many years of bacon grease and heavy cream have spread her spots across her immense and awkward body; her stomach hangs so low to the ground now that she can only waddle, throwing one hip at a time out and around her stomach, and dragging most of her weight forward by planting one of two rickety front paws.

Suzette has happily accepted her role as family repository for all fattening foods. She is, after all, a city cat who never did much exploring anyway, even when she was thin. She didn't really chase her tail even when she could have caught it. My parents are happy now to lift her to the places she used to like to get to under her own power: the sideboard in the dining room or the middle of their king-sized bed. Suzette has already disproved all the veterinarian's warnings about eating herself to death, about my parents killing her with kindness. This year, as I turn thirty-two, Suzette turns seventeen.

The cat and I were always friends until I left home and fell in love with men who raised dogs and smelled like foreign places. Now when I come home for a visit the cat eyes me a little suspiciously, territorial, like an only child.

I don't have any true memories of my parents touching each other. I have seen pictures of them the year before I was born when they look happy enough, look maybe like two people who could actually have sex, but in my lifetime I've never even seen them hug.

"Everything was perfect with your father and me before you were born," my mother has told me over and over, confusion in her voice but not blame. "I guess he was jealous or something," she says, "and then all the best parts of him went away. But it has all been worth it," she adds, her voice turning gay as she fixes the cat a plate of sour cream herring chopped up fine, "because of you."

When I was growing up there was never anything like rum raisin ice cream or amaretto cheese spread in the refrigerator. My mother has always eaten next to nothing: a small salad sprinkled with lemon juice, or a few wheat thins with her martini at the end of the day. (One of my childhood nightmares was of my mother starving herself to death, one bony hand extended like those Ethiopian children on late-night TV.) My father ate big lunches at work and made do at night with whatever there was. When I came home from school I was offered carrots and celery, cauliflower and radishes, and sometimes an orange as a special treat.

I have forgotten many things about my childhood, but I do remember how terrified my parents were that I would become overweight. I remember long tearful conversations with my mother about what my friends and teachers would say, what everyone in the world would say, behind my back if I got fat. I remember my father slapping my hand at a dinner table full of company (one of the few times we pretended to eat like normal people) when I got caught up in the conversation, forgot the rules, and reached for a warm roll. I remember my mother buying the family clothes slightly on the small side so we were always squeezing and tucking and holding our breaths. My mother said that feeling the constant pressure of our clothes would remind us to eat less.

What I know now is that I was never fat, that none of us was ever fat, and I have assembled years of photographs to prove it. The first thing I did when I went away to college was gain fifteen pounds that I have never been able to lose.

After college, when I left home for good, my father, in a gesture so unlike him that my mother attributed it to the onset of senility, began to listen with great regularity to the waltzes of Johann Strauss, and my mother, for reasons which are for me both unclear and all too obvious, started overfeeding the cat.

In my real life I live in California and volunteer twice a week at a homeless shelter, where I stir huge pots of muddy-colored stew and heap the plates with it, warm and steaming. My friend Leo stays over at my house every Saturday night and we watch movies until daylight and then we get up and work all day in my garden. I love watching the tiny sprouts emerge, love watching them develop. I even love weeding, pulling the encroaching vines and stubborn roots up and away from the strengthening plants, giving them extra water and air. I love cooking for Leo entire dinners of fresh vegetables, love the frenzy of the harvest in August and September when everything, it seems, must be eaten at once. I love taking the extra food to the shelter, and at least for a few months, putting the gloomy canned vegetables away.

What I love most of all is lying in bed on Sunday mornings thinking about the day in the garden and hearing Leo puttering around making coffee. It's never been romantic with Leo and I know it never will be, but still, on those mornings I feel a part of something. With the moon sliding behind the sunburnt hills, the sun up and already turning the tomatoes from green to red, the two of us get our hands dirty together, pulling out the dandelions, turning the rich dark soil.

Aside from the weight issue, which always gets us in trouble, my mother and I are very close. I told her the first time I smoked a cigarette, the first time I got drunk, the first time I got stoned, and at age sixteen when I lost my virginity to Ronny Kupeleski in the Howard Johnson's across the border in Phillipsburg, New Jersey, I told my mother in advance.

"It's just as well," my mother said, in what I regard now as one of her finest moments in parenting. "You don't really love him, but you think you do, and you may as well get it over with with someone who falls into that category."

It wasn't the last time I followed my mother's advice, and like most times, she turned out to be right on all counts about Ronny Kupeleski. And whatever I don't understand about my mother always gets filed away behind the one thing I do understand: my mother believes she has given up everything for me; she will always be my harshest critic, she will always be my biggest fan.

81

My father has had at least three major disappointments in his life that I know of. The first is that he didn't become a basketball star at Princeton; his mother was dying and he had to quit the team. The second is that he never made a million dollars. Or, since he *has* made a million dollars if you add several years together, I guess he means he never made a million dollars all at one time. And the third one is me, who he wanted to be blond, lithe, graceful, and a world-class tennis champion. Because I am none of these things and will never be a world-class sportsman, I have become instead a world-class sports fan, memorizing batting averages and box scores, penalties and procedures, and waiting for opportunities to make my father proud. Fourteen years after I left home sports is still the only thing my father and I have to talk about. We say, "Did you see that overtime between the Flyers and the Blackhawks?" or "How 'bout them Broncos to take the AFC this year," while my mother, anticipating the oncoming silence, hurries to pick up the phone.

My mother believes that her primary role in life has been to protect my father and me from each other: my rock music, failed romances, and teenage abortion; his cigarette smoke, addictive tendencies toward gambling, and occasional meaningless affairs. My mother has made herself a human air bag, a buffer zone so pliant and potent and comprehensive that neither my father nor I ever dare, or care, to cross it.

The older I get, the more I realize that my father perceives himself as someone who, somewhere along the line, got taken in by a real bad deal. I am not completely unlike him—his selfishness, and his inability to say anything nice—and I know that if it were ever just the two of us we might be surprised at how much we had to say to each other—that is, if we didn't do irreparable damage first. Still, it is too hard for me to imagine, after so many years of sports and silence, and he is ten years older than my mother. He will, in all likelihood, die first.

My parents, I have noticed in my last several visits, have run out of things to say to each other. They have apparently irritated and disappointed each other beyond the point where it is worth fighting about. If it weren't for the cat, they might not talk at all.

Sometimes they talk about the cat, more often they talk to the cat, and most often they talk *for* the cat, responding to their own gestures of culinary generosity with words of praise that they think Suzette, if she could speak, would say.

On a typical afternoon, my mother might, for example, drop everything to fry the cat an egg. She'll cook up some bacon, crumble the bacon into the egg, stir it up southwestern-style, and then start cooing to Suzette to come and eat it.

The cat, of course, is smarter than this and knows that if she ignores my mother's call my mother will bring the egg to her on the couch, perhaps having added a spot of heavy cream to make the dish more appetizing.

At this point my father will say, in a voice completely unlike his own, "She's already had the milky-wilky from my cereal and a little of the chicky-chick we brought from the restaurant."

"That was hours ago," my mother will say, although it hasn't been quite an hour, and she will rush to the cat and wedge the china plate between the cat's cheek and the sofa. My parents will hold their breath while Suzette raises her head just high enough to tongue the bacon chips out of the egg.

"We like the bak-ey wak-ey, don't we, honey," my father will say.

"Yes, yes, the bak-ey wak-ey is our fav-ey fav-ey," my mother will say.

I will watch them, and try to search my conscious and unconscious memory for any time in their lives when they spoke to me this way.

The more years I spend living on the other side of the country, the better my mother and I seem to get along. It is partly an act of compromise on both our parts: I don't get angry every time my mother buys me a pleated Ann Taylor skirt, and my mother doesn't get angry if I don't wear it. We had one bad fight several years ago Christmas Eve, when my mother got up in the middle of the night, snuck into my room and took a few tucks around the waist of a full hand-painted cotton skirt I loved, and then washed it in warm water so it shrank further.

"Why can't you just accept me the way I am?" I wailed, before I remembered that I was in the house where people didn't have negative emotions.

"It's only because I adore you, baby," my mother said, and I knew not only that this was true, but also that I adored my mother back, that we were two people who needed to be adored, and the fact that we adored each other was one of life's tiny miracles. We were saving two other people an awful lot of work.

When I am at home in California I don't communicate with my parents very much. I live a life they can't conceive of, a life that breaks every rule they believe about the world getting even. I have escaped from what my parents call reality by the narrowest of margins, and if I ever try to pull the two worlds together the impact will break me like a colored piñata, all my hope and humor spilling out.

One Saturday night, when Leo and I have stayed in the garden long after dark, planting tomatoes by the light of a three-quarter moon, I feel a tiny explosion in the core of my body, not pain exactly, or exactly joy, but a sudden melancholy relief.

"Something's happened," I say to Leo, though that's all I can tell him. He wipes the dirt off his hands and sits down next to me and we sit for a long time in the turned-up dirt before we go inside and get something to eat.

When the phone rings the next morning, so early that the machine picks it up before Leo—sleeping right beside it on the couch—can get to it, and I hear my father say my name once with something I've never heard before in his voice, something not quite grief but closer to terror, I know my mother is dead.

I hear Leo say, "She'll call you right back," hear him pause just a minute before coming into my bedroom, watch him take both of my hands and then a deep breath.

"Something bad?" I say, shaking my head like a TV victim, my voice already the unfamiliar pleading of a motherless child.

Later that day, I will learn that sometime in the night my mother woke up my father to ask him what it felt like when he was having his heart attack, and he described it to her in great detail, and she said, "That isn't like this," and he offered to take her to Emergency, and she refused.

But now, sitting in my bed with the sun pouring in the skylight and Leo holding my hands, I can only see my mother like a newscast from Somalia, cheeks sunken, eyes hollow, three fingers extended from one bony hand.

My mother was scheduled to go to the dentist that morning, and my father tried to wake her up several times, with several minutes in between—minutes in which the panic must have slowly mounted, realization finally seeping over him like a dark wave.

On the phone he says, "I keep asking the paramedics why they can't bring one of those machines in here." His voice loses itself in sobs. "I keep saying, why can't they do like they do on TV?"

"She didn't have any pain," I tell him, "and she didn't have any fear."

"And now they want to take her away," he says. "Should I let them take her away?"

"I'll be there as soon as I can get on a plane," I tell him. "Hang in there."

"There's a lady here who wants to talk to you, from the funeral home. I can't seem to answer her questions."

There is a loud shuffling and someone whose voice I have never heard before tells me, without emotion, how sorry she is for my loss.

"It was your mother's wish to be cremated," the voice goes

on, "but we are having a little trouble engaging reality here, you know what I mean?"

"We?" I say.

"Your father can't decide whether to hold up on the cremation till you've had a chance to see the body. To tell you the truth, I don't think he's prepared for the fact of cremation at all."

"Prepared," I say.

"What it boils down to, you see, is a question of finances."

I fix my eyes on Leo, who is outside now. Bare-chested, he has started the lawn mower and is pushing it in ever-diminishing squares around the garden and in the center of the yard.

"If we don't cremate today, we'll have to embalm, which of course will wind up being a wasted embalming."

I count the baby cornstalks that have come up already: twenty-seven from forty seeds, a good ratio.

"On the other hand, you have only one chance to make the right decision."

"I don't think she would have wanted anyone to see her, even me," I say, maybe to myself, maybe out loud. I want only to get back in bed, wait for Leo to bring me my coffee and replan my day in the garden. I think about the radishes ready for dinner and the spinach that will bolt if I don't pick it in a few days.

"In this heat, though," the voice continues, "time is of the essence. The body has already begun to change color, and if we don't embalm today . . ."

"Does she look especially thin to you?" I ask, before I can stop myself.

I cannot leave, I think suddenly, without planting the rest of the tomatoes.

"Go ahead and cremate her," I say. "I can't be there until tomorrow."

"They're going to take her away," I tell my father. "It's going to be okay though. We have to do what she wanted."

"Are you coming?"

"Yes," I say, "soon. I love you," I say, trying the words out on my father for the first time since I was five.

There is a muffled choking, and then the line goes dead.

I hang up the phone and walk out to the middle of the yard. I say to Leo, "I think I am about to become valuable to my father."

After a lifetime of nervous visits to my parents' house, I walk into what is, I remind myself, now only my father's house, as nervous as I've ever been. I can hear Strauss, "The Emperor's Waltz," or is it "Delirium," streaming from my father's study.

The cat waddles up to me, yelling for food. No one ever comes to the house without bringing a treat for Suzette.

"I thought cats were supposed to run away when somebody dies," I say, to no one.

Run? Leo would say if he were here. *That?*

My father emerges from his study, looking more bewildered than anything else. We embrace the way people do who wear reading glasses around their necks, stiff and without really pressing.

"Look at all these things, Lucille," my father says when we separate, sweeping his hand around the living room, "all these things she did." And he is right, my mother is in the room without being there, her perfectly handmade flowered slipcovers, her airy taste in art, her giant, temperamental ferns.

"I told the minister you would speak at the service," my father says. "She would have wanted that. She would have wanted you to say something nice about her. She said you never did that in real life."

"That will be easy," I say.

"Of course it will," he says quietly. "She was the most wonderful woman in the world." He starts to sob again, lifetime-sized tears falling onto the cat who sits, patient as Buddha, at his feet.

The night before the funeral, I dream that I am sitting with my mother and father in the living room. My mother is wearing my favorite dress, one that she has given away years before. The furniture is the more comfortable, older style of my childhood; my favorite toys are strewn around the room. It is as though everything in the dream has been arranged to make me feel secure. A basket full of garden vegetables adorns the table, untouched.

"I thought you were dead," I say to my mother.

"I am," my mother says, crossing her ankles and folding her hands in her lap, "but I'll stay around until you can stand to be without me, until I know the two of you are going to be all right." She smoothes her hair around her face and smiles. "Then I'll just fade away."

It is the first in a series of dreams that will be with me for years, my mother dissolving until she becomes as thin as a sheet of paper, until I cry out, "No, I'm not ready yet," and my mother solidifies, right before my eyes.

On the morning of the funeral, all I can think of is to cook, so I go to the market across the street for bacon and eggs and buttermilk biscuits, and come back and do the dishes that have already begun to accumulate.

"If you put the glasses in the dishwasher right side up, I discovered, they get all full of water," my father says.

I excuse myself, shut the bathroom door behind me, and burst into tears.

I fry bacon and eggs and bake biscuits and stir gravy as if my life depends on it. My father gives at least half of his breakfast to the cat, who is now apparently allowed to lie right on top of the dining-room table with her head on the edge of his plate.

We talk about the changes that will come to his life, about him getting a microwave, about a maid coming in once a week. I tell him I will come east for his birthday next month, invite him west for a visit next winter. We talk about the last trip the three of us took together to Florida. Did I remember, he wants to know, that it had rained, like magic, only in the evenings, did I remember how we had done the crossword puzzle, the three of us all together? And even though I don't remember, I tell him that I do. We talk about my mother, words coming out of my father's mouth that make me believe in heaven, I'm so desperate for my mother to hear. Finally, and only after we have talked about everything else, my father and I talk about sports.

Before the funeral is something the minister calls the "interment of the ashes." My father and I have our separate visions of what this word means. Mine involves a hand-thrown pot sitting next to a fountain; my father, still stuck on the burial idea, imagines a big marble tomb, opened for the service and cemented back up.

What actually happens is that the minister digs up a three-inch square of ivy in an inconspicuous corner of the church garden, digs a couple of inches of dirt beneath it, and sprinkles what amounts to little more than a heaping tablespoon of ashes into the hole. I can feel my father leaning over my shoulder as I too lean over to see into the hole. Whatever laws of physics I once knew cannot prepare me for the minuscule amount of ashes, a whole human being so light that she could be lifted and caught by the wind.

The sun breaks through the clouds then, and the minister smiles, in cahoots with his God's timing, and takes that opportunity to refill the hole with dirt, neatly replacing the ivy.

Later, inside the parish house, my father says to the minister, "So there's really no limit to the number of people who could be cremated and inter . . . ed," his voice falling around the word, "in that garden."

"Oh, I guess upwards of sixty, eighty thousand," the minister answers with a smile I cannot read.

My father has that bewildered look on his face again, the look of a man who never expected to have to feel sorry for all the things he didn't say. I pull gently on his hand and he lets me, and we walk hand in hand to the car.

After the reception, after all the well-wishers have gone home, my father turns on the Strauss again, this time "Tales from the Vienna Woods."

People have brought food, so much of it I think they are trying to make some kind of point. I sort through the dishes mechanically, deciding what to refrigerate, what to freeze.

It has begun raining, huge hard summer raindrops, soaking the ground and turning my mother, I realize almost happily, back to the earth, to ivy food, to dust. I watch my father amble around the living room, directionless for a while, watch a smile cross his lips, perhaps for the rain, and then fade.

"Listen to this sequence, Lucille," he tells me. "Is it possible that the music gets better than this in heaven?"

Something buzzes in my chest every time my father speaks to me in this new way, a little blast of energy that lightens me somehow, that buoys me up. It is a sensation, I realize, with only a touch of alarm, not unlike falling in love.

"She would have loved to have heard the things you said about her," my father says.

"Yeah," I say. "She would have loved to have heard what you said too."

"Maybe she did," he says, "from . . . somewhere."

"Maybe," I say.

"If there is a God . . ." he says, and I wait for him to finish, but he gets lost all of a sudden as the record changes to "The Acceleration Waltz."

"I love you so much," my father says suddenly, and I turn, surprised, to face him.

But it is the cat he has lifted high and heavy above his head, and he and the cat begin turning together to the trimetric throb of the music. He holds the cat's left paw in one hand, supporting her weight, all the fluffy rolls of her, with the other, nuzzling her coffee-stained nose to the beat of the music until she makes a gurgling noise in her throat and threatens to spit. He pulls his head away from her and continues to spin, faster and faster, the music gaining force, their circles bigger around my mother's flowered furniture, underneath my mother's brittle ferns.

"One two three, one two three, one two three," my father says as the waltz reaches its full crescendo. The cat seems to relax a little at the sound of his voice, and now she throws her head back into the spinning, as if agreeing to accept the weight of this new love that will from this day forward be thrust upon her.

Three Lessons in Amazonian Biology

The River

I'LL ADMIT I PICKED Ecuador for its symbolic possibilities. I wanted a place where things were reliable: twelve hours of darkness, twelve hours of light. It was the end of the old year, two weeks before my thirty-third birthday, the age my Catholic friend Tony said all things would be revealed to me. Thirty-two's highlights included three busted friendships, two bogus photography assignments, and a lover turned stalker. I wasn't holding my breath.

Balance, I thought, New Year's Eve at the Equator. I called every magazine I'd ever shot for until somebody paid me to go.

My guide's name was Renato, and he was Catholic too, sweet and serious, a broken-in Pittsburgh Pirates cap on his head, fresh out of guide school and looking for plants to identify, rare butterflies, tropical birds.

First Renato took me to Mount Cayambe, a hairsbreadth short of nineteen thousand feet above sea level, its summit smack dab on the Equator and covered always with ice caps and snow.

"This is the highest point on earth along the Equator," Renato said, "and the only place in the world where the latitude and the temperature reach zero degrees simultaneously."

I framed Cayambe in my camera and snapped the shutter. Renato and I were going to get along fine.

Renato said he would take me to the north coast to see the remains of the ancient culture of Agua Blanca, to the Isla de la Plata to see the blue-footed boobies, to the cloud forests near Mindo to see the atta ants by the hundreds of thousands, each one carrying a piece of a leaf over its head like a parasol.

I told him I wanted to lay my eyes on the Amazon Basin, wanted to feel her dark waters underneath me, figured she might have something to tell me that I needed to know.

"The jungle is a magic place," Renato said, "like a temple. We will waste the trip if we go too soon."

"It can't be too soon," I said. "Not for me."

"Going straight from your America to the jungle," he said, "is like going from the brightest sunlight into the darkest cave. If you don't take time to adjust your vision, it doesn't matter what the cave holds for you, you will never be able to see."

The rivers had been my place once, Colorado Plateau rivers that tumbled through the Sawatch and the San Juan mountains, that carved through deserts of slickrock and sand. But I hung up my oar blades over a year before, moved myself to a city next to an ocean, saying *water is water* as I drove toward the coast. I traded in my life jacket for halogen sensor lights and an electric garage-door opener, told myself that one life story was as good as the next.

I thought if I went to enough art museums and unrated movies I'd stop thinking about the sound the river makes when a hot June day has brought a foot of snow down from the highest peaks and I'm lying in my sleeping bag beside it, listening to the boulders roll.

I'd heard too that city men were different, that I might find one there who read books and cooked with spices and didn't save all his passion for class-five rapids and narrows and chutes. What I found when I got there was the same man with different excuses, enough rancor in him to bring me to my knees.

I'd sworn off the whole species for a while after that, at least till I knew how to pick one better. When I went to Ecuador I hadn't had anything resembling a date in six months.

I had an idea in my head about going home for the first time to the biggest river system of them all, more massive than all the Colorado Plateau rivers I'd been on at high water put together and then some, a river as thick with life as the Colorado was barren, as torpid as the Colorado was fierce. I wanted to remember what it was like to float down something that wouldn't try to swallow me. I wanted to see if after a year-long flirtation with tidal pools and breakers, Big Mama River would take me back in.

"I will take you first," Renato said, "to the river of riches, Aguarico, which flows into the Napo, which picks up the Curaray and then becomes the Amazon that you see on the maps. But you must understand it is all the Amazon, in the same way that every part of the cow is beef."

"I do understand," I said. "I told you I know about rivers."

"I will take you to the Lagarto," he said, "to Imuya, the place of the howler monkeys." He fingered the bill of his ball cap. "I will take you," he said, "to the Filet Mignon."

But first we went to the ocean, to a town called Puerto Lopez where we ate seviche for lunch and dinner and slept in windowless rooms above the Spondylous Bar. We drank pitchers of Caipirina, made from vodka, sugar, and lemon, listened to the music of Eros Ramazotti and Franco de Vida on old vinyl disks. Renato taught me how to dance salsa, cumbia, and ballinato, and when the music allowed it, which wasn't often, I taught him how to country swing.

The bar was run by three Colombians—Alberto, Abel, and Jimez—three of Peter Pan's lost boys who danced all night with the local girls and swam in the ocean all day. I was the first tourist in the bar since the end of October and they went out of their way to show their appreciation, to make me feel at home.

"Woodstock," Abel, who knew no English, said, pulling another battered album from behind the counter. "Eric

Clapton, Crosby Stills and Nash." He pronounced each sylla-
ble like a class in English diction. "Janis Joplin," he said.
"Steppenwolf, the Byrds." Jimez traded me my belt buckle for
his switchblade. I was the only one Alberto had permission to
dance with other than his wife.

"There are thirty-eight hundred vertebrates in Ecuador,"
Renato said, after our third pitcher of Caipirina, "fifteen hundred and fifty birds, four hundred reptiles, twenty-five hundred fish, over a million insect species, twenty-five thousand
varieties of vascular plants."

"Biodiversity," I said. "Do you know that word?"

"Of course," he said, and frowned a little. He always said *of
course* when the answer was no.

The next day we went by boat to the Isla de la Plata to see the
nests of the blue- and red-footed boobies, the flight pattern of the
frigate and tropic birds, and a crab called Sally Lightfoot who
made her ghostly way across the beach's rocky dividers and ran
across the surface of the water like Jesus when the tide came in.

"A woman like you," Renato said, "pretty and smart. Why
do you come to Ecuador without . . . someone?"

"How I can't get that right," I said, "is almost uncanny." I
saw the frown crease his brow. "Do you know that word?"

"Of course," he said.

We watched the sea urchins wave their spiny selves back and
forth in a tidal pool.

"In the Amazon," Renato said, "there is a tiny catfish called
a candiru that will swim right into a man's penis, and lodge
itself there by erecting sharp spines."

"And you are telling me this . . ."

"To amuse you," he said, "to give you something to wish on all those bad men." He held out a picture of a dark-haired woman holding a child. "Anyway," he said, "it amuses my wife."

"She's lovely," I said. "They both are." I handed him back the picture. "So I can swim in the river, then, worry-free."

"Yes," he said. "Except for the piranha . . . and the six hundred volts of electric eel."

"You won't scare me off the Amazon," I said, "so don't even try."

"I want to go there even more than you do," he said. "But you mustn't think it is all pretty birds and lily pads. There are things that will hurt you there, like here," he said, and a stingray jumped from the water as if in service of his words.

"Like everywhere," I said. "It isn't Paradise."

"That's where you're wrong," Renato said. "It *is* Paradise." He shook his head. "Is this what they tell you in your America," he said, "that Paradise is a place without pain?"

"Tonight," Renato said, "Carmita has something very special for you to eat."

"Steak?" I said, because I knew that was his favorite.

"Only in your country," he said, "do they eat steak near the ocean. This is better than steak. You wait and see."

We were back from our boat trip, sitting on the porch of the town's only restaurant watching Alberto and Abel run into the water with inflatable rafts and ride the small waves back onto the beach, their skin glistening with salt water, their hair slicked smooth and black. They tumbled together like porpoises, like harbor seals, laughing like creatures born in the sea.

"They are amphibious, those boys," I said to Renato. "Do you know that word?"

"Of course," he said.

"Like the grand cayman," I said, and snapped my arms together like jaws.

"Amphibious," he said, trying to save the word in his mouth for later.

The sun hovered on the horizon, unsure whether or not to set. Abel ran up the beach and made his hands into a megaphone. "Blood Sweat and Tears," he called out. "Procol Harum."

I gave him the thumbs up.

"In my America," I told Renato, "there is more light in the summer than there is in winter. The days are shorter now than they are in June."

He squinted his eyes first at me and then at the sunset. "I think," he said, "that this is not possible."

"No," I said, "it is. In Alaska, in fact, there is a town called Point Barrow that is so close to the North Pole that the sun goes down one day in November and it doesn't rise again until February first."

"You have seen this place?" he said.

I shook my head.

"Then you do not know if it is so."

"I *do* know," I said, "because it happens where I live too, just not as dramatically. In the summer our days are fifteen hours. In the winter they are only eight or nine."

100

"No," he said, shaking his head, frowning. "It is not as you say."

"It isn't something *I* made up," I said. "There are reasons for it . . . theories."

"I do not know these theories," he said.

"Then you have to take my word for it," I told him, "until you go and see for yourself."

Carmita's husband came to the table and set a plate in front of us covered with something that looked a lot like the creature from *The Little Shop of Horrors*: a crusty brown body with no head and a dozen gray spongy legs, all of them ending in black-and-red claws.

"*Percebes*," he said proudly. "You must have *cojones* to catch them. Do you know this word *cojones?*"

"Oh yes," I said.

"It is *mucho* dangerous," he said. "The *percebes* live in the place where all day long the ocean pounds into the rock." He slapped his left hand against his right palm, hard.

When he'd gone back to the kitchen I picked the thing off the plate by its largest claw, let the body and the other claws dangle. "This is a test," I said, "to see if I'm ready for the Amazon."

Renato smiled. "It is not a test," he said. "It is a delicacy."

"Okay," I said, "then you take the first bite."

On our last morning in Puerto Lopez I woke up to find the balcony next to the Spondylous covered with papier-mâché heads. There were at least a hundred of them, some black-haired, some brown, some male, some female, some pink-skinned, some brown-skinned, some mustachioed, some with glasses; a whole town full of people cut off at the necks and stuck on wooden pegs nailed to the balcony's rail.

Renato came outside to find me in the street taking pictures.

"On New Year's Eve," Renato said, "Ecuadorians burn life-sized puppets in the street . . . loved ones who have died, failed politicians, sports heroes who have let us down."

The biggest pig I'd ever seen in person was making his way toward us on the street.

"It is not a happy New Year, like it is in your America," Renato said. "On New Year's Eve we are crying. On January first we are happy again."

The pig walked right up to me, rubbed its bristly hair against my bare leg.

"We will be in Quito on New Year's," Renato said. "Thousands of puppets will be burned, even George Bush, even Lorena Bobbitt." He scratched the pig behind the ears and it made a noise like a cat purring.

"Perhaps," he said, "you should make a puppet or two of your own."

On the way back to Quito we stopped first at Agua Blanca, where excavation had begun on the ruins of a culture that thrived in 500 A.D. and whose people are remembered first, Renato said, for trying to become more beautiful by deforming their skulls and removing their teeth.

From a boy on the street I bought a necklace of tiny clay human figures, half of them pregnant, the rest of them men, turned on.

Then we went to Mindo, and got the van stuck in the cloud-forest mud along the side of the road. While Renato dug with the shovel, I walked two miles to town, drank a *cerveza* with the local boys while the bartender ran around trying to see if the one truck in town would start. In the end the bar crowd pulled us out with an ox so thin his rib cage looked like a weapon. That night we stayed in the Hostería El Bijou for a dollar per person. The rooms had mosquito netting, and not much else.

I was watching the biggest spider I'd ever seen in my life systematically devour giant mosquitoes by candlelight when Renato knocked on my door.

"How's your netting?" he said.

"Absolutely nothing bigger than a small dog will get through," I said, sticking my head through one of the bigger holes to smile at him.

"Mine's no better," he said, "or I'd trade. Did you hear them say there is no water?"

"To drink?" I said.

"To drink, to flush, to wash your hands." He started to close the door. "I'm sorry about this, Lucy," he said. "We should be in Quito by now, eating steaks and drinking good Chilean wine."

"But I'm getting extra credit for this," I said, "aren't I."

"Two days in Quito," he said, "and the Amazon is yours."

In Quito he took me to the Church of the Basilica, where all the gargoyles were water creatures: turtles, iguanas, dolphins, and snakes.

"No *percebes*," I said, pointing to the decorated buttresses.

"As you can see, the church has not been completed," he said. "They obviously haven't gotten to the *percebes* spire yet."

Inside, the altar was decorated with coral and sea stars and mother-of-pearl. The bells pealed in loud rapid halftones, a gentle waterfall reaching the sea.

"For the people of my country," Renato said, "water is everything: love, life, religion . . . even God."

"It is like that for me too," I said. "In English we call that a metaphor."

"Of course," said Renato, "and water is the most abundant metaphor on earth."

Outside my window in downtown Quito a hundred thousand people were burning puppets in the street. Renato had gone home at ten p.m. to be with his family. It was the first time I'd been alone in nearly a week.

"Happy New Year," I said when Tony answered.

"Where the hell are you this time?" he said.

"You have to guess," I said, "but I'll give you good hints."

Tony and I had been friends for years, lovers one brief weekend in the middle of them. He was a triathlete, and he read poetry; to my friends I called him the most beautiful man in the world.

"Australia," he said, after two hints; "Thailand," he said after a third.

He'd been an alcoholic, had stopped drinking long before I met him; his sobriety day the same as my birthday: January 8th. He told me once that New Year's Eve was the most difficult day on his calendar. I called him each year, from wherever I was.

Ecuador was his fifth guess; the clue: *Here it's the equinox, every single day.*

He said, "Lucy, I want you to stop in Ann Arbor and see me on your way home. We've never been together when we're both single. We ought to do it this time, see what we've got."

I felt the last lonely six months change in my head from an eternity to an instant. I counted all the ways Tony was different from the others.

"It's your day, angel, and mine too," he said. "I want to show you my house, want you to meet my great new dog. Let's lavish a little affection on each other to start the new year. Come on, Lucy, what do you say?"

The distance hummed in the line between us. "Did you say ravish?" I said.

"Yeah," Tony said, laughing his easy laugh. "That too."

"I'm going to the Amazon in the morning," I said. "I might not be able to change my plane."

"Just try," he said. "I can feel it this time, Lucy, it might just be our year."

I walked out into the streets where heaps of half-burned puppets and garbage smoldered. It was only a few minutes after twelve but the city was deserted. All the Ecuadorians had gone home to have a midnight feast with their families. The only people left on the street were the foreigners, the homeless, and me.

An old woman in rags handed me a shot of something that tasted like rotten peaches and made my head spin right after it went down. I threw the paper cup onto one of the fires. Across the flame I saw another woman sobbing, holding her sides.

I went back inside and called the airline. It cost six hundred dollars to make the change.

Renato and I raced down the Río Aguarico all day in a speedboat to get to a camp called Zancudo—mosquito in Spanish—that doubled as a border base for the Ecuadorean army. The Peruvian army was stationed on the opposite bank, not a hundred yards downstream.

"When we are not at war with Peru," Renato said, "we play football with them on Sunday. But now we are at war, so you may hear gunfire in the night."

He was walking me to my cabin, making sure I could find the bathroom in the dark.

"We have an informal agreement with the Peruvians not to aim at the tourist cabins," he said, "but I wouldn't sleep in the window bunk, even so."

When the shots came loud and close and in the middle of something good I was dreaming I sprang awake so fast I nearly hanged myself in my mosquito net. I hit the floor and crawled under my bed, pulling the netting down with me. There were five or six more rounds of gunfire; then the night went silent again.

The next morning we took a canoe with an outboard motor farther down the Aguarico and made a hard left turn up the Lagarto River, which was smaller and clear and the color of weak coffee. Everything else, from the banks of the river to the top of the canopy, was a rich and relentless green. Jungle sounds were all around us, the wild music of lunatic birds.

"Today we go to Imuya camp," Renato said. "Imuya means place of the howler monkeys in the language of the people who have always lived here."

"Will we see them?" I said.

"We will see all manner of monkeys today," Renato said, "spider, woolly, titi, capuchin, squirrel, tamarins, marmosets, three-toed sloths. No one ever sees the howler monkeys. But when they call you can hear them from five miles away."

We saw a flash of pink just under the surface of the water, and then again just above.

"Pink-bellied river dolphins," Renato said and shut the motor off. "You can swim with them if you want."

One dolphin surfaced and rolled over slowly. The skin on his back was brown tinged with pink, the same color as the boys from the Spondylous Bar.

I slipped over the side of the boat and into the water.

"They are shy, you know," he said. "It won't be like . . .

"Flipper?" I said.

"Yes," he said, laughing, "that's right."

The water was warm and turned my skin chocolate. The dolphins made big arcs, keeping their eyes on me from some distance away.

I tried to imitate their dives and Renato laughed harder.

"Stay away from the edges," he said. "There are cayman, fer-de-lance, water moccasins . . . did I tell you about the can-diru?"

"Yes," I said, "and don't tell me again."

We walked the two-mile boardwalk across the floating rain forest to Lake Imuya carrying our gear, our water, our food. The jungle around us was thick and green and brimming with life sounds, teeming with them. Every time we took a step off the boardwalk I thought *I am killing at least a thousand different species at one time.*

When we got to the lake two Siona Indians, Rojillio and Lorenzo, were waiting in a rough-hewn canoe, hand-carved from a single tropical tree. Renato puffed out his chest, carried his load a little higher.

"You will take my picture with Rojillio," he said, and I did.

"He is a wise man," Renato said. "Has learned every lesson of the river."

Renato sat in the very front of the canoe, then Lorenzo with a paddle, then me. Rojillio sat in the very back holding the big paddle he used to steer. Rojillio spoke in a language that was not quite Spanish. Lorenzo grinned, started to laugh.

"He says the last few days they have seen a grand cayman near here," Renato said. "Thirteen feet long. He says she may have babies. He says we mustn't make her mad."

Rojillio made a noise in his throat three times, a low guttural croaking like a frog. Lorenzo giggled again, but soft this time, like a breeze.

"That is the noise," Renato said, "of the baby cayman."

Rojillio made the sound again, didn't even get to the third croak when the big cayman's head popped up above the surface of the water.

"There," Lorenzo said, his first English word spoken.

I got the cayman in my viewfinder and clicked off a couple of shots. She was coming toward us slowly, toward the front of the canoe, not making even a ripple in the water, her eye fixed, it seemed, only on Renato.

She came closer and closer, till I had to back off from my zoom to get anything but her eye in the shot.

I backed it off as far as it would go, realized in that split second that the lens distance had met reality, dropped my camera to my chest just in time to see the cayman rear up and out of the water, propelled by the muscle that was her tail like nothing I'd ever seen before and silent. Her two front legs and eight or nine feet of her thirteen-foot body were in the front of the canoe and she was snapping her three-foot-long jaws hard at Renato.

Rojillio barked out a command that in any language could only have been "Don't fall into the water," and Renato made a move around Lorenzo, out over the water on the opposite side but somehow not in it, prettier than a wide receiver with the goal line in his sights.

The cayman stretched her neck at Lorenzo and Renato, who were now more or less both in my lap, and we all high-sided to keep the boat from tipping toward the cayman, till she got tired of the balancing act and slipped back down into the water.

Her head stayed above it though, her one eye fixed on me this time, so close I could have scratched her head without extending my elbow.

For several minutes we floated that way in the dead silence of Imuya's high noon. Then Lorenzo took his paddle and put it in the water as smooth as a spoon in fresh whipped cream, and pushed us, just slightly, away from the cayman.

We were twenty yards past her when Lorenzo and Rojillio exploded into laugher. Renato smiled, but I could see he was still shaking bad.

"In guide school," he said, "they told us grand cayman are nonaggressive."

Later that day I took Renato's photo with his head inside the jaws of a skeletal cayman, the camp's biggest trophy, nowhere near the size of the one that had jumped in our boat.

"I keep thinking," Renato said, "of my wife, my son, my mother, how they would be feeling right now if things had gone the other way."

He scraped a speck of dirt off one of the teeth of the cayman with his nail. I stared off the dock down into the dark water, then up into the thick canopy of green above. A tree frog dropped from a branch onto my upturned neck, and I brushed it away without so much as a squeal.

"It must be strange for you, as well," he said, "to think that no one would be grieving."

"It's not quite as bad as all that," I said. "I do have friends."

"Still," he said, "to be alone is unnatural. Look around you." He motioned to the trees above us, the lake below. "There isn't an animal in the jungle that doesn't have a mate."

A pair of scarlet macaws flew past us at eye level chattering to each other.

"How do you do that?" I said. "Is the entire animal community at your beck and call?"

"No," he said, "I am at theirs."

"Besides," I said, "finding a mate is no problem; finding a good one is where I go wrong. I guess I'm a little fussier than a scarlet macaw."

"And why do you think she is not fussy," he said, "just because she knows how to choose better than you."

Something big crashed in the water and Renato flinched more than he wanted to.

"Why haven't you been paying attention?" he said, touching first his eye, then his earlobe. "Why haven't your rivers taught you how to live?"

I thought about the rivers I'd left behind in my America, remembered their golden mornings, the delicate surprise of a midsummer frost. I remembered how from above the desert rivers gleamed like emerald necklaces, the only green for hundreds of miles of driest buttes and steepest mesas, of broken rocks and blowing sand. I remembered thinking that if the Amazon were flat and green it would have no way to hurt me. I had forgotten the first lesson I ever learned on the river: the place that makes you vulnerable is the place that makes you strong.

Just then we heard a sound like the wind through a culvert on the coldest day of an inner-city winter, though the temperature in Imuya couldn't have been much under a hundred degrees. It was the most hollow, the saddest, the loneliest sound I'd ever heard.

Renato motioned with his head to the rope ladder and we climbed to the camp's thatched lookout spot. The sound was louder up there but the trees weren't moving. Even the top of the canopy was still as the first breath of dawn.

111

"It is the howler monkeys," Renato said, "calling from four, maybe five miles upriver."

"It's the wind," I said. "An animal could never make that sound."

"It is the monkeys," he said, "and they are no bigger than well-fed parrots." He held his hands together to indicate their size. He said, "I told you the jungle is a magical place."

"How do you know it is not the wind," I said, "if no one ever sees the monkeys?"

"It is like your three months of night in Alaska," he said. "You have to take my word that it is so."

Renato drove me to the airport as the sun rose on my last morning in Ecuador, as it always did, at precisely six a.m.

"My head is swimming," I said, "with all the things you've shown me."

"It is my country that has shown you," he said. "I only drove the car."

At the airport he adjusted his cap and stood straight, almost at attention.

"I feel," he said, "as though we have become *compañeros*." He grinned like a boy. "Do you know that word?"

"Of course," I said.

"More than friends," he said, "less than brothers. It is . . ." He shook my hand. "Almost uncanny."

"Yes" I said, smiling, "it is."

"When you come back to Ecuador," he said, "we will see how much the river has taught you."

"And if I come back alone?" I said.

"Then next time we will give your eyes even longer to adjust."

The Lessons

The traveling time to Ann Arbor was seventeen hours, counting a mad dash across the parking lot at Kennedy, several deicings, and fifteen circles in a holding pattern around Washington, D.C. Tony wasn't at the gate when I got off the plane at Detroit International. Nor was he at baggage claim, nor in the parking lot, nor in his office, nor on his cellular phone.

After two hours I called my friend Henry in Chicago because he was in the next time zone and that was as close to human contact as I was going to get after midnight.

"You've come all the way today from a different hemisphere," he said. "Go get yourself a nice hotel room and call me in the morning."

I was on the phone to the Marriott when Tony walked in.

"I'm sorry," he said. "I must have gotten the times confused."

Back in Ann Arbor I admired his new furniture. I petted his handsome and young black dog. It was three in the morning in Michigan; in Quito, I knew, the sun was about to rise. I said, "Tony, I've got to go to bed."

"We need to have a little talk first," he said, patting my hand like I was an old person. "I'm sorry, Lucy, but I've met someone new."

My eyes felt like the insides of a clothes dryer. "Since Friday?" I said. "In only five days?"

"Yeah," he said. "I guess I should have called you. Her name is Beth"—he let go of my hand when he said it. "I saw her in a shop window on Tuesday, and it feels really healthy so far."

"It's okay," I said, and meant it. "I'm fine right here on the couch."

"Well, that's the other thing," he said. "Beth has kind of a problem with you being here. I guess I should tell you it caused our first fight."

"I'm sorry, Tony" I said, "I'm not going anywhere till I get some sleep."

When I woke up Tony was sitting on the couch looking down at me. Outside the window everything was glazed with a fresh ice storm, blinding in the sun.

"I don't think I handled last night very well," he said.

"I've slept," I said. "Now you can take me to the airport."

"I don't need to," he said, stroking his dog. "I went to Beth's last night and patched everything up and now she's dying to meet you."

"Tomorrow's my birthday, Tony," I said, "and all I want to do is go home."

In the car on the way to the airport Tony said, "You know, I could still turn this car around at any moment."

I looked out the window at the frozen trees, the branches heavy with icicles ready to snap.

"I would probably do the same thing you are doing," he said. "Of course, later I'd feel like a total jerk."

114

LESSON #1:

"Monarch butterflies," Renato had said on our first day in Imuya, "make blue jays throw up. That is how monarch butterflies keep from being eaten. But over the years, by a process known as Batesian mimicry, several other butterfly species have learned how to color themselves to look like the monarch every time a blue jay comes around.

"The problem arises," Renato said, "when a blue jay's first experience is with an impostor butterfly. If the blue jay doesn't throw up that first time, he will spend the rest of his life not knowing which are the safe butterflies and which are the ones that will make him sick."

I put my head against the little window while they once again deiced the plane.

"Whoever the hell he was," a voice said above me, "I'd bet my front teeth he wasn't worth it." She was small and black and sexy, stuffing her bag in the overhead bin above me and pulling her skirt down, adjusting her thirty or forty gold rings.

"Ecuador," she said, eyeing the tag on my carry-on. "Now there's a place I've always wanted to go."

"I just got back," I said.

"And the guy," she said. "Was he in Ecuador?"

"No," I said, "Ann Arbor."

"Well," she said, "if you'll excuse the expression, then fuck that shit."

She settled in next to me, stuck out her hand. "My name's Charisma," she said. "What's yours?"

115

"Lucy," I said. "Lucy O'Rourke."

"Well let me ask you something, Lucy O'Rourke, do you know where I'm going tonight?"

"Oakland, I guess," I said, "if you're on the right plane."

"That's right," she said. "That's where my ex lives . . . my first ex . . . God knows where the second one is . . . but the first one called me up last week and said, 'Charisma, you just fly yourself out here and bring an empty suitcase 'cause we're going shopping.' That, my girl, is what to look for in a man."

A boy of eighteen or nineteen paused in the aisle beside us, held up his ticket, shrugged, said to Charisma, "I think you're in my seat."

"Another pick of the litter," she said, and then to the boy, "This is a great big plane, darlin', I know you can find another."

The boy hovered there for a minute, shifting his weight from seatward to backward; then he moved on.

Charisma said she was a writer, and a painter, and she ran an antique store her third husband bought her, and she also sang on weekends in a Detroit club, blues and a little jazz, though I couldn't tell which thing she did for pay.

"Do you write novels?" I said.

"Novels, Lord no," she said. "I can't even stay married." She pulled out a nail file, scissors, polish, decals of tiny gold stars.

"Now you tell me all about Ecuador or the man in Ann Arbor," she said, "whichever you need to talk about more."

When I got home there was a phone message from Steven, a carpenter turned massage therapist and tantra expert I'd met back in the summer when I'd sat in Oakland's Café Roma drinking my first macchiattos and looking for friends. At that time Steven was stinging from a breakup with a woman who he said was so uptight she wouldn't talk about her bowel movements. Going to India for two years, he said, had forever changed his life.

He said that if Capricorns would only embrace their goatish nature they could be the most successful people on earth. He said Mercury was coming out of retrograde soon, and then everybody's problems would be solved.

I hadn't heard from Steven since that day, but he had remembered my birthday all that time, had called to see if he could take me out. I looked at the pile of bills and the empty refrigerator, took a shower, and called him back.

He took me out for sushi, said that because it was raw and because it was art it was food in its purest form. I drank enough sake to choke down even the flying fish eggs, even the shrimp heads. He said there was no bad karma with sake as long as you drank it out of a box.

Back at my apartment on opposite sides of my couch he gave me a coupon book for five free massages. He told me about his family, his Mormon roots, the years he spent on the Big Island, how he and his second wife took sex to such an art form that sometimes the neighbors came by to watch.

Then he said, "I think I'd like to give you a big birthday kiss."

"That would be nice," I said.

When we were finished he said, "That was a little bigger than I anticipated."

117

"Oh," I said, "I'm sorry."

Then he said, "Tell me something, Lucy, have you ever thought about you and me having sex?"

"No," I said, because I hadn't, and I didn't tell him the rest of it, that I hadn't thought of him at all since that day at Café Roma when we met.

"Perhaps," he said, "you could think about it now."

I fingered the coupon book and tried to imagine it; I thought about his Hawaiian neighbors, how I didn't even know what tantra was.

"Well," I said, "it's been a lovely evening . . . and I feel like we're becoming friends, and everybody says that's the place sex should come from . . ." His eyes wouldn't let mine wander. He nodded like he hoped there was more. "I do have a kind of a passion for men who can build things," I said, "and I know you can, though you don't anymore."

"But I could . . ." he said, "if we were together and there was something you wanted."

"So I guess," I said, "it might be nice, it being my birthday and all."

Steven lifted his hand off the place it had fallen, between our knees. I counted off through thirty seconds of silence.

"And what do *you* think, then," I finally said, "about you and me getting together?"

"Well, frankly," he said, drawing a big cleansing breath, "I just don't think you are spiritually advanced enough for me."

LESSON #2

On the second day in Imuya we saw all the hummingbirds: the green-tailed golden-throat, the fawn-breasted brilliant, the amethyst-throated sun angel, the spangled coquette.

"The spangled coquette," Renato had said, "got its name because the males of the species are pugnacious and territorial and they won't let the females get close to the flowers to drink the nectar they need in order to live. So the female has learned to go into a false heat, a false blush of her mating colors. When the male hummingbird sees her he becomes very generous, he lets the female eat whatever she wants. When she has stuffed herself sufficiently, the female hummingbird turns dull again, and flies away."

A week after my birthday I broke down and picked up a copy of the *Bay Guardian* just to look, I said, through the personal ads. After spending the better part of the night reading them, I settled on a man named Mitchell Wagner whose ad was benign and funny, focusing mostly on his six-year-old son.

We made a date for the following Friday—Mitchell, me, and Willy, dinner at his house, trout with lemon and parsley, broccoli, potatoes, and German chocolate cake for dessert.

I negotiated the six-year-old well, I thought, watched *Snow White and the Seven Dwarfs* with him, and played teepee under the table until my back was sore.

Mitchell fired one question after another at me: what was the best and the worst thing about me, what was the character

119

of the last three men I dated, where did I expect to be living in five years, and in ten.

In between questions he talked about his ex-wife, her addictions, how he'd left her in Baltimore one middle of the night, taken Willy with him, got ready for the police or the FBI to find him, for the investigation that never came.

"She didn't even call my friends to see what had happened," he said, "not even my mother." He moved his hand around Willy's head in giant circles. "I mean does that sound like natural motherhood to you?"

"No," I said, though I knew nothing about motherhood, natural or otherwise.

"You wouldn't ever pull a stunt like that," he said, "would you?" and his eyes got narrow like he was expecting me to lie.

"No," I said, "I can't imagine."

"You know," he said, when I told him it was time I should be leaving, "I was going to say this to your answering machine, but after some reconsideration I think I'll say it to your face."

I braced a little against the arm of the couch.

"Never before," he said, "have I spent three hours with anyone who took less of an interest in me."

"I'm sorry," I said, "It was all I could do to . . ." *keep up with the questions*, is what I was going to say, but then he had his hands around my neck in something I at first believed was strangulation, and only later—when his tongue went down my throat—understood to be a kiss.

"I'm having a hard time," I said, backing to the door, grabbing my purse as I moved down the landing, "keeping up with the turns this evening has taken." I moved my eyes back and forth between Mitchell and Willy. "Thanks for dinner," I said.

Willy made tiny fists at me inside his too-big pajamas, and said a soft "Bye-bye."

LESSON #3:

"The loudest bird in the jungle," Renato had said on the third day, "is known as the screaming pehah."

He stuck two fingers in his mouth and made a sound indistinguishable from a wolf whistle on a construction site. A few seconds later the bird answered back, almost as loud.

"The screaming pehah is an interesting bird," Renato said, "because he spends over seventy-five percent of his life looking for a mate."

"Not like anybody else we know," I said. Either Renato didn't hear me or he decided not to smile.

"And the reason he has to scream so loud," he said, "is because he is just a plain bird, small and brown . . . and living in this jungle with so many beautiful birds—blue and yellow parrots, ruby-throated hummingbirds, scarlet macaws—he knows he is made superior only by his scream."

The phone rang at two a.m. and it was Mitchell Wagner.

"I can't stop thinking about you," he said in a voice that was half croak and half whisper. "In one night you've changed everything I'd come to believe about women."

"I don't know what to say," I said.

"Say you'll see me again," he said. "Say you'll come for dinner tomorrow."

"No," I said, "Never," and hung up the phone.

Long before daylight the phone rang again.

"Darling," the voice said, "this here's Charisma. I was just calling to see if you're feeling as beautiful as you are today."

"Yes," I said, "thank you, Charisma. I think maybe today I am."

"There are two basic kinds of birds in the jungle," Renato had said on our last day in Imuya, "the ones who eat fruit and the ones who eat bugs."

"You make it sound so simple," I said.

"It *is* simple," he said, taking both my hands so I'd listen. "The ones who eat fruit have more time to sing."

On the 747 from Quito to Miami I'd been amazed by the graceful curve of the South American continent, by the way the biggest waves shimmered before they crashed on the impossibly long virgin shore. *In the beginning*, Renato had said, *all of the world was America.*

I stayed awake until the sky started to lighten. Even in Point Barrow the sun would be rising soon. I fell into sleep and dreamed about taking my life back to the river. For the rest of the morning the howler monkeys cried in my dreams.

The Moon Is a Woman's First Husband

HENRY THOUGHT WE COULD beat the bad weather.

We'd heard all about Gordon over our poor excuse for a two-way radio, twenty miles off Cuba and blowing itself into a bigger frenzy every minute we rigged the boat. But it was going west, they said, heading straight, as the late storms often did, for the Gulf of Mexico, and we were going east, to the Bahamas.

I was running through the rigging, making sure we had all the line and cable and hardware we needed to get the boat under full sail. We had to be off the dock by nine a.m. if we were going to make the sixty miles to Bimini by nightfall. Bimini's harbor entrance was tricky even in daylight, and impossible in the dark ever since Hurricane Hugo had picked

123

up the lighted entrance buoy like it was a rubber duck and smashed it back down near an old airstrip in the middle of the island.

"I can't find the winch handles," I called down the companionway to Henry, who had his head in the bilge and was banging on the generator with a pair of channel-locks.

"They're here somewhere," he said, "but we aren't going to need them if I can't get this engine to turn over."

"To the contrary, Captain," I said, but not loud enough for him to hear.

The boat's name was *Phaedrus*, after *Zen and the Art of Motorcycle Maintenance*, and, I always said, *The Dialogues of Plato*, even though I knew Henry hadn't ever read those. She was a fifty-two-foot ketch, double-masted, and so big across the beam you could hold a square dance in her main cabin. She was a boat designed for cookouts at the dock and Inland Waterway cruises, but Henry had a taste for open water he couldn't quite control.

Carter Thompson was on deck with me, testing the anchor lines. He had thrown both big hooks into the water and run out their full length of rope just to make sure.

"Will that generator being down have any effect on using the windlass to raise those anchors?" Carter asked, wrapping the first of the anchor lines around the big silver wheel designed to haul it in.

"None whatsoever," I said. "That windlass hasn't worked since the boat's belonged to Henry."

I got up to help Carter haul in the five hundred feet of stiff and heavy anchor line.

I said, "The captain believes in raising anchors the old-fashioned way."

Henry and I had been sailing together about ten times in the five years we'd been friends. He was a southern boy, raised in central Florida drinking Coca-Cola out of bottles with peanuts stuffed into their necks and taking potshots at alligators with BB guns. His family was way too poor to send him to college, but he'd made a million dollars anyway, three times, he was fond of saying, and lost it at least two and a half. I liked him because he was generous with money when he had it, because he gave me advice without needing me to take it, and because he'd let me paint the name *Phaedrus* on the boat's transom in big black letters freehand, hanging upside down over her stern, and he didn't even stand on the deck to watch.

We had planned this trip for the tail end of hurricane season, and Henry thought we'd be shorthanded if the weather got bad so I called Carter Thompson at the last minute and he had gotten free.

Carter and I had met in Baton Rouge earlier that year eating stand-up creole, my shrimp gumbo to his étouffée, and though not much had happened in the way of romance I had fallen a little for his high cheekbones, his crazy gold hair that went every direction, and the soft honeyed voice of his Martin guitar. His eyes were neither green nor blue, nor even quite hazel. They had softness in them, and some laughter that I thought was kind.

Carter had a fiancée in Los Angeles who was scowling in every picture of her he carried and a best friend in St. Louis named Ubiquitous Al who he said no one had ever met. And

125

even though he was known as the best location scout in the movie business, the first thing he'd said about himself in Baton Rouge was that he was a sailor.

Henry wasn't the easiest person in the world to get along with, but I thought he and Carter might do okay. They had met one time when we were all, by chance, on business in Chicago, where Henry sells real estate. We'd gotten stoned and gone up to the top of the John Hancock building and stared out the windows, and it was like one of those magic-eye pictures except in reverse.

Then we'd gone to an Italian restaurant where the waiters sang opera and we pretended it was my birthday so they'd come right to our table and sing for me. Henry bought a bottle of pricey champagne and when the waitress asked if we'd like another I said yes, like I'd forgotten it was all just a game.

Henry was about to get married for the fourth time to a girl half his age named Candy, who said *no ways* and *youse guys* and worked at a Piercing Pagoda in the middle of a shopping mall. Henry had been knocked down by love only once, but hard, and had never recovered. I didn't know why Carter wanted to marry the girl who scowled.

I got to go sailing with Henry so often because all his wives didn't want to go so much that they didn't mind if I did. Henry said I was different from the women he married because I didn't whine and I didn't scare easy and I didn't have to pee every ten minutes and I didn't get sick. You would have thought he might aim for those qualities in a wife, living part of his life on the high seas the way he did, but the women he chose were stamped out of cardboard, each one exactly the same as before.

Henry had sat me down early that summer in the center square on Georgetown, Great Exuma. It was Regatta, the biggest party of the year on the island, and reggae music and the smell of gin and coconuts filled the air.

"Do you want me to tell you why I'm marrying Candy and not you?" he said.

"No," I said.

"It's really very simple," he said.

"No," I said, a little louder than before.

"It's because you're not always nice to me," he said.

"Is anybody *always* nice to anybody?" I said.

"Candy is," he said, "to me. Always."

Carter also said things to and about me that I didn't understand, metaphors in which I could find no meaning. "We are in the press box together," he said once on the phone, "looking down at the playoff game of my life." And before that, in Baton Rouge when we'd parted at the airport he'd given me a little kiss and said, "I am the dance floor here, Lucy, but you . . . you are the taps."

Phaedrus didn't like to come to the wind much, and was still and slow on anything less than the broadest reach, but she could keep up with boats twice her fair market value surfing down the rollers in a following sea. She was a tough old girl, wasn't sound so much as she was stubborn, and in five years of sailing with Henry, she'd always got us back to the dock, often without running lights, once without a propeller, always without radar and a windlass, but home safe nonetheless.

Henry called her the K-car of sailing vessels, but he loved her as much as a man can love a boat. He said the way she took good care of him and all the rest of us was proof she loved him back.

I'd worked on sailboats in my early twenties, on the Great Lakes and in the Caribbean, worked for one asshole after another who'd have a list of rules to follow as long as religion and who'd scream *I'm giving it one pulse of forward!* every time we tried to come to a slip as if we were docking the space shuttle *Discovery*.

Henry was the opposite of those captains. He believed that one of the functions of a dock was to stop a moving vessel, and *Phaedrus* had the battle scars to prove it. Sometimes we got underway without something important—a bumper or a bowline, butter or a life raft—but we always had plenty of rum-punch fixings and enough duct tape to fashion any piece we forgot.

There was only one rule on board *Phaedrus* that I knew of: the videocassette tapes could not be stored in their proper boxes. I'd seen Henry kick a man off the boat in Georgetown once, a Frenchman who couldn't stand the disarray. Henry woke up one morning to find the videos not only boxed correctly but alphabetized. The Frenchman had done the CDs too, and was working on the reading library when Henry walked in.

"In France," the man had said, "our apartments are small, like a ship's cabin. It is important to stay organized."

"Well, this isn't France," Henry had said, picking the man up almost by the scruff of the neck and setting him down in the middle of the cabin where he couldn't touch anything. "The name of this country is Phaedrus," Henry said, "and I'm the king."

The Frenchman was off the island before cocktail time that evening.

We raised all three sails as soon as we hit the Gulf Stream. I was the unofficial helmsman on all trips, partly because I could hold a tighter course than anybody Henry knew, and partly because I got seasick the minute I took my hands off the wheel.

Henry said it was a control thing and he tried one day to hypnotize me out of it but I threw up all over his Sperrys. He never let anyone challenge me for the helmsman's job again.

Carter and Henry had a hell of a time getting the sails up without the winch handles, which we had determined once and for all were not on the boat just as the Miami skyline dipped below the horizon to our stern. I said getting the sails *down* would be even harder, especially if the wind picked up, but Henry said we'd cross that bridge when we came to it.

"What do you say we kill the engine," Carter said, stretching his back after raising the sail, "and let Nature do with us what she will."

"I forgot to tell you," I said, "Henry doesn't ever turn off the engine."

"You're kidding," Carter said.

"It's a little agreement," Henry said, "between sweet *Phaedrus* and me."

Carter gave me a look across the cockpit that said *Why doesn't he just buy a powerboat* but I pretended not to notice. I didn't like the noise or the diesel fumes either, but I also knew the odds she wouldn't restart were better than two to one.

Henry made a batch of rum punch and we all settled into our positions, me behind the wheel, the men stretched out in the cockpit one on either side of me.

Henry and Carter started swapping lawyer jokes, and then sailing stories, and then, of all things, wedding plans.

I said, "You two sound like a couple of Junior Leaguers."

"And you sound like an old maid."

"Go to hell, Henry," I said.

"And a foul-mouthed old maid at that," Henry said.

"For your information," I said, "I'm getting married this summer myself."

"No shit?" Henry said.

"No shit," I said.

"She's lying," Henry said. "I'd bet the boat on it."

"Are you lying?" Carter said.

"Of course I am," I said, "but I had you going there for a minute."

"Less than a minute," Henry said.

"Anyway," I said, "it's not the very most far-fetched idea in the world, is it?"

"It makes the top ten," Henry said. He turned to Carter. "Lucy's expectations put most mortal men out of the running."

"Some days," I said, "I think I'd go home with anybody who whistled."

"And what *do* you hear from Josh lately?" Henry said.

"He called to tell me he's sleepwalking into walls and furniture," I said, "that he gets up in the morning covered with bruises. I told him to get help, to go see Janice, you know, my old therapist."

"And he said, 'Lucy, I can't go see Janice,'" Henry said.

"How is it that you know everything?"

"You think you are the first person whose boyfriend went to bed with her therapist?"

"Now you sound like my father," I said.

"Thanks a whole lot."

"And the other days?" Carter spoke up, and we both turned to face him. "The days you wouldn't go home with anyone who whistled?"

"The other days I want to hold out for rapture and fireworks. Other days I'm just not willing to settle."

"Like I am," Henry said.

"I didn't say that," I said.

"Like I am," Carter said, and we both turned again to look at him. "I am," he said, and we waited for him to tell us, but he didn't say anything more.

"I've had fireworks," Henry said, "and land mines and mortar shells and fucking H-bombs. Now I just want someone to talk to, and touch, and screw."

"Interesting choice of words," I said.

"What's that supposed to mean?" Henry said.

And I said, "What do you think?"

Three hours and eighteen miles out of Miami we hit a series of little squalls one right after another. One minute it would rain so hard we couldn't see the bow dipping into the water from the cockpit, the next we'd be baking in the midday sun.

Carter got up and did a rain dance, which he turned into a sun dance when the clouds broke apart. We were happy and excited as kids that morning, cut loose from our real lives and set free on the ocean. The wind was steady at twenty knots, just far enough off our nose to allow us to sail. The swells were ten feet, sometimes cresting to fifteen.

"What I'd like to know," Carter said, "is when we are gonna grow up enough to get over the idea that there's some perfect person out there for each of us who's gonna make every day of our lives like Paradise?"

"In Nassau," I said, "there's a toll bridge to Paradise, and it only costs a buck."

"My idea of Paradise," Henry said, "is being the guy who owns the bridge."

"This is Paradise," I said. "The three of us and *Phaedrus*, out on the wild wide sea."

"*Phaedrus* is my true love," Henry said and leaned over to kiss the winch that gleamed silver and bright in the intermittent sun.

"I've been doing some reading about the original Phaedrus," I said, "in Plato. I think you'll be interested in what I found."

"Tell me everything," Henry said, because he knew I wanted to.

"It's one of the dialogues," I said. "Phaedrus asks Socrates whether it's better to spend your life with someone who you're compatible with, like a friend, or someone who you're crazy for, someone who'll make your life a living hell."

"And what does Socrates say?" Henry said.

"He says you should be with someone you can get along with, and he spends thirty pages proving it . . . logically . . . like a theorem." I watched the shadow of relief cross the faces of both men.

"Then," I said, "he changes his mind."

"And says you should be with the person who makes your life a living hell," Henry said.

"What he says," I said, "is that when we fall full tilt in love with somebody, it's because our soul recognizes another soul that it was mingled with on some previous plane."

"Socrates says *full tilt?*" Carter said.

"He says, *but what is man's logical reasoning, compared to the power of divine madness?*"

"Divine madness," Henry said. "I like that."

"He says when we're in love we're like a charioteer driving two giant horses," I said. "One lunges forward, pulling the chariot like a bat out of hell, the other plants all four feet in a screeching skid, and the charioteer has to stay on top, has to keep them together."

"Been there," Henry said, "done that."

"The point is," I said, "even Socrates says we shouldn't set-tle."

"Of course we must bear in mind," Henry said, "that all those boys were talking about being in love with each other."

"Socrates was queer?" Carter said.

"It's not like it makes any difference," I said.

"Maybe not to you," Henry said.

"Unless Socrates was trying to seduce Phaedrus," I said.

"Which he was," Henry said.

133

"Right," I said. "But Phaedrus said it was better that they weren't lovers, because it allowed them more freedom to talk about love."

"Like us," Carter said.

And Henry said, "Exactly."

Right about then I noticed that the squall we were in was lasting longer than all the others.

"Henry," I said, "does it feel to you like the wind is up?" And I'd no sooner said it than a gust came whipping across the beam of the boat, making the rigging sing sharp and loud and straining the furling lines hard against the winches. The prevailing winds across the Gulf Stream were easterly, and anytime they clocked to the south it meant a front was coming through.

"It appears we are suddenly on a broad reach," Henry said after a minute. "Let's try to get a reef in that mainsail." And before we could move to do it the first of the big waves crashed over the bow.

"You got any life jackets on board?" Carter asked. Henry ignored him, which I knew meant the answer was no.

The wind had doubled itself again by the time we got the mainsail reefed down, and seemed now to come from everywhere, one minute over the bow, the next across the beam; occasionally a gust would even lift my hair from behind. We furled the genoa in as close as we could to the starboard stay and secured the mizzen sail in the dead center for balance. Each wave that came over the bowsprit was bigger than the last. Thunder rumbled somewhere to the south of us. Gordon, I thought, clearing his throat.

Henry played with the GPS satellite navigator to make sure we were still on course. The current in the Gulf Stream would set us more than two knots to the north in normal conditions, and it was anybody's guess how many knots a big wind would add to that.

"It says we're down to five knots," he said. "We'll never make Bimini in daylight doing that. I could ask her for a few more rpm's, but I don't want to piss her off." He smiled the old-salt smile he saved for special occasions like hurricanes. "I've known a sailor or two who've made that cut at night."

"That was when there was a light there," I said.

"Details," Henry said.

"The book says *never* attempt Bimini harbor in strong onshore conditions."

"And where would you be today, my dear," he said, "if you had lived your whole life by the book?"

Nobody said what we all knew, which was that if Gordon had changed his course and we had just hit the moving edge of him we'd be lucky to get anywhere near Bimini, let alone safe inside the harbor.

Phaedrus wasn't built for the conditions we were fast approaching. She had too much beam, too little structural support for the flex she needed, too much open space below to hold fast in a great big sea. Henry had told me once to think of her as a giant animal whose wooden rib cage was in no secure way connected to its fiberglass skin. Already we could hear the strain around the big main cabin; it creaked each time we dove off the front of a wave.

The thunder no one had admitted hearing was getting too

close to ignore. I counted seconds from the flashing of lightning to the next clap. Seven, and then six, and then four.

"That's quite a little wind that's blown up all of a sudden," Henry said. Carter was as quiet as I'd ever known him to be.

"In West Africa," I said, raising my voice, "the people believe that the sun is a field and in it lives the ram of god. When the ram strikes the sun with his hooves, thunder roars, and whenever he shakes his tail, lightning flashes. Rain is caused by tufts of wool falling from the ram's fleece, and when the wind blows it is because the ram is galloping."

Carter looked somewhat blank. Henry, I knew, had his mind hard on something else, the structural specifications of the boat, maybe, or the foresail that was straining near to the point where it would tear.

I was getting pretty queasy and worse yet, I had to pee. But that would mean not only giving up the helm but also going below, and that combination would make me move quickly from the stage of seasickness where you're afraid you're going to die, straight into the one where you wish you would.

"Tell us a story," I said to Henry to get my mind off my bladder. "Tell us the story about the hole."

"A man gets up, walks out the door, and steps into a hole," Henry said.

"I love this one," I said. "Listen to this, Carter."

"He thinks to himself, *Goddammit, why didn't I see that hole*," Henry said, reaching down between his feet to make sure that the scuppers were draining. We were taking water in the face by the bucketful now, our skin stinging and stiff from the salt.

"Then the next day the same guy gets up," Henry said,

136

"walks out the door, and steps into the hole. And he says, *Goddammit! How the hell could I step in the same hole two days straight?*"

A bolt of lightning struck so close it made the air sizzle. I looked seventy-two feet up to the top of the mast, then down at my hands on the big chrome wheel.

"The next day the guy gets up again," Henry said, "walks out the door, and steps into the hole. Now he's really pissed off."

Henry fiddled with the GPS. "See how much you can cheat her to the southern side of ninety, Lucy," he said.

"Aye-aye, Captain," I said.

"And so . . ." Carter said.

"So it's the fourth day, right?" Henry said. "And the guy gets up, walks out the door, and steps in a hole."

"She won't let me have much over ninety-five," I said.

"Take what she'll give you then," Henry said.

"And *then* what happens," Carter said.

"I appreciate your continuing interest," Henry said. "So the next day the guy gets up, goes out the door, but he doesn't step into the hole."

Henry furled the genoa in a little tighter.

"And so . . ." Carter said.

"That's it," Henry said. "That's the hole story."

"He doesn't step into the hole," Carter said.

"Right," Henry said.

"He steps over it," Carter said.

"I guess," Henry said. "Or around."

For a few minutes we sat without talking, listening to the

sound of a thousand gallons of water crashing over the bowsprit, the sound of fatigued nylon moving more wind than it could bear, the sound of the hull stretching, and then stretching a tiny bit farther, all that stiff fiberglass moving against the warp and wind of the wood.

"If it were dark right now," I said, "the stars right above us would be Delphinus, the dolphin."

"Tell us more about him," Henry said.

"There was a poet and musician named Arion sailing back to Greece. The ship's crew turned against him, were going to kill him, but he summoned up a dolphin with his lyre, jumped into the sea and onto the dolphin's back, and was carried safely away."

"That's a happy story," Henry said, "for you."

"I know some happy stories," I said.

The GPS said we were down to making less than two knots. The wind was squared in our face again and gusting to more than fifty knots. The waves were more than thirty feet and coming faster all the time. Still no one had said the word *hurricane*.

The mainsail had torn along its halyard so far it was useless, and Carter had bundled it around the mast with bungee cords just to keep it out of my face. We had the genoa furled in so close she *had* to tear before too long; the only questions were *how* soon and *how* bad.

"We maybe should try to get that genny down," Carter said, "in case we need it later."

Henry nodded slowly, but didn't make a move. Even if they

got her furled, without a winch handle they might not get her out again, and if the engine crapped out, the genoa would be our only chance to make any headway at all.

The storm was full on us, the wind howling so loud, the thunder so close, the flashes of lightning so bright that I thought we wouldn't even hear the engine if it sputtered, but then I felt it under my feet, felt it cough once, twice, and level out again. My eyes met Henry's and I knew he'd felt it too.

I was so sick by then that the only thing making me stay on my feet was how hard it was to keep *Phaedrus* pinched up on the ninety-five-degree heading. Even so, something in me wasn't going to let Henry see me puke.

Then, when it seemed like things couldn't get any worse, a fluky wave came at us broadside, so big and fast we put the top of the mainmast into the sea. Water rushed into the low side of the cockpit and I heard what I thought was a long split of wood running forward to aft. I clutched the wheel and stared at the compass and then we were upright again and only taking waves over the bow.

"The singular disadvantage of the sea," Henry said, his voice rising over the pitch of the storm, "is that after successfully surmounting one wave you find behind it another one, equally important and equally interested in doing something effective in the way of swamping boats."

"Who said that?" Carter said. He too had to shout to be heard.

"Stephen Crane," Henry yelled. " 'The Open Boat.' "

"That crack . . ." Carter said.

"It wasn't what you thought," Henry said. "Not this time,

139

not yet. At this point it's just the fiberglass arguing with the wood and losing." I thought I heard Henry laugh a little. "We'll know right away," he said, "if a wave breaks her open. Can you get her any tighter to the wind, Lucy?"

"A hundred," I said. "Maybe a hundred and five."

"Do what you can," he said. "I'd like to have a better angle for the next one of those laterals that hits us."

And no sooner were the words out of his mouth than the next one did come, and two more after that. The cracking, whatever it was, got louder each time.

I took advantage of the chaos the third wave brought to throw up, fast and silent into a cup that had been rolling around in the cockpit, and when we were heeled way over I tossed the cup into the sea. It was the most demure puking the high seas have ever known, but damned if Henry didn't catch it anyway.

"That's my girl," Henry said.

"We're fucked this time, Henry," I said. "Aren't we."

"No, darlin'," he said. "We're gonna be fine."

And I knew our words were reversible. That I could have said, *Are we gonna be okay, Henry*, and Henry could have said, *No, we're fucked*, and in the end the meaning would have been exactly the same.

Carter looked as though he wished he'd never met me that night in Baton Rouge. Then one more of those mast-dunking waves caught the side of the boat.

"Carter," Henry said, "get your lyre out and start calling for that dolphin."

"What kind of shape is your life raft in?" Carter said.

140

"Decent shape," Henry said, and I prayed he wasn't lying. Then he said, "How long you think you're going to last in a dinghy out there?"

"Tell us the story about the monkey," I said.

"You know that one by heart," Henry said.

"Tell me again," I said.

"You put a monkey in a box, give it a food pellet every time it presses the lever, it'll learn real fast how to get its food."

"I do know that story," I said, not to stop but to encourage him.

"Then you change things around on him," Henry said, "and instead of a food pellet when he presses the lever, you give him a shock."

"But that's not how you make the monkey crazy," I said, taking the biggest wave so far full in the face.

"No," said Henry, "that's not how you make the monkey crazy."

"Okay," Carter said, "I'll bite again."

"You make the monkey crazy," Henry said, "by giving him a shock sometimes, giving him a food pellet sometimes, and not giving him any way to determine which it is he's gonna get."

We were soaked through now and cold and caked in dried salt, more than fifteen nautical miles to travel at an average of two knots, while we listened to our only sail tear itself into ribbons and waited for the boat to split apart.

Then it got dark, and it was harder than ever to imagine our progress. There was just the endless wind blowing sixty knots, and then seventy, right in our faces like out of some unseen tunnel, and the black waves that tried again and again to swallow us, and the lightning, every few minutes, showing us each other's faces, scared and exhausted, and the absurd and ever-changing angles between *Phaedrus* and the sea.

Then, just when it seemed like the storm had gone on and would go on forever, the wind got a little lighter, the waves got a little smaller, and we were in the lee of Bimini Island.

"I see lights," Carter said. "Watch now, when we get on top of the next wave."

And sure enough there were lights, enough lights to be Bimini jumping up above the waves on the eastern horizon.

"Okay, Captain," I said, "now what do we do?"

There was more than one problem with trying to come into Bimini harbor at night. First there was a shoal that ran the full length of the west side of the island, a piece of coral so tough and so shallow that it had ripped open the hulls of enough boats of every kind to earn Bimini its reputation as one of the great wreck-diving islands in the world.

There was one break in the shoal midway down the island, but how we'd find it in the dark was anybody's guess. If we made it through the break we'd have to ride the narrow inland passage a couple miles north to the harbor entrance by listening to the waves breaking against the shoal with one ear and the waves rolling up the beach with the other, and trying to keep *Phaedrus* between them.

In the daytime, with no wind whatsoever, the tides could rearrange the sandbars enough to make the entrance tricky. The guidebook didn't even bother to say not to try it in the dark.

"Take her down a thousand rpm's, Lucy," Henry said. "Carter, let's you and I take down the genoa."

There was hardly any point. Only two or three feet of shredded nylon strips remained near the top of the forestay. Hardly enough to catch the wind.

"I want you to get as tight to the wind as possible," Henry said. "We don't want to come up on that reef without our brakes on."

"Maybe we should just stay out here till morning," I said. "Sail up and down the coast until first light."

"It could be blowing a hundred knots by morning," Henry said. "Trust me, Lucy, I can smell my way in."

For the first time in hours it felt like we were having fun again.

Carter lashed himself to the bowsprit, looking and listening in the dark for waves, his yellow rain gear glowing up there like some misshapen moon. I kept one hand on the wheel and one hand on the throttle, ready to throw it into reverse the second Carter yelled. Henry fiddled with the GPS, kept his flashlight trained on the navigational chart, which was soaked through and in pieces, looked up every once in a while to try and read the island lights.

"I've got waves breaking at eleven o'clock," Carter yelled.

"Throttle back," Henry said, but I'd already done it.

"Not too far," we said together as *Phaedrus* coughed and choked.

"Fall off to the south," Henry said. "Give me one hundred and fifty degrees."

"There," I said, when she'd made her slow turn.

"Good," Henry said, "Now back up to ninety."

"Waves," Carter said. "This time ten o'clock."

"What do you see dead ahead?" Henry yelled up to him.

"The beach," he said. "And I've got waves now at two o'clock too."

"Okay, Lucy," Henry said, "let's drop her real nice and easy into reverse."

I pulled the throttle back and the engine made a horrible noise, metal on metal, gears grinding so loud that they could have heard it on Bimini. I slammed it back into neutral and the noise stopped.

"We don't have reverse, Henry," I said.

"No," Henry said. "Pity. Okay, let's try a little forward again."

"I've still got waves breaking at ten and at two," Carter yelled.

"We'll know in the next thirty seconds," Henry said. "We're either right smack dab in the middle of the cut, or about to do some serious ecological damage."

I could see the waves now, big and breaking white and on both sides of us. I lined up the boat's nose in the space I thought I could see between them, and braced myself for the crash.

"We've got the cut," Henry said.

"We've got the cut," Carter screamed. "Unfuckingbelievable!"

"Okay, helmsman," Henry said, "a nice easy turn to the north."

The blue-water passage between the shoal and the sand

beach had probably never been rougher in the history of Bimini Island, but it felt like a bathtub to us. Carter stayed in the bow and yelled out his guesses at the distance from each set of waves but I could hear them perfectly even from where I stood, and Henry said later I ran the line between them as well as a computer could have done.

By the time we got into the harbor there was plenty of town light to show us the way to the Customs House dock, and I made a beeline for it.

"The wind's gonna push us against that dock so hard you won't be able to do a thing to stop it," Henry said. "Just try to make sure you keep her in line."

Getting *Phaedrus* secured to the dock was no problem, but keeping all thirty-six tons of her from walking up and over it was. The wind was well over seventy knots now, even inside the harbor. We lined her side with all the big black bumpers we could find on board, doubled her spring lines, went to bed, and hoped for the best.

The next morning Henry and I were up early. The storm was even worse and we needed more bumpers, but we had to wait for the customs official to come and take us out of quarantine before we could leave the boat. Carter emerged from his cabin just before noon in a T-shirt that stopped above his belly button, nothing on underneath. I opened my mouth to say something funny, but the combination of the happy-to-be-alive adrenaline that lingered in my body and the elegant lines of his was leaving me speechless. Henry was intent on the preparation of one of his specialties—pork loin à la Jack

Daniel's—and Carter was up the companionway and on deck before Henry looked up.

"Close your mouth," Henry said, and I did, and pointed, and we both put our heads up the hatch. Carter was up there bare-assed and beautiful, checking the bumpers and coiling lines.

"Carter," Henry said, "I don't want you to think me prudish, but we're in the middle of what passes for a big city in the Bahamas, and the Bahamians take a rather dim view of the white people coming in here and breaking their laws."

I could see the customs official in full government regalia rounding the corner at the far end of the long dock.

Carter looked stalled out, his hands stopped mid-coil.

"Cover yourself," Henry said. "Now!"

Carter grabbed the towel I'd hung the night before in the rigging, and leapt for the companionway before the customs official had raised his eyes. He gave me a look that said *Old fart,* or something just like it, then he disappeared into his cabin and for the first time shut the door.

We walked up the hill to Opal's for dinner—grouper and conch fritters—and stopped at the End of the World Saloon for a Kalik beer on the way home. I got interested in a bar game, a stainless-steel ring hanging from a string that you had to swing just hard enough to catch on a peg that came out of the wall, but Henry said we shouldn't leave *Phaedrus* alone longer than we had to, so we went back to the boat and made it an early night.

The next morning I opened up the companionway wide enough to stick my head and shoulders out and a bucket's worth of water hit me square in the face, lifted off the bay by

146

one big gust of wind. "It must be blowing eighty now," I said, "gusting higher than that."

"The highest point of this island is only fifteen feet above sea level," Henry said. "If it keeps raining like this it may not be here in the morning."

"The Quest for Atlantis expedition met here five years ago," I said. "There's a whole lot of boulders off Paradise Point. They say that it's a fallen temple."

"Maybe they just got here a few years too early," Carter said.

It started raining hard again and I slammed the companionway closed.

"Nothing to do, I guess," Carter said, "except talk some more about love."

"Your turn, Carter." I said. "Up till now you've been off the hook."

"There's not much to tell," he said. "I've been with Sarah off and on for twelve years. I love her," he said, "just not in all the right ways."

"You mean she doesn't turn you on," Henry said.

"Sarah's a very beautiful woman," Carter said. "I proposed to her two years ago Groundhog Day . . ."

"Groundhog Day!" I said.

"The end of winter's kind of a big deal for me," Carter said. "But anyway, I can't make myself set a date."

"So you're making Sarah crazy like a monkey," Henry said, "and you haven't had sex in twelve years."

"I didn't say that," Carter said.

"Twelve years," I said. "I've been thinking twelve months is like to kill me."

"Or twelve days," Henry said.

"Nobody said I haven't had sex in twelve years," Carter said.

"Henry did," I said.

"Why all this mystery?" Henry said. "Let's hear it Carter, how long?"

Carter stared hard at Henry for a minute, then opened the companionway and stepped out into the storm.

Henry looked at me, a little sheepish. He said, "I guess that wasn't a very seamanly thing to say."

It was an old joke, from our very first year of sailing. We'd hit the anchorage off Stocking Island, Exuma, right at sunset and it was as packed with boats as we'd ever seen it, but it was too late not to go in. We wedged ourselves between the shore and a smaller boat called *Penny Pincher* that Henry said was taking his half out of the middle anyway. Henry had a real thing about people who stayed at anchorage so long they thought they owned the space.

The wind was out of the west when we dropped our hook, keeping us well away from *Penny Pincher,* but at midnight it went still as a confessional and we wound up with our stern bobbing only a few feet from their bow.

The guy on *Penny Pincher* and his wife woke up, came on deck, and started to yell at us. He said we were getting a little too close, and Henry said we were on top of it, which we had been, taking up line as we needed it, then letting it out when we swung on by. Then the guy said he thought it hadn't been very seamanly of Henry to drop anchor there in the first place, and that now the seamanly thing to do would be for us to pull up anchor and move on.

The guy was right, of course; he just blew it with his choice of words.

"I might consider moving," Henry said, "if you could be seamanly enough to ask me nice."

"Are you crazy?" the wife screamed, the moonlight showing through her gauzy nightgown. "All our worldly possessions are on this boat."

"And where are your nonworldly possessions," Henry said, "in Cleveland?"

"Come on," the guy said, "be a man about this."

"Look, pal," Henry said and I thought they were going to fight, but there was no way they could get to each other across those three or four feet of open ocean.

"Captain," the guy said, "would you please move your vessel?"

"With pleasure," Henry said, and we did.

"I'm bored," I said on day number four of life at the dock with the hatches all closed. "There's something resembling the sun out there today. I'm going for a swim."

"You be careful," Henry said. "That sea's not going to be what you're used to."

"I'll go with you," Carter said, though I didn't know whether it was to get away from Henry or to be with me.

We went to the town beach on the northeast side of the island, which was normally crowded and a little crummy, though the hurricane had scoured it clean of both people and debris. I threw my towel down and leapt for the water with nothing in my head except how it would feel.

The waves were breaking about a hundred feet from shore, every fifth or sixth one running well enough for me to catch a short body surf. Henry was right, the waves were big for the Bahamas and much stronger than in any year before. Carter was easing in more slowly, holding his hands above his head, letting the waves crash against his thin torso, making funny faces each time they did.

I felt like I could stay in those waves forever, so I floated on my back till a big wave swamped me, and dove through as many in a row as I could. I swam out to the place just beyond where the waves were breaking, where there was nothing between me and Greenland, say, except one or two islands and a million miles of sea. Then I swam up and down the beach along the leading edge of the breakers. I did somersaults till I was dizzy. I floated again, this time with my eyes closed, then tried to guess when I'd be lifted by each surge of the sea.

I looked back at the beach and saw a sight at first I didn't understand: Carter, in the sand on his hands and knees. *A contact lens,* I thought, *a jellyfish bite, a shark attack.* I swam hard for the beach to see what was wrong.

Slowly it dawned on me that hard as I was swimming, I wasn't getting any closer to the beach. The ocean would let me get just inside the breaker zone, but it wouldn't give me anything more. *Rip current:* the words formed in my head bright as the marquee from a bad movie, followed immediately by *Don't panic,* that from my first-ever swimming instructor at the YMCA. And I knew then that what I saw in Carter's posture was exhaustion, that he had fought the sea with everything he had and beat it, just barely, and that he'd be no help whatsoever to me.

I stopped fighting for a moment and tried to breathe deeply, thinking *conserve your energy*, thinking *Carter should run for help and quick*, thinking *what were you thinking*, again, and again.

"Carter!" I screamed, and he either didn't hear me or he was still too shaken to look up.

I was being dragged sideways too. In a hundred more yards I'd be at the end of the beach, at the end of the island. Well on my way to Greenland without a boat. Panic rushed through me fast and true for the first time then and made my already tired limbs go even weaker.

"Carter!" I screamed again, and still he didn't look up.

I looked back behind me and saw a big wave coming in, the biggest of the day maybe, a wave I would never in my right mind try to ride, and decided in a split second that my only hope was to sacrifice myself. I let myself be lifted into it, swimming to catch it for all I was worth, and it did pick me up for a moment, high above the beach and all the rest of the ocean, and when it started to curl I curled with it, and it tumbled me over and over until I smashed headfirst into the gloriously solid sand.

As soon as I hit I dug in with my fingers and toes, my arms up to my elbows, anything that would hold me in the shallow water while the undertow tried to pull me back out. I crab-walked a few feet up the beach before the next wave came, and when it rushed around me I dug in again.

It took three more rounds of between-wave crawling till I

knew I had it licked for sure. Down the beach Carter had gotten himself to a sitting position. He gave me a tired thumbs-up and I returned it. It took half an hour to gather the energy to walk back across the island to the boat.

"The part of the story I don't get," Henry said when I had told him what happened and Carter had gotten into the shower, "is why if it was so hard for Carter to get himself in he didn't figure you'd be in trouble too."

"He couldn't have done anything even if he had," I said. "He was exhausted, he wouldn't have even made it onto his feet."

"You're being way too easy on him, Lucy," Henry said.

The shower stopped running and I put my finger to my lips. Carter stepped out of the head buck-naked and walked across the main cabin to the galley to get a cold beer.

"I don't suppose you have any personal rules about nudity in the absence of Bahamian officials," Carter said to Henry.

"No," Henry said, "but I am getting sick and tired of looking at your hairy ass."

Carter crossed the room again and pulled on a pair of sweatpants.

"*Phaedrus* doesn't like to come to the wind," Henry said to me, "but she'll find a way to do it for you whenever there's a need."

Carter and I were stoned and lying on our backs at the northernmost tip of the island. The sun had burst through the clouds that afternoon for the first time in five days, and you would have thought it was the face of Jesus the way the people of the island came out and danced in the streets.

The wind was still howling, all the roads several feet under water, but the sky had been clear for the few hours before the sun went down, and it was clear still, fifteen minutes past dark.

The Milky Way was above us, adding stars at the rate of a couple hundred per minute. Behind us the hurricane waves still crashed on the sand. Henry was back on the boat making mashed potatoes with coconut milk and my favorite of his island recipes: guava duck.

"I told Sarah I'd use this trip to get my head sorted out," Carter said. "Told her I'd know whether I wanted door number one, number two, or number three."

"One is marrying her, I take it," I said. "Two is the wild life. What's three?"

"Finding someone I am physically attracted to, and trying to make it work with her."

He rolled up on his elbow, his body toward mine. I couldn't see the color of his eyes in the dark, but I saw what I thought was hope in them.

"What makes you think you wouldn't be the same way with the next woman as you are with Sarah?" I said.

He rolled back onto his back and put his hands over his eyes. "If I thought I would," he said, "I'd have to kill myself."

"Let's go the bar," I said, "and have ourselves a Goombay Smash."

"Which is?" Carter asked.

"The Bahamian remedy for anyone who starts talking about killing himself."

"Lucy," he said, "are you going to get me drunk and try to take advantage of me?"

"We're going to start with the getting drunk part," I said. "We'll wait and see what happens after that."

Carter and I woke up together in my big aft cabin to the sound of Henry playing Italian opera, loud all over the boat. Carter had gotten good and drunk on the Goombay Smashes, admitting to me only after downing three that he was a lightweight and shouldn't be allowed more than one.

He'd fallen sound asleep in my bunk before I'd gotten out of the head, and when I looked down at him, his sweet face and lovely long limbs, I couldn't resist crawling in beside him. I'd slept like a baby all through the night, but I noticed that at some point Carter must have taken off his pants again.

"Hey crew," Henry said, "I got johnnycakes on the grill. The wind's under thirty for the first time this week and we sail for Nassau at sunset."

"We're coming," Carter said, without looking at me, but when I made a move to rise he grabbed my hand.

"And before we leave, Carter," Henry said, "I want you to look at that generator one more time, make sure it's gonna run the bilge pump in case the weather turns on us again."

"Aye-aye, Captain," Carter said. He wrapped his long fingers around the back of my hand, kept his body horizontal.

"And what do you think," Henry said, "about my jerry-rigged keyway in the driveshaft?" His voice was close now, right outside the cabin door. "Do you think it'll hold up if we need to do a little reversing to get out of this harbor?"

Carter put my hand on the sheet that lay across his stomach, palm down, ran it down the front of him until it sat on top of his erection, then he closed his hand around mine, around the sheet, around it, so tight I couldn't move.

"I think so," he said to Henry, "but we might want to take a minute this morning to try and find somebody who's got welding tools."

His hand was still on my hand. I closed my fingers even tighter, tried to wiggle them a little; he pressed his hand down harder, holding mine there and also dead still.

"Yeah," Henry said, "I think I'll let you do that while I sump pump that engine compartment one more time." I heard Henry's hand on the door latch, saw it make a quarter turn.

Carter removed his hand; mine lay there, a bird flown into a clean piece of glass.

"Are you guys getting up," Henry said, still outside the door, "or what?"

"Yeah, right now!" Carter said and bolted out of bed.

It was my favorite sail in all the world, the overnight run across the Banks, no water deeper than sixteen feet, no boats, no reefs, no channel-marker light since the *Blackhawk II* had wiped it out one careless New Year's Eve, and now twenty knots of wind behind us, surfing down the shallow waves of a blue-green Bahamian following sea.

Orion gleamed above us, so bright and clear that I could have had his photograph if I'd had a steady place to mount my camera. On the other side of the mast the Pleiades, the seven daughters of Atlas, sparkled like a tennis bracelet fallen on a cloth of black silk. In the early-morning hours Leo would be up, the meteors they called the Leonids falling out of him at the rate of up to a hundred thousand an hour.

"Orion was the most beautiful man the world has ever known," I said. "Maybe he still is."

"I thought Carter said *he* was the most beautiful man in the world," Henry said.

"And he was so tall," I said, "that he could wade through any sea with his head above the waters."

"Shawn Bradley could walk across *this* sea with his head above water," Henry said.

"Who wants rum punch?" Carter said.

"I want the Pleiades," Henry said, "all seven sisters at once."

"So did Orion," I said. "That's why Zeus turned them into stars. To give them a break.

"Orion's first wife was so vain she was banished to the underworld," I said, "and his second wife's father was so jealous he made Orion blind."

"This sounds more like Henry all the time," Carter said.

"Then Artemis, the virgin goddess of hunting, fell in love with him and sicked Scorpio on him in a jealous fit," I said, "and that was the end for Orion."

"I thought a pack of love-crazed women tore him limb from limb," Henry said.

"That was Orpheus," I said.

"How do you guys know all this shit?" Carter said.

"And in the end all the Pleiades married gods," I said, "except for one, who married a man. She's the dim one. I mean, she's the one you can hardly see."

We were coming into Nassau harbor, the moon fat and full in the west now, dawn breaking over the fish market, over the Paradise Island Bridge. Orion was setting in the west with the moon. On the eastern horizon, his enemy, Scorpio, was on the rise.

Henry had left me at the helm all the way from the tongue of the ocean into the busy harbor. I kept waiting for him to take the wheel from me, but he never did.

"I wish I'd brought my moon map," I said. "It's so close tonight we could name all the seas."

"You mean you don't have all those committed to memory too?" Carter said.

"I remember that the Sea of Crisis lies halfway between Tranquility and Fertility," I said.

"As it does on earth, my dear," Henry said, "as it does on earth."

Even at that hour boats were hurtling in and out of the harbor, and the currents were making it hard to keep all the channel markers in line.

"After the princess's father blinded Orion," I said, "an oracle told him to gaze at the dawn to regain his sight, and he did, but then Aurora, the dawn goddess, fell in love with him too. I think that's what made Artemis so mad."

"It's hell to be beautiful," Henry said. "Isn't that right, Carter?"

"It beats the alternative," Carter said.

I was keeping my eyes on the harbor buoys, trying to tell if any of the cruise ships were moving.

"We almost got married," Henry said. "Didn't we, Lucy?"

"We did?" I said.

"Last summer," he said, "right before Candy and I got engaged."

"I must have missed that," I said.

"I'm gonna call Sarah," Carter said, "as soon as we tie up to the dock and say *Groundhog Day. Marry me. Aloha.*"

"A guy gets up one day and steps in a hole," Henry said.

"Every morning a celestial cow gives birth to a golden calf," I said, "and every night the woman of the sky opens her mouth to swallow him."

"Who said that?" Carter said.

"I don't remember," I said. "I read it somewhere."

"Lucy," Henry said, "do you ever get your head out of your stories?"

"The moon," I said, "is a woman's first husband."

Moving from One Body of Water to Another

THIS STORY BEGINS WITH Carlos Castaneda. In February, at LAX. I had missed the only plane I'd ever missed in my life, and let me tell you, I shave it finer than OJ, week in, week out. I do it for the adrenaline—these days I'm not out in the wilds as much as I'd like—but never before had a plane actually left without me.

That day the buses and taxis were gridlocked like I'd never seen them coming into the Loop, so I left my rent-a-car running by the curb at Terminal One and made a break for it across the parking lot to Terminal Three. I went screaming through security and along the moving sidewalk figuring I had it made. The gate agent admitted that the plane pushed back four minutes early.

159

It wasn't like it mattered. I was going to New York City. There was another flight in less than an hour. I had no business there until the next day. But I was mad anyway. In those days I'd use any excuse to scowl, which is what I was doing when Carlos Castaneda walked up.

Now let me make it clear right off the bat that I was never a groupie. Sure I read the books when I was twenty. The first three anyway. But I don't remember much.

I was living in those days from campground to campground in the national parks: Arches, Canyonlands, Capitol Reef. The Grand Circle Tour is what they called it. Twelve national parks in ten warm Winnebago days.

My then boyfriend and I lived there a whole year, pulling up United States Department of the Interior survey stakes and digging out guardrails, moving camp every two weeks according to the rule book, going to town for groceries and a shower—that's right—whether we needed it or not.

We didn't have any peyote to test Castaneda's theories but we found the next best thing: Boone's Farm Strawberry Hill and homegrown marijuana. The combination made those big desert rocks get right up and stand in your path.

But that was ten years ago; the boyfriend is an attorney now, and I take pictures for adventure magazines, which doesn't exactly make me an ecowarrior but it sure beats the hell out of law. What I'm trying to say is that it had been a long time since I'd even thought about Carlos Castaneda, and even if I had I'm not sure that what I thought would have been good.

"Excuse me," he said, and I looked up into the face of a compact Chicano man with electric eyes and laugh lines deep as arroyos running away from them. "My name is Carlos Castaneda," he said, "and I have one or two things to tell you."

What everybody says now is, *How do you know it was really him*, like that is the pertinent question. *It was him*, I say, like I learned in graduate school, *or another man by the same name*. I mean, is it less interesting if it was just some guy who thought he was Carlos Castaneda, or more?

"Hello," is what I said to Castaneda.

"Please forgive the intrusion," he said. "I can see that you are angry."

"No," I said, "I'm not. I just missed my plane."

The laugh lines in his eyes got even deeper.

"I am the reason you missed your airplane," he said.

"No . . ." I said, "I don't think you even make the top ten."

"Listen to me," he said. "I have come here to tell you that your life is about to open up in ways you never could have imagined." He took a step toward me and took both of my hands in his. "You won't be able to stop it, so you mustn't try; you must surrender to it, or be lost."

There was something about his eyes. I know it's not like me to say this. But I couldn't have looked away if I tried.

"Spend at least an hour a day in the sight of open water," he said. "It is also important that you move to a house that has hardwood floors." *Move?* I thought, *not again*, but he tugged on my hands and I nodded. "You will meet a man," he said, "who thinks with precision. You would do well to love him."

I nodded again.

"I'm afraid that's all I have to tell you," he said. "I have to go to Mexico City now."

161

He held my hands for one more moment. "You mustn't get upset about missing airplanes, Lucy," he said. "That should be the very first step." He sparkled his eyes at me one more time, and then he was gone before I could ask how he knew my name.

The first thing I did when I got to the hotel in New York was call my friend Henry in Chicago.

"I've got the most amazing thing to tell you," I said.

He said, "As I recall, *The Bridges of Madison County* begins something like that."

"Just listen," I said, "for once in your life."

"Okay," he said and I began.

"I just don't get how he knew my name," I said, when I had told him, "how he knew that's where I'd be. Am I supposed to believe he altered the entire air and ground transportation schedule of an international airport on my behalf?"

"This is what Carlos Castaneda does, Lucy," Henry said. "I mean, this is the man's line of work."

"So what do you think I should do?" I said.

"I'd go find yourself some open water," he said. "I'd look for an apartment with hardwood floors."

"You're making this sound like the kind of thing that happens every day," I said.

"It does," he said, "to somebody." I could hear him channel surfing in the background.

"Don't let me keep you with my petty miracles," I said.

He said, "I thought you were going to tell me something really amazing. I thought you were going to tell me you got a free cab ride in New York."

The phone rang again before my hand was off it.

"You are a national treasure," Carter said into the telephone, "and I'm the nation."

"Well, well," is the thing I'd started to say to all the Carterisms I didn't understand. "You sure found me in a hurry this time."

Carter Thompson was prouder of his command of the information superhighway than he was of anything else. Fax phones, car phones, cell phones, voice mail, webs and nets and modems. He was so well connected that sometimes he knew the next city I'd be in even before I did. His most prized possession was his brand-new headset. He could be on the phone all day long, he said, and never have to use his hands.

"I'm doing a six-day shoot on the beach in Oregon," he said. "Is Oregon on your way to anywhere soon?"

"Not really," I said. "But I suppose I could swing by on my way back to Oakland."

The way I described it to my friends was that Carter was what I'd had for the past several months instead of a relationship. We'd worked our way up from talking on the phone once a month to once a week to once a day when his forever girlfriend Sarah finally got sick of waiting for him to propose and dropped the ax.

He sang seventies songs to my answering machine and sent me a teddy bear that said *I love you* in French when you squeezed it, made from an over-the-phone recording of Carter's very own voice. I named the bear Chip and hugged him to me night after night while Carter flew from one end of the country to the other looking for the landscapes in which the biggest stars in Hollywood would talk to aliens, scale mountain tops, wage war, and fall in love.

He sang "Fire and Rain" from a hotel room in Minneapolis, "Time in a Bottle" from a seaside inn in San Diego, "Anticipation" from a cellular phone on a set just west of Washington, D.C. If I was home and his room had the capability we'd both switch onto speakerphone and sing the songs together, me piecing them out on my piano, him strumming away on his guitar.

So far our face-to-face time consisted of one long weekend in Baton Rouge, one stoned night in Chicago, one sailing trip with Henry through a hurricane, and three near misses in West Coast cities, all three due to Carter's tendency to overcommit.

We hadn't ever had what I would call a real live kiss. Carter told me on the phone one time that he'd never had sex with anyone that was as good as his fantasies and I couldn't tell if he was kidding or not. Behind his back I called what we had virtual love.

"How long since you've been in your apartment?" Carter said.

"Eight weeks," I said, and he said, "Going on nine."

"You're an animal," he said.

"Animals have burrows," I said, "or dens or nests or caves."

"Do you know how many housewives in America would trade their lives for yours?" Carter said.

"I don't know any housewives," I said. "I don't even know the people who live next door."

"Two days in Oregon," Carter said. "Think about it. We'll have fun."

I hung up the phone and walked down Eighty-ninth Street to Riverside Park to watch the sunset over the Hudson. The sky was an entirely different color than it would have been in California, where the light was blue and sultry, or back in the Rockies, where it was golden and crystal clear. Back *home* in the Rockies I almost said, but caught myself just in time.

Home was a word that was making me choke up with such increasing regularity; it no longer even depended upon the context: an ad for discount home furnishings could do it, or the lit-up scoreboard at a baseball game.

I had tried everything I could think of to make Oakland my home. I bought expensive pots and pans so I'd want to stay home and cook dinner. Last Valentine's Day I had gone to the florist to buy myself purple tulips and once I'd got them in my hand I thought they would look great on top of a shiny black piano, so I walked straight to a music store and went into debt to buy one of those too. But I never changed my driver's license or my vehicle registration when I left the Rocky Mountains. I still did my banking from a thousand miles away.

I pulled a handful of baggage-claim checks out of my jacket pocket. Chicago, Vancouver, Honolulu, Anchorage, L.A. One job had piled up on top of another until I'd backed myself right up against my yearly trip to see all the photo editors I worked for in New York.

I didn't live in the best neighborhood in Oakland so I'd started carrying my portfolio around with me from city to city, negatives and originals, everything I had to show for the last five years of work. It was fine until I got to L.A. and got paranoid, afraid someone might come into my hotel room while I

165

was on a shoot, or in the middle of the night while I was sleeping, and take it all away.

I'm not proud of what I did next, but I'm afraid it's part of the story. I spent a couple hours of my only day off driving around the suburbs of Los Angeles looking for a storage unit in a good neighborhood. Then I spent another hour walking among the hundreds of identical cement units to see which one was the very most safe.

I wish you could have seen it. The big 10x20 cement storage unit, my little gray portfolio leaning up against one long and barren side.

What I probably should have done next is check myself into a mental hospital. Or at least one of those places California is famous for where it seems like a resort with pools and pastel colors but it turns out all the aerobics teachers have Ph.D.s in stress-related disease.

What I did instead was work my fifth hundred-hour week in a row. Driving back out to the storage unit to get the portfolio was one more reason I was late for the plane.

I walked to the section of Riverside Park where I could see the open water of the Hudson and waited for it to give me a sign: a leaping sea creature spelling words with his tail perhaps, or a glimmering light shooting skyward. Maybe the Hudson River would part and I would walk across it, straight into a walkup with hardwood floors and a man who fixed watches sitting by the fireplace in an intricately hand-carved chair.

I turned back to the east, back toward the city, the lights of the buildings making the sky so bright it looked as if there was another even brighter sun setting behind them. The world began to spin 180 degrees in the wrong direction, and I got confused for a minute about which coast I was on, but in the next moment the illusion faded, and I was just looking at a big city that would never in my lifetime be dark enough to see the stars.

I remembered one time when I was taking my river boat down Westwater Canyon, on the Colorado. It was highwater, seventeen thousand cubic feet per second of river forced between the walls of a canyon so narrow you could reach out your oars and almost touch both sides. The terrible teens, they called it at that level, for all the crazy lateral waves and hydraulics it caused in the river.

The rapids come at you nonstop for a three-mile period and I was trying to keep my nose pointed at each of those waves coming from every direction, and read the river map and bail water all at the same time.

I'd been looking down at the river map next to me only for a second or two when a hydraulic so slick I didn't feel it turned my boat right around and when I looked up to take the next wave I didn't realize that I was facing back up the river.

What I remember most about that day is not the chaotic and crazy water, but the sensation of that moment, how when it dawned on me a few seconds later that I was pointed in the wrong direction, it was the canyon, and not me, that whirled around to catch up.

The next morning, I had to be at Madison and Fifty-seventh by nine-thirty. The day was dank, gray, and rainy, indis-

167

putable proof that the groundhog had seen his shadow only two days before. The driver of the cab was Pakistani and we talked about his mother and brothers and sisters at home, how he had to send them more than half his money, how he would never be able to improve upon his new life in America because they depended on him and always would.

He pulled over to the curb in front of the address I gave him. The fare was seven dollars and eighty cents. He turned halfway around to look at me through the opening in the plastic that separated us.

"I have something to tell you," he said.

"Okay." I said. You can bet by now I was all ears.

"Do you see my hand?" He held it in front of me.

"Yes," I said. His eyes were flat and the color of gunmetal.

He said, "Do you know what this hand is capable of?"

"No," I said.

He put his hand inside his jacket like Napoleon. "Now can you see my hand?" he said.

"No," I said.

"Now do you know what my hand is capable of?"

"No," I said.

"Do you know the size of my hand?" he said. "Do you know its color? Do you know if it is damaged in any way? Do you know if I have all of my fingers?"

"No," I said.

He pulled his hand out of his jacket, brown, intact, empty. He said, "Now can you see my hand?"

"Yes," I said.

"Now do you know what my hand is capable of?"

"No," I said.

He snapped his hand against the Plexiglas that separated us so hard we both felt it, the whole cab vibrating with the force.

"Is there really any difference between when you can see my hand, and when you can't see it?" he said, his gun-colored eyes no longer flat.

"Not much," I said.

"Do you understand what I am trying to tell you?"

"No," I said.

"You will," he said, "you will," and turned back around to face the wheel. I held nine dollars up to the window, saw one dark eye flash in the rearview mirror.

"Don't be ridiculous!" he said. "Get out of the cab!"

"No, please, take it," I said.

"Get out!" he said, and out I got.

The first thing I did was go to a phone booth.

"Henry," I said, "I got a free cab ride in New York."

If you've never really had a home, even if you decide you want one, it's harder than hell to know where to start. My father worked around the clock and around the country; my mother was a person whose life had left her more confused than anything, and she drank water glasses full of vodka to make the confusion go away.

My mother ran away from the Colorado mountains to Broadway when she was thirteen years old and made it, marginally, in the theater. Then she met my father and gave up everything she loved, as she was fond of saying, to have me.

My grandmother never forgave my mother for leaving the

west, never forgave her for choosing my father, the most eligible bachelor in Trenton, New Jersey. She hated that he couldn't fix a fence if his life depended on it, hated that he didn't know the difference between a posthole digger and a manhole cover, was ignorant enough to ask her one time what a cattle guard was for. Most of all she hated the things my father said to her, and hated my mother for letting him say them.

On my parents' last visit to Colorado, when I was only a baby, my father walked around the farmhouse worrying that he or I would catch something, mumbling under his breath words like *fat-ass redneck* and *white dirt trash*. My grandmother told my mother that if she couldn't get him to control his mouth they could come next time without him, and my father said over his dead body and they bundled me up and we drove away. After that my mother and my grandmother had no communication, my mother loyal to my father as a tick on a hound, my grandmother too proud, I always figured, to try to break the feud.

I tried to get in touch with my grandmother a couple of times during the years I lived in the Rockies, but there was no response to the letters I sent. It felt too much like sneaking around behind my mother's back to make more of an effort than that. Then the two women died the same year without either of them knowing it. They hadn't spoken, at that point, for more than thirty years.

My father and I talked more often than we had before my mother died but never with much more success. He had called me a few days before I left Oakland the last time to tell me that he'd just realized that there was no scenario in which he was going to reap the rewards of his life insurance policy, and that if I wanted the money after he was dead I'd have to start paying the premiums next month.

On my third morning in New York the sun came out again and I had three appointments to make in four hours. I probably couldn't have swung it under the best of conditions, but then I got stuck in a nonexpress elevator. Fifty-six floors . . . and I swear we stopped on every other one. Models, secretaries, computer heads, construction guys. You could have populated a whole season of sit-coms with the people who came and went in that one long ride.

Finally it was just me and the Rastafarian messenger boy I'd started with on fifty-six—primary colors from head to toe, dreadlocks to the middle of his back.

"Do you know what time it is?" I said, afraid to hear the answer.

"It is time," he said, smiling bigger than an Osmond, "to go to the beach."

"That would be nice," I said.

"Anything is possible," he said. "You only have to believe." He stepped out on the second floor, and the door closed behind him.

"What?" I said to elevator's mirrored ceiling. "What?"

The doors opened on the lobby level and I stepped out, and then out again, into the sun.

"Are you coming to Oregon tomorrow," Carter said into the phone, "or what?"

"I'm sorry," I said, "I thought I'd know by now the right thing to do."

"You mean a little bird would have told you?"

"Or a cab driver," I said, "or a messenger boy."

I thought of Carter's lovely long hands, I thought of our first night in Baton Rouge, him singing songs to me under the stars. Then I thought about all those hours waiting for nothing in Baggage Claim. His voice on my answering machine, apologetic, contrite, never more full of love.

"How much time would you have?" I said. "How long would I stay?"

"You know I never know the answers to those questions in advance, Lucy," he said.

"But what are we talking," I said, "minutes, hours, or days?"

"Hours," he said, and when I didn't say anything he said, "At least. You wouldn't love me," he said, "if you saw me every day."

"Who said I love you?" I said.

"So," Carter said, "are you coming or not?"

"I'll call you back in fifteen minutes," I said, and I hung up the phone and called Henry.

"Henry," I said, "do you think that Carter thinks with precision?"

"I think Carter thinks very precisely," he said, "about whatever it is that will make Carter happy."

"I knew you were going to say that," I said.

"Then why did you bother to call?" he said.

"It's weird," I said. "I can't tell whether or not we're a couple."

"Please don't make me say a couple of what," Henry said.

"Henry," I said, "do you think I'm in love with Carter?"

"The odds, I'm afraid, would support it," he said.

"But clearly you would not," I said.

"Has he kissed you yet?" Henry said.

"Not exactly," I said.

"What about Sarah?" he said.

"They're history. Carter says it's her doing this time. She sent him a postcard from Paris, *having a wonderful time, glad you're not here.*"

"Lucy," Henry said, "has it ever occurred to you that *you* made Castaneda come to the airport?"

"You mean that I made him up?" I said.

"I mean," Henry said, "that you are the one with the power, and not him."

I swung the last coach seat on the only nonstop to Portland, one of those late-afternoon flights where the sun keeps on setting for almost three hours, where you almost keep up with it while you fly.

I watched yellow fade to orange, fade to red, fade to magenta until the whole sky was a purple so deep it looked eternal, a single band of red back-lit and on fire inside. I stared out at that sunset so long and so hard that it lost itself somehow in its own beauty, became purer than anything I could affix with a word. I stared until I wasn't sure if there had been a sunset at all out that window or if it, too, was something I had made, from the inside of the airplane, using only my eyes.

I'd called the rent-a-car company in advance, and asked for a car with a tape deck. If Carter and I were going to start something actual, I wanted the soundtrack to be under my control. But it was a big weekend in Portland, antique car shows and cowboy conventions. The agent said I was lucky to get an economy car, some had am/fm, some had nothing at all.

The guy at Alamo was Lithuanian, small, dark, and friendly.

"And you are in town," he said, "for business or for pleasure?"

"Pleasure, I hope," I said, "but I'm not holding my breath."

"And what is your business?" he said, fingers poised on the keyboard.

"I take pictures," I said.

"You take pictures like with a Kodak Instamatic?" he said. "Or you take pictures like Avedon and Stieglitz?"

"Somewhere in between," I said, smiling now. "You are a fan of Avedon and Stieglitz?"

"To name only a few," he said. "I have dedicated my life to studying the photographic masters." He looked up for a moment, hard into my eyes. "Do you believe what I have told you?" he said.

"Sure," I said. "Of course."

"Well, in that case," he said, "I'm going to give you a mid-size convertible for the price of an Escort. Unlimited mileage as well." He shoved my credit card back across the counter. "Now," he said, "would you like a tape deck?"

When I got to my hotel in Cannon Beach my mail had

caught up to me and there was a letter asking me to call a lawyer in Colorado.

"At long last your grandmother's estate has been settled," he said from there the next morning, "and much to everyone's surprise she left you the ranch near Hope, Colorado."

"The ranch near Hope," I said, "the ranch on the Rio Grande?"

"Practically *in* the Rio Grande, is what I hear," he said, "but it's a beautiful piece of property."

"I don't understand," I said. "We barely even met."

"Your cousins don't understand either," he said, "but it's probably a blessing. Nobody on the other side of the family would have the money to dig it out of the hole."

"It's in a hole?" I said.

"A tax hole," he said. "Seems nobody's paid taxes on it since 1982. It'll go up for auction this summer, unless you need a project that'll take all your time and drive you crazy. You could put it on the market yourself, of course, maybe come out a few bucks ahead in the end."

"Wait a minute," I said. "Do you know if this ranch has hardwood floors?"

"I think maybe you are getting the wrong mental picture . . ." he said. "It's a cabin, a shack, been for years in disrepair."

"But the floors are made of wood, surely," I said.

I could hear him rustling papers on the other end of the line.

"I want it," I said, before he could answer, "and I don't want you to do anything until I've seen it for myself."

"No," Henry said before I'd even gotten to the part about the back taxes. "Absolutely not."

"It would be mine, Henry," I said, "my place in the world."

"Come to Chicago." he said. "I'll make you a great deal on a dream home in Sanctuary II."

"Come on," I said, "what's the worst thing that can happen?"

"You spend all your money to make the place livable, you don't have a hundred dollars to get on a plane, it snows six million feet and you can't get out your driveway, the days get shorter and shorter and you shoot yourself in the head."

"See," I said, "that doesn't sound so bad."

"I bet it comes with built-in back taxes," he said.

"No," I lied, and laughed a little, "at least I lucked out there."

"I want to say, don't come crying to me," Henry said, "but you'll need to."

"Thanks," I said, "for everything, I mean it, Henry. I'm feeling good."

The next day was the sunniest in the history of Oregon Februaries and warm. The offshore rock remnants northwesterners called sea stacks gleamed where they rose from the water, the winter light washing them in deep shades of amber. Carter came by my room midafternoon and we went straight to the beach. He wanted to walk, apparently thought that would be the best way to avoid whatever was about to happen, but I wanted to stand at the water's edge, so he stood there too.

After all the winter storms the sea was violent, moody, a

slightly different color than usual, bluer than green and tinged with silver.

Behind us people moved past in clusters like stories. An Hispanic girl and her new boyfriend, both of them supple and brilliant in the first blush of love. A family—was it just one family—a merry-go-round of children and Chihuahuas and cockers and strollers. A couple in their eighties moving slowly, holding hands.

"Fifty years together," Carter said, "maybe more."

"No way," I said. "First date. I saw him in the personal ads." The tide was coming in and the waves rolled down toward us through the pockets between the sea stacks, tumbled over themselves and crisscrossed like rapids in a river, but this was no river, there were no banks, a million miles square of continuous motion; only the sea stacks were solid, hiccups of figure in an unfathomable ground.

But there was something about those sea stacks, the way they made a dark backdrop for the water. They made the waves look as though they were falling from an incredible height. And those waves *were* high, after the storm, but they couldn't be as high as they looked, ten or twelve or maybe fourteen feet above us, and close. And when they reared up like they did, full of themselves and the backwash of the ones that had come before them, they looked as though they would surely swallow us, and all the people around us, and the beach and even a few of the houses, the ones that sat low in the dunes. But as they raced toward us after crashing, there was some undetectable moment when the illusion faded, and they became the right size for waves again.

"I'm usually very demonstrative in a relationship," Carter said, and I took my eyes from the tumbling water long enough to hold his gaze. "Even with Sarah, even after all those years, we still held hands."

"A relationship, Carter," I said, "is that what we're in?"

"Virtually," he said, and I might have laughed at him then, but I didn't.

"Let's walk," he said again, and this time I moved away from the edge with him.

We stopped at a jewelry counter a bearded guy had made out of a wrecked lifeguard stand, but I was feeling too restless even to look down.

"Look at this, Lucy," Carter said. "It might be something you'd like." It was an amber ring, a pretty stone, a little too big and clunky for me.

"*That's* not the ring *you* want," the jeweler said and I looked up at him then. His eyes were intense, and black like the seagulls.

"Oh, no?" I said. "And what ring is it that I do want?"

"Here," he said, reaching into the case and handing me a ring. It was a flat silver circle with a little mountain range of raised bronze. Two tiny stick figures were carved into the side of the mountain. Two lines of tiny dots led from their heads up into the sky. It was a silly ring, a kitschy ring. "No thank you," I said and tried to put it back in his hand.

"Those two little men on the side of the mountain are Don Juan and Carlos Castaneda," he said, not taking the ring. "See the deep thoughts coming out of their heads?"

I turned the ring over in my hand. I looked closely at the lines of deep thoughts.

178

"You're right," I said. "That's the ring I want."

"What's the matter?" he said, his black eyes bouncing from my hand to my face. "You got some synchronicity happening in your life right now?"

"So much so," I said, "that's it's threatening to fuck with my normal level of cynicism."

He backed away from me then, took the thirty dollars out of my hand. "Don't worry," he said, "that always comes back."

I took the ring and slipped it on the small finger of my left hand.

"What was that all about?" Carter said when we left the jeweler, and I got ready to tell him, but he started combing his hair in the middle of my first sentence, and I knew he didn't really want to know.

I turned my head back to the water, watched how high and crazy it was there in front of the sea stacks, how calm and regular the waves on either side.

We'd had a talk on Henry's boat one late windblown evening where I'd told Carter I'd never kissed a man first and he said his sisters taught him something like fifteen hundred tests that he should do to make sure a woman wanted to be kissed before he kissed her. He said he would get so caught up in the tests that he'd still be going through them long after the moment passed.

But this was a different kind of test, so I kept my eyes on the water, which was crashing harder now into the sand in front of us. And I wanted to say, "Carter, would you just look out there and tell me that those waves right in front of the sea stacks are higher than they are everywhere else in this ocean."

179

Because those words *optical illusion* were slipping farther and farther from me, just the way *sunset* had the night before.

The tide was coming in and the waves crashed harder still and I watched them falling. I wanted to catch them in the act of getting small, of tumbling back into what we could all agree was reality, but then one I watched didn't get small, and it hit the beach running and lapped hard around our ankles, a tease from the other side.

"The ocean is higher right there than anywhere else," I said finally. "I know that it can't be, but it is."

"Maybe we should walk," he said, and touched the side of my face, and I thought again about the sunset on the airplane, the way it had stopped being a sunset, and started becoming something else entirely, some more authentic form of beauty than anything I could name.

"I met Carlos Castaneda in an airport last week," I said. "He tried to tell me some important things."

"Really, Lucy," Carter said. He put his arm around my shoulders and tried to guide me away from the waves that were getting bigger and closer still, but I wouldn't move.

"You don't think this is like God or something, do you?" At that he backed, just slightly, away. I was getting close to something then and I could feel it, like maybe I had jumped, for a moment, onto the wheel that makes everything turn, and at any second it might send me flying backwards, and I didn't want to miss anything in the moment I was there.

And I didn't know, exactly, why I couldn't stop looking at the place where the water fell from the sea stacks, or why I needed so badly to make that big flat ocean into a river. I'd made things up all my life that way and believed in them. I thought love was like that, too, that you could frame it like a photograph, according to your need.

It was that part of me that stared at the water, the very same part that knew that for every positive image there was a pure and perfect negative, that right on the other side of the thin piece of paper called *making things up*, was a whole nother story, and that story was about learning to believe in the things that had been there all along. It was no different from believing in the sunset, really; the translation of object to offering, a simple matter of faith.

And I understood finally what the Pakistani driver had meant—was it a week ago to the day—when he smacked his hand against the Plexiglas window that separated us and said, "Is there really any difference between when you can see my hand and when you can't see it?" I knew the answer now. It was that there is every difference in the world—and none. It was that intuition is nothing more than the most likely junction of the thing called will and the thing called chance. It was that belief is a firework: precarious, marvelous, momentary, and bright.

And it was at that moment that Carter Thompson gave me the first real live kiss I'd ever had from him, long and hard, but soft in a way too, full of all the feeling he had inside him, though whether it was love or only gallantry I couldn't say for sure.

And no sooner had he kissed me than he broke free of my arms and went running into the water, sweatshirt and pants and shoes and socks soaking, and he ran back out again shaking and dripping like a dog with a Frisbee, looking at me for all the world like he was waiting for a treat.

"And now the bad news," he said, looking at his watch. "I didn't want to tell you earlier, didn't want to ruin the day, but I fly in an hour to Amarillo, Texas. Cows. Really big ones. Taking over the world."

"You'll miss the sunset," I said, "among other things."

"You must see it alone, Lucy," Carter said. "It is Carlos Castaneda's will."

I almost laughed along with him. Then I almost smacked him across the face. Then I put my hands on either side of his high and beautiful cheekbones the way I had imagined it a thousand times and his skin was soft and warm and flawless, just the way I knew it would be.

And I knew then for sure that I did love Carter Thompson but not very much and that I wouldn't continue to love him for very much longer. That first I would watch the warm February sun sink into this icy West Coast ocean and then I'd go back to California to my books and my world-class pots and pans and my shiny black piano, but that I would not stay there very much longer either.

I knew, as well, that my time at the ocean was almost over, that open water could also be a river, that home might be a broken-down shack with hardwood floors and somebody else's furniture, a place that could forgive you all your years of expectations, a place that could allow you—in time—to forgive yourself.

And I knew I would be alone in Hope but not forever. I'd done harder things than be alone before in my life; an awful damn lot of them. And I knew that when the alone time was over I'd never need again to try to save my life by locking it into a 10x20 cement block container, that there was a man out there somewhere waiting for me who thought with precision, and that I'd be way too smart by that time to settle for anybody's virtual love.

Then Carter was gone and I stood alone and watched the sun fall into the ocean and I watched the light show all around it, the way the sand glowed, translucent, like the surface of the brain of the world.

Two little girls, just shy of thirteen, long-limbed and long-haired, moved down the beach between me and the water, the glowing sky, perfectly fluid, perfectly free. They were silhouettes, nothing more, so when the one closer to me threw her head back in laughter I wasn't even slightly surprised to find myself laughing too.

And I made the earth spin 180 degrees again, just like I did that day on the river, just like I did that night in New York, only this time I was standing on the brink of a whole new ocean, and the sun wasn't setting this time, it was coming up.

Like Goodness
Under Your Feet

HOPE IS A PRETTY TOWN, stuck right at the mouth of a big box canyon, two rock walls standing on either side of Main Street like sentinels. There isn't much more to it than the one street: the Kentucky Belle grocery, the True Value Hardware, the Crooked Creek Saloon, the Hope Hotel, the First National Bank of Hope with bars still on the windows, a shop that sells jewelry made from silver and braided horsehair.

Willow Creek runs right behind Main Street, through a cement flume that used to carry the silver down from the mines above town in the old days. A faded historical marker says that a hundred years ago, three hundred people a day were moving into Hope to crawl all over the country with

184

pickaxes and gunny sacks, and the silver was pouring out of the mountain by the trainload.

"If you want the real stories," a voice says behind me, "you've got to talk to the locals."

I turn to face a thin woman with sharp brown eyes and a lot of freckles.

"And you would be one of those," I say.

"B. J. Blair," she says. "Twenty-nine years here and I'm still not talking to myself, too often."

"I'm Lu . . ."

"Please don't insult my intelligence. You're Marge Cunningham's granddaughter Lucy come to take over the ranch upriver. Anybody with eyes could see that."

"Is that right?" I say, but not without a little twilight-zone tingle in my stomach.

"The resemblance is uncanny," B.J. says, "but surely I'm not the first person to notice."

"I didn't know her," I say. "She and my mother had a fight more than thirty years ago."

"Must have been a big one," B.J. says.

A UPS van comes screaming onto Main Street, right out of the commercial. It's the first vehicle to come into town since I pulled in a half hour ago.

"She spoke well of you," B.J. says, "was always bragging on you winning this or that award."

"I had no idea," I say. "I tried to meet her, a couple of times."

"People are proud," B.J. says. "Then they die. Come on up to the Café. I'll make you some lunch."

I get lunch and the short version of Hope's history to go with it. How Rutherford B. Hope found the first silver practically by accident up at the Holy Moses Mine a thousand feet above town, how brokers as far away as Paris and Madrid knew the town by name after that, how during the mining boom the town burned down to the ground three times in fires set late at night by drunkards, and how each time the merchants were so eager to make money that they had it up and working again by noon the next day.

B.J. tells me how the mine stayed open when so many others closed at the turn of the century, stayed open through the twenties and thirties, decade after decade, sizing down until the hippies came in the sixties and took over at least half of the houses that belonged to the miners who were starting to die.

When the mine finally shut down the last of its operations in the late seventies, the population dipped to less than two hundred and Hope almost became a ghost town, almost lost its school. A group of townswomen, my grandmother among them, fought with the state to keep the school open and won.

"The population has leveled off at around three hundred," B.J. says, "but the realtors still look more kindly at you if you have a pack of kids in the car when you arrive. You got any plans to bear children?"

"Not immediately," I say.

"Too bad," she says. "At least you're of child-bearing age. Maybe you should start with a dog."

"Maybe I should start with a houseplant," I say. "I'm not known for how well I take care of things."

"A dog first," B.J. says, "then a friend, maybe," and her face is as blunt as an invitation.

186

"From what I hear," I say, "my grandmother's place might not be in any shape to receive company."

"Wait," she says, "you mean you've not seen it?"

"No," I say, "I just drove in."

"Then don't waste your time talking to me," she says, "get out there this minute and see your place."

"Is it a wreck?" I say, and brace for her answer.

"Oh no," she says, "it's magic. It's one of those places that seem like they have always been there, like it was there when the rocks first came out of the ground."

I drive north out of town, up the Rio Grande Valley where the river makes two small turns in the sandstone-colored bluffs and then one big one north before making a straight-line run east again to its headwaters near the Continental Divide.

I am here, I keep telling myself, as an experiment. I have come to get away for a while from the sharp edge of the continent, to see if maybe I am done with edges generally. I have come because a meadow at the base of the high backbone of America is the most secure place I can think of, and also because I know I could be back in the city in forty-eight hours if and when I realize I have made a terrible mistake.

My car isn't as full this time as it was the last time I crossed the Great Basin going the other direction. People are supposed to accumulate, I thought, as they get older, but I seem to be sloughing off, like a person wrapped in a hundred layers of cellophane, tearing one layer off at a time, trying to get down to me.

I have my cameras, my tools and most of my outdoor gear,

187

and a box of letters from a dead woman I am not related to, a woman I haven't let myself think about five times in the three years since her death, a woman who may have been the only person in thirty-four years whom I've ever really loved well. I have her ashes in a coffee can on the seat beside me. She told me not to scatter them until I found the right place.

My grandmother's ranch is sitting right where B.J. said it would be, in the center of the biggest bend of the river, the Divide turning itself like a horseshoe behind it. It is not a house that sits on the land as much as one that sits in it: a log cabin built over a century ago with logs cut from a forest even higher than this place and floated downstream strapped together like a raft.

There is a barn, a hundred years old and burnt by the sun the colors of autumn, with a huge gable and a hayloft. Buck-and-rail fences run as far as the eye can see. The prairie grass gone years without being grazed is tall and green topped with gold, and thick with wildflowers, lupine and paintbrush and skyrocket gilia. Sunbeads jump across the surface of the river and pairs of the bluest birds I've ever seen hop from one fence post to another.

Ponderosa pines and aspen groves line the property along the edges that climb upwards toward the Divide, which crests in a round-top mountain, three ridges down the front of it so symmetrical it looks like it has been scratched by the claw of a grizz.

The door to the house is propped open with a coffee can and inside is the kitchen, old and worn, but neater than I expected. There's an old-fashioned meat grinder attached to one end of the counter, and a cutting board shaped like a pig over the sink. The refrigerator is old and trimmed with chrome, and right in the middle of the door a picture of me from a God-knows-how-old issue of *Photography,* winning the Ansel Adams Award my first year out of school.

The feeling that started in my stomach when B.J. recognized me has grown into butterflies at the sight of my picture all these years in my grandmother's house. Then I go into the living room, and things really start to spin and I sink straight down into what I realize as I'm doing it must have been her favorite chair. Above the careworn furniture, hung from walls desperately in need of painting, are five—no six—Lucy O'Rourke originals: a snow-covered barn near Layton, Utah; a couple dancing close at a gypsy wedding in L.A.; a small dark horse in a blinding snowstorm in South Dakota; an old man tuning a fiddle near Grass Range, Montana; clothes blowing on a line in a summer thunderstorm in Iowa; my mother wide-eyed, applying makeup before a magnifying glass.

I sit in her chair for a long time, and think hard about the woman I didn't know, who seemed to show no interest in meeting me, who spent a small fortune on my photographs while her house gently slipped toward the river, who died God knows how many days before someone came to find her, and whose decision—which is seeming less and less arbitrary all the time—has left me the owner of this ranch.

The next morning I walk to the top of the hill to find the family cemetery B.J. told me about: no headstones, only markers of hammered silver, all the names except my grandmother's too far gone to read.

"This is the most blessed piece of ground I've ever seen," I say, but no one is there to hear me. It isn't a ranch without a ranch dog, I reason, so I get in my truck to drive to the pound.

The nearest animal shelter is in Durango, more than two hours away, so I stop by B.J.'s on the way through town for moral support. She hangs the "Away on emergency . . . back in a few hours" sign on the door and makes the drive with me.

"I've been in Hope twenty-six years," she says. "Sometimes I think it's the best place to live in the universe, and other times I think it's just a hideout for stray dogs and lost souls, for people who couldn't get their life right the first time and are too scared to try it again."

When I don't say anything she says, "That's me I'm describing, by the way. I don't know anything about *your* story."

We surprise a small herd of elk that have come down to the edge of the river to drink and they bound across it, away from the road, nine-tenths grace and one-tenth clumsiness.

"Some days I'd use the words other people use to describe my life," I say, "like independence and some degree of success. Most days it seems like one false start after another, way too much up and down to keep winding up at the very same place."

"I think," B.J. says, "there's a time in your life when all the ups and downs start to look like a straight line, and the straight line starts to look like an adventure."

She points at an immature bald eagle sitting on a log in the river, waiting on a fish. "I think that's how people live to be old."

At the pound the dog B.J. picks for me won't even come to the door of the cage, stays balled up coyote-style against the back wall while the racket of a hundred dogs as they leap and howl and try to outcute each other goes on around her.

The yellow card says she is eight months old and that it is her last day before euthanization and when I pick her up her back end is so caved in from starvation she can't even stand. She's got a face that Rin Tin Tin would give his last bone for, every color of brown, white, and gray freckles increasing in intensity the farther away from her eyes, as if they've been drawn by a brush.

"The Lana Turner of dogs," B.J. says.

"Some dogs won't eat in here," the warden says. "This one won't even drink."

When I lift her into my arms she goes stiff the way wild dogs do when they're handled.

"I don't reckon she's had much contact with people," he says. "We picked her up near the reservation. There's a lot of dogs just run loose out there."

I carry her out to what they call The Yard, a twenty-foot-square area of dirt chain-linked all around, even across the top, a place to see how a dog acts once you get her outside of her cage.

I set her down in the middle of the yard and go to one corner and sit down myself. She's frozen for a moment with her paws almost spread-eagled, then she crawls straight over to me, like an Army grunt expecting an air raid, crawls right onto my lap and makes another perfect nose-to-tail ball.

"I guess that settles that," B.J. says.

I decide right that minute to call her Ellie the dog.

The first Ellie had blond hair and brown eyes and a smile so big her mouth had to open like a flower to contain it. We met in a shopping mall the day she rescued me from the people who work for *Consumer Reports*.

Sometimes they just asked a few questions about something I didn't ever buy—diet soda or processed cheese spread—but sometimes they got me into one of those little white rooms that exist in the deepest belly of the malls where they hand out the tasting samples.

That day it was mayonnaise, and Ellie must have heard me saying I didn't even use it and I was in a big hurry and couldn't they please let me pass. The clean-cut young man assured me it would only take a minute and put his hand, the way they always do, right in the crook where my arm meets my elbow, and that's when Ellie approached us, a bit like a defensive end.

"No, no, no, no, no!" she said, startling the young man nearly out of his politeness.

"I beg your pardon," he began.

"No, no, no, no, no, no, no!" Ellie said and dragged me away from him and didn't stop until we were well around the corner in front of an Orange Julius sign.

"That," she said, "is the only way on earth to deal with those people."

"Thanks," I said.

"My name's Ellie," she said, and I shook her hand.

The second time I saw her was on a hike she had planned

near her home in the mountains. She invited me, she said, along with all her favorite women—a painter, a poet, a teacher, and a witch. We hiked up a trail called the Pathway of Angels, that ended in a waterfall that when back-lit by an afternoon sun looked like it was raining diamonds.

It was September, and I remember how the aspens held the last of their green like a breath, how a tiny bird washed herself near the steep wall of water, how Ellie sang on the trail, but only to herself, a song without words and nearly without music, like she was somehow giving voice to the blood pumping in her veins.

All the other women are a blur to me now, a snapshot I have somewhere of permed hair and defined thighs and all-cotton clothing. I remember how carefully I took that photo, my goal, even then, to make Ellie proud of me.

Ellie was tough as nails and fiercely independent, but there was a fierceness in her love too, and if you were the object of that love, as I was for a while, you would come to understand the power it had to hold you up and keep you together, a love so fierce it wouldn't let you let her down.

She scared everybody a little, nobody more than her parents, who had her committed when she was sixteen. She always said the one thing of value she accomplished during the year she was inside (and she loved that word, *inside*) was that she held a red car convention, and everyone came.

She made all the arrangements from the hospital, the flyers and programs and the media ads, and smuggled them out with a psych tech who was sweet on her. Before you knew it there was a poster on every telephone pole in Evanston, Illinois.

She offered prizes for the biggest red car, the smallest red car, the reddest red car, and invited restaurants and craftspeople to set up booths. She would always tell the story in such a way that you thought the turnout was going to be fifty or a hundred people, and then she'd sit back with that flower-blossom smile all over her face and say just one sentence: "Sixteen thousand two hundred and thirty red cars."

Back in Hope, Ellie the dog doesn't move a muscle the whole time Doc Howard examines her. He drives all the way up here from Gallup, New Mexico, once a week, he says, because nobody else will. He leaves his office open on the other days so if you need dog food or painkillers or a shot of one thing or another you can come get it yourself and write your name on a pad.

He says he thinks Ellie is older than they told us at the pound, probably a little over a year. He says she'll need to gain twenty pounds to be at her ideal weight. When he looks at the red rims around her eyes he says he thinks she has distemper.

"There is no cure," he says. "If she's going down you'll know it in two weeks. She'll start coughing, wheezing, it won't be very pretty, but you can hope it will be fast."

I buy her a bag of immune-boosting dog food and a chew toy, and we make our way back to the ranch.

When we get there, it is almost as hard getting Ellie out of the truck as it was getting her in it. And for the first two days she won't come near the house.

On the third day she tiptoes cautiously across the threshold, sits at my feet, and smiles up at me, her tail thumping the rotted floorboards. She sneezes, almost imperceptibly.

"No, no," I say. "Don't you dare go getting sick on me."

I was an only child, a lonely child and I called myself a loner, but the broad flat fields of the ranch and the way the Divide sweeps around it give a whole new meaning to the word *lonely* for me, like what the word meant when the word was invented.

"You could be dead a long time out here before somebody would notice," I say to Ellie. "We all could."

A mouse scurries across the floor and Ellie is into the air and on top of it in a pounce so graceful and effortless she confirms my belief that she is half coyote and maybe even a little more. She lays the lifeless mouse at my feet, untouched, it seems, except for a broken neck, and waits to see what I'll do with it.

The days go by and we settle in, Ellie the dog holding the fort—since our day of arrival she won't go near the truck—and me making daily trips to town for groceries, light bulbs and plumbing parts, and anything else I can think of we need.

Ellie can hear my truck coming long before I hit the end of the driveway, and that's where she meets me, a big coyote grin on her face. She bounds back to the house along with me, a run-run-run-spring, run-run-run-spring pattern where on every fourth stride she throws her legs straight out on all sides of her, as though she just cannot contain her joy at my arrival.

At night we listen to the real coyotes yip and howl and I watch Ellie prick up her ears and then steal a glance at me to see if I am watching. When she sees I am, she picks herself up and lies down again, but on top of my feet this time.

Don't worry, is the rhythm she thumps out with her tail. And the look in her eyes says *I won't ever leave.*

It's the best time of day in my kitchen, the sun just up and over the Divide and pouring in my windows when Ellie jumps up and flies out the door with a growl in her throat. B.J. gets out of her pick-up with a bag full of bagels in one hand and a rawhide chew in the other, which she drops for Ellie who can hardly believe her eyes.

"Damn distributor always brings me more of these than I know what to do with," she says. "I hope it's not too early for you. I won't stay if you're busy."

I take the bagels from her hands, the cream cheese out from under one arm, the coffee thermos from under the other.

"Little by little, huh?" she says when she sees the portion of the walls I've repainted, the length of floorboard I've scrubbed clean.

"I can clean all I want to," I say, "but it's not gonna help if this roof caves in or the house slides into the river."

"You need a man out here to mess with that stuff," B.J. says. She's got my oven lighted and is toasting enough bagels for a junior high school.

"I need a man," I say, "like I need a hole in the head."

"That's just what your grandma used to say." She sinks down in a kitchen chair. "I just think it's a crime against the universe that you two never met."

"It was her choice," I say.

"The fight was about your father, you know," B.J. says. "She didn't care for him at all."

"That hardly puts her in an exclusive category," I say.

"She would have loved to have raised you right here by her-self."

196

"Then she should have," I say. "I'd have probably been a lot better off."

I set two mugs down in front of her.

"People in town said you wouldn't come," B.J. says. "They said it wouldn't mean anything to you at all."

"It was almost like that," I say, "It could have been. I guess it still could be."

"Your mother must have flipped when you told her you were coming."

"My mother's dead," I say. "They died the same year, within days of each other, within weeks of my best friend, the one I named the dog after."

"And you haven't had a real friend since," B.J. says.

"I've had friends," I say. "No one like Ellie. There was a woman named Thea who came close, and I tried to drown her in the Colorado River."

"I doubt that," B.J. says. She dips her cream-cheese-covered bagel straight into her cup of coffee. "So," she says, holding the bagel up for me to bite it, "what are you doing here?"

I came because Carlos Castaneda told me to, is what I might have told her. Or *I came because it's the place from which my mother ran away*. Or *I came because a part of me was dying in the city*. "Ellie would have liked this," are the words I finally use. "I have her ashes, and her letters. I had to find the right place for them before I could let her go."

The first Ellie wanted me to have a home more than she wanted me to have anything. She didn't approve of any of the men I dated. "He's not lyrical enough for you," she said one time. And "There's nothing I can do for you until you lose your taste for prototypes." And "Sometimes, Lucy, I swear you were put on earth just as confirmation of my comparatively good mental health."

She said she couldn't understand how a landscape photographer could have such a problem with figure/ground relationships.

"Find yourself a place you belong in the universe," she said, "a place where the dirt feels like goodness under your feet. Take the right picture and a man will walk into it. If you can bear him even a little, then for a while let him stay."

What I loved most in the world was sitting at the table in Ellie's kitchen while she cooked pot roast or white beans or honey-glazed ham. She had a garden big enough to feed a battalion, though her husband and sons seemed to always eat out. She could can her way through a ton of peaches so fast it would make your head spin. She could make pesto and salsa and a caseful of Ball jars of pickled green tomatoes all at the very same time.

Even after the diagnosis, no one could keep her out of the kitchen. She wore a bright kerchief around her bald head and her hands flew from the oven door to the refrigerator to a ten-second rub of my shoulders.

"Suppose I die before the next canning season," she'd say as she leveled a hard look at me. "What the hell is everybody around here going to eat then?"

When winter came she went away to die, to Tulsa, Oklahoma. There was a man there who said he could heal her by talking to her feet. He would hold one herbal remedy after another up to her soles and her feet would tell him, he said, which ones her body needed.

She had called and written me letters from her ranch almost daily and from the hospital in Albuquerque where she had all the bone marrow taken out of her body, treated for malignancy, and then put back in. For three days she had been in the world between the living and the dying and on the fourth day she wrote me a letter. When she got to Oklahoma, though, all the calls and letters stopped.

In the end she wouldn't even talk to me when I called; she wouldn't talk to anybody. She cut a deal with her hospital roommate to lie to everyone. By the time I got the truth it was way too late to get to her. She died while her husband and sons and I were in a plane over western Oklahoma, the roommate still maintaining that Ellie hadn't wanted any of us there.

During our second week at the ranch Ellie the dog starts to spend more and more time under the porch and I hear her coughing in the morning and try not to cry. She stays under there, too, when the thunderstorms come, huge and silent in the afternoon until they work themselves up first into thunder that rolls over in waves sometimes as long as fifteen seconds, and eventually into lightning that dances across the mountaintops and leaves us looking for fires.

By evening though the storms have usually passed and I beg Ellie to come out and have something to eat. She wags her tail and her eyes flash at me but she has no intention of coming.

The porch is high enough for me to get half my body under and get ahold of one of her paws, which I do. After that she doesn't resist me, lets herself be pulled by the paw like some kind of doggy Gandhi, lets me heft all fifty pounds of her and carry her to the food bowl and feed her, one morsel at a time out of my hand.

Later, when we are sitting on the couch together, she'll extend that same paw—a little like a lady who's just dropped her hanky—and wait for her belly to be rubbed. So I'll rub it for a while and maybe pick up my guitar and sing the kind of songs people commit suicide by and wonder what I am doing in the middle of nowhere, more alone than I've ever been except for a half-wild coydog named after my dead best friend who probably won't live to see Friday.

"I'm calling the phone man tomorrow," I say to Ellie. "I don't think it's cheating for us to get a phone."

The only person I can think of to call is my friend Henry in Chicago.

"I'm glad you're having fun," he says. "I just want to know when you are going to get over all this earth mother shit and come back to civilization."

"They like you better here if you have babies," I tell him. "I decided to start out with a dog."

"A dog is a good thing," Henry says.

"I think she has distemper," I say.

"And your new boyfriend is a Jehovah's Witness," he says. "Honestly, Lucy, would it kill you to set yourself up *one* time so that the odds are in your favor?"

"I don't have a new boyfriend," I say.

On the tenth day at the ranch Ellie the dog digs herself a

place under the porch where I can't reach her and stays under there solid for two days and nights. I crawl under as far as my body can go and listen to her wheezing. The coughing is incessant now, her breath ever more labored and ever more slow.

I bring her water and anything else I can think of—chicken broth, hamburger, even canned tuna—and leave it there for her so she won't think it's a bribe, but she won't touch it even after I leave.

Her eyes have gone dull and her gums are white and pasty. I try not to think about what I'll have to do to get her out of there in the morning if she dies in the middle of one of these long dark nights.

On the second morning I hear nothing at all and I think she's dead, but when I get underneath her tail still thumps weakly between the dirt and the floorboards.

Then the big storms come. Clouds that are lit as if from within, every shade from purest white to deepest indigo, they build up on all sides of us, some from up on Red Mountain, some from the La Garita range, some from upriver in the sky we can't see beyond Bristol Head.

Most days the storms that come by the ranch come from the west, drop their moisture on the top of the Divide and then struggle along to the La Garita, but this one sits over us hour after hour. It drops its rain or its hail and then rests for a minute and starts up again, swirling and swirling right over the ranch as if it didn't have anywhere else to be.

When night falls things get all the more spectacular, the thunder coming from all directions and the lightning lighting the fence line like it is something electric, lighting Red

Mountain, lighting the river, lighting the barn and the cabin and the whole ranch, making it brighter than it is in the day.

Wrapped in blankets, I sit on the porch right above the place that I know holds Ellie, and pray to the lightning and God and Carlos Castaneda to please not take her away from me.

It was the third time the first Ellie and I were together, cross-country skiing in a too-early snow. The aspen leaves were red and gold and even green in places, and they fell onto the carpet of heavy white wetness like crayons scattered on a freshly washed sheet.

We'd been silent for the better part of an hour but for the sound of the skis and the crunch of the powder.

"I love you already," were the words that she said.

When we got back to the car she said, "I'm not like the others. I won't ever leave."

A month to the day later, the doctor found the first lump.

For three months after Ellie died I saw her everywhere. She was one of the backup singers at the James Taylor concert, the girl who took my money at the car wash, a woman in a lingerie ad plastered all over France. This happened so often and with such uncanny resemblance that after a while I was sure Ellie was making it happen, letting me know she wouldn't be going anywhere as long as I needed her around.

I read her letters several times daily and I would dream of her every time I closed my eyes. Her voice was in my head to the exclusion of all others. I got pulled over one night for speeding, and when the cop came to the window the natural thing seemed to blame it on her.

Then one day her voice stopped its speaking, I slept hard and dreamless, and no one I passed on the street looked like her. Nothing had prepared me for the emptiness that followed. I folded all her letters and put them safe away.

I wake up on the porch with the sun beating through the blankets and Ellie the dog sitting at attention and staring at me. Her eyes are bright and her gums are red and she jumps straight in the air when I sit up to greet her.

"Now that you are well," I tell her, "it's time to make a decision about whether or not we are going to stay here."

She wags, not so much her tail as the whole back half of her body, spins on a dime and kills another mouse, just before it gets to the threshold.

"That one's yours," I say, and she cocks her head at me and bites down once and swallows.

When she starts to get her strength back Ellie and I begin the tradition of our daily walks. Ellie starts out right at my heels like some kind of cattle dog, but the farther we get off the property and the better the smells, the bigger and bigger circles she makes, until three or four minutes go by and there's no sign of her.

I call her then, not too loud in case she is hunting, and more often than not she pops back over a ridgeline, waits for me to make an eye-contact check-in, and then she's off and after something else. If she is gone for five or six minutes I yell louder still and wait in the echo for the sound of her panting—I always hear that before I hear her footfall—and she comes tearing down the hill and throws herself into my arms and gets petted until one of us gets tired of it and then she's off and running again.

I don't mind having to call her so much because after so many years of missing her I love having Ellie's name in my mouth.

Almost a whole week later, after the storms have gone and the rain has stopped and I'm sitting on the porch, I pick up the old Larrivee guitar I bought for Carter Thompson but for once in my life had the good sense not to give him, and I start strumming the chords for "Brown-Eyed Girl."

Ellie the dog comes straight out from under the porch and sits down next to me like she's just paid her money and has a front-row seat.

While I sing the words she looks at me intently, but when I get to the Sha-la-la-la-la-la-la-la-la-la-la-ti-da part she throws her pretty head back and sings right along. It is not a howl or a bark or a sound that a dog makes, but the exact sound a human makes when she doesn't know the words.

I sing Leonard Cohen's "Suzanne" after that, which she sits through patiently, appreciative, it seems, but she doesn't make a sound. But next I sing "The Boxer," and when I get to the Li-la-li, Li-la-li-li-li-li-li, Li-la-li part it goes just as I suspect it will and she joins in.

She is, I'll admit, a little heavy on the R's, so we sing it Ri-ra-ri instead of the other way.

"I love you," I say, and she cocks her head sideways.

"Rri rrove rooo," I say, a little slower this time.

"Rri rrove rooo," she says, her tail thumping behind her.

"Rrrred, rrrred rrrrrobin," I say.

204

"Rrrred, rrrred rrrrrobin," she says, and licks her lips and lies down.

"Gerrrallldo Riverrrra," I say before she gets tired of the game.

"Rerrrallldo Riverrrra," she says, but I know I'm about to lose her.

So I pick up the guitar and we do "Bobby McGee," Janis's version with lots of Ra-ra-raing at the end, and after that I add an Ellie sing-along chorus to whatever song I play until after ten or twelve of them she lays herself down on a piece of sheepskin to let me know her set is done for the day.

I put the guitar down and look up at the sun, bright now on the Divide. Then all of a sudden it seems like the right time to me, so Ellie the dog and I walk with the coffee can to the top of the hill and I open the box of Ellie's letters.

She wrote:

This morning the horses, thirteen of them, have been running along the ridge at the far end of the pasture. They string out in a line, galloping, disturbed by our presence. Two old white mares lead the herd.

She wrote:

I have taken to wearing my bald hats again. They are quite ridiculous and yet I take great pleasure putting them on my head.

She wrote:

It has rained and rained and rained here since Thursday. Clouds and mist move through the canyon like women carrying great baskets on their heads.

She wrote:

I am still holding the ground, the earth, in that way that is peculiar to me and I feel grateful for it.

She wrote:

I feel like I am going underwater for a while. I need to swim with those submerged creatures.

She wrote:

I know now that it is true that I carry you with me because I can feel you on the front of my body up by my face and chest where my breath warms the hollow of my neck. Which is nice but it makes me miss you even more.

In her last letter she wrote:

I'm thinking it must be very strange for you to have a friend like me.

I open the coffee can and before I even know what I'm doing the ground around my feet is covered with ash. The ground is soft after the rain, and the dark clouds in the west mean more rain is coming. Tonight it will fall on Ellie and take her back into the ground, and she'll be food for the skyrocket gilia and the purple lupine, the prairie grass and the ponderosas, every wild thing that grows on my grandmother's ranch.

Ellie the dog looks up at me, extending her paw, like she's requesting more singing, winking her coydog eyes at me like saying *thank you for giving me the right name.*

"We've been here a month," I say. "Time to move if we are moving."

Ellie curls herself in a tight ball right over the tops of my feet. If the first Ellie heard me talk about leaving this place, she'd have flattened all my tires.

B.J. told me there wasn't a person in town who didn't try to talk my grandmother into leaving the ranch near the end, about going down to Durango where she could be cared for properly, put her feet up for a year or two, maybe extend her life. But she stayed on the ranch till the end, kept it up in her fashion, and my mother never let anyone help her put down the bottle, and Ellie, hiding out with that crazy doctor in Oklahoma, never even picked up the phone.

They were all alone in the end as it happened, Ellie by design, my mother even though my father was right beside her, my grandmother because that had been the condition of her life. I have done so many stupid things in my life to avoid being alone and now I've written myself a full-time prescription. I think it is necessary. I can hope that it's temporary. I've started with a dog. Next, maybe a friend.

The sun is climbing steadily up the face of Red Mountain and the air is so clean after the rain I can count the new leaves on the branches of aspen.

I start strumming some chords and Ellie the dog sits at attention. If the first Ellie were here this morning, she'd sing the song without words that she sang at the waterfall. She'd say that one of the biggest problems in my life so far is all the times I said I love you when what I really meant was Geraldo Rivera. She'd tell me why she made it so hard to come through for her those last few weeks she was living. She'd say I'd finally found the place I didn't know I needed, the place where Ellie the dog and I were meant to hold our ground.

Then You Get Up and Have Breakfast

"I'M GONNA FIND a man in this town who'll have sex with me this weekend if it's the last thing I do," I said and I let the door to the Glory Hole Cafe close with a smack behind me.

B.J. wiped the mayonnaise and mustard from her hands onto her apron, poured two cups of coffee, got the phone book from behind the soda fountain, and sat down.

There are 283 people in Hope. It takes up only two and a half pages of the Alamosa Regional phone book. Men outnumber women almost two to one here, but B.J. could only come up with four live bodies, even so. One was in the middle of a nasty divorce that included babies, one was up cutting wood and hadn't been seen in over a month, and the other two I'd met several times already and let me just say that the sparks didn't fly.

208

"Everybody'll be at Paul's party tonight," B.J. said, "this year's crop of summer people too. Take a big bath, put on something sexy, then take your pick."

Paul Stone had a Fourth of July party every summer. He also built a float each year for the parade. This year he was going to dress like a Green Beret Special Forces member and roll down Main Street firing a Gatling gun that shot three-bean salad and had signs hanging from the trailer saying "Bomb clinic, 3:00 p.m." His floats were never "authorized" by the town fathers, but he always managed to sneak them in anyway. He's been pretty big on gun control since three years ago when his baby brother blew himself away.

"Take my pick," I said, and tried to believe it was possible. But we both knew my record was at a brand-new all-time low.

"There'll be fire in the sky tonight in every shape and color," B.J. told me. "You just go have yourself a little dance in the flames."

Carter Thompson had said goodbye to me for good not three whole days earlier, taking his backpack and his high-pitched laugh and his traveling Martin guitar case with him.

"I thought that boy was way too pretty," was all that B.J. had said.

And he was. All curly blond hair, laugh lines, and cheekbones. Hands that moved like poems as they rose and sculpted the air.

I had thought for a while he was the one I'd been waiting for, thought it was a good sign that unlike all the others, the first thing we did wasn't jump in the sack.

209

Carter liked my grandmother's ranch and since I'd moved back to the Rockies he flew through Denver whenever he could arrange it, but the visits were so short that sometimes we didn't even get out of the airport. I was on the road too those days shooting pictures on assignment for adventure magazines. If we had a weekend at the same time we'd get ourselves outdoors wherever we were: skiing or hiking or floating down a wild river. Five months went by like that before I realized we hadn't had sex.

Carter had a big house I'd never been to somewhere in Los Angeles. Most years he wasn't there a total of thirty days. When we met I was in Louisiana on my own nickel shooting the lunar eclipse over the Mississippi Delta for a coffee-table book I have in the back of my mind. He was scouting a location for a remake of *The Swamp Thing*, where the "Thing" becomes a member of the LSU football team.

It was a couple of years after my photographs had made a name for themselves, my specialty night stuff: moonlight bouncing off metal barn roofs and northern lights and color patterns in the stars.

The night we met we drove Carter's rented convertible out into the bayou and took pictures of the glimmering fenders. Then we sang "Peaceful Easy Feeling" and "Red Rubber Ball."

I left B.J.'s and wandered up to Paul's house to help him with the Fourth of July decorations and to make sure he didn't live up to his reputation for cooking the chicken too slow.

He was working on a new sculpture called *Virtual Reality*,

an old-fashioned penny gumball machine filled with bullets, with a .357 Magnum attached on the front, hanging by a silver chain. Not everyone in town understands Paul's humor, which is, he says, one of the primary reasons why he stays.

Hope had been my home base for the three months since my grandmother died and left me the homestead. She'd lived there by herself and hadn't kept up with it or the property taxes. After she died the bill came straight to me.

I had been living in the city, spending grant money I wasn't sure I deserved, and trying to take photographs good enough to earn another one. I thought if I gave up my apartment and started taking more assignments I could pay the back taxes and still have time to keep the ranch house from slumping down the hill and into the river. After three months and a hundred plane flights I was making progress with the taxes, but the house and the river were gaining on me, fast.

I sat down and watched Paul paint the porcelain sides of the gumball machine baby-doll yellow. *Solace* was the name printed on top of the can.

"I pick my paints by name rather than color," he said. "The kitchen is *Elusion*, the hallway is *Madness,* and the downstairs bathroom there is called *Fun Blonde*."

"Who'da thought madness would be all one color," I said.

"That's what you think at first," Paul said, "but then it starts to make sense."

He put the paintbrush down, picked up the silver revolver, and put it, for just a moment, inside his mouth.

"And speaking of madness," he said, "my best friend's com-

211

ing out from Kansas this weekend. I'm trying to get this done for him to see."

His name was Erik Sorenson, and I knew him only by the inventions he'd brought and left behind in Hope: a beer-can launcher with two barrels, one for Coors beer, one for all others; a rocket rigged to shoot lit fluorescent light tubes; an air gun that shot rolls of toilet paper so that they unrolled on the fly.

"He's outdone himself this time," Paul said. "He's coming with ninety thousand fireworks, and a cannon that shoots a bowling ball farther than a mile."

"Is he single?" I asked him, and Paul made a noise in his throat that was not quite a laugh.

"Is he an asshole?" I said.

"He's a prince," Paul said, "the brightest and the best. Off the charts in the IQ department, sweeter than a man ought to be." He stared for a minute at his hand that still held the silver revolver. "The world gets to be a little much for Erik sometimes, and he's had more than his share of shitstorms. He keeps it together to the tune of a fifth and half of tequila a day."

"Too bad," I said. "I have a rule about alcoholics."

"That's what's funny," Paul said. "So do I."

Carter Thompson would get passionate every now and then, most often out of doors, in public places and fully clothed. Airports seemed to turn him on especially, the imminent departures and scenic overlooks, sparkling city skylines and serrated silhouettes of mountain ranges, the horizontal expanse of great salty lakes. But when we got home he'd stay up singing till the sky started to lighten, and more often than not I'd conk out on the couch. On the rare nights we ended up in bed together this was the protocol: he in a T-shirt, always, with no bottoms, curled tight and away from me, the dark hairs of his backside pressed prickly into the curve of my womb. If I moved, even the slightest bit against him, he'd ball up even tighter.

One night, I dreamt a down-and-dirty dream and must have gotten ahold of his leg with mine in my sleep and went after it. The next morning his face: pitying and ashen. I learned without a word being spoken all the things I'd never be allowed to ask.

The first time I saw Erik Sorenson he was standing in front of a burning cauldron of gasoline with a couple thousand fireworks wrapped in his big Norwegian arms. Paul stood a few steps behind him with the garden hose trained in his direction while Erik made trips back and forth to his pick-up and dumped the fireworks, two armloads at a time, into the flaming pit.

It was the night of the Fourth, the town fireworks long over and no match for the spectacle on Stone avenue: two middle-aged men enveloped first in huge clouds of black-powder smoke, then in showers of sparks, in bottle rockets, whirligigs and doodads, in flying paper tanks and airplanes, in twirling friendship lanterns and exploding Tequila Sunrises.

I watched Paul and Erik throw their heads back in laughter, half witches in that instant, half schoolboys. Paul wiry and

213

quick, Erik huge and lumbering, a Sasquatch of a man, a Clydesdale; I thought, *one of his hands is the size of Paul's head.*

Right then a bottle rocket flew into Erik's mouth and he turned toward the spectators, huddled as we were behind big plates of safety glass in Paul's shop. His face curled into a huge sideways grin.

"It went right into my mouth," he said, pointing and laughing, and his words were a shower of red and golden sparks.

The first thing I asked him was why he liked to get so close to the fire and he said, "Because my granddaddy told me it's the only place to be."

Later that night, down at the Crooked Creek, I forgot my own rule long enough to challenge Erik to a shot-drinking contest. I'm not much of a drinker, but the stuff that came out of my mother's breast was one-tenth milk and nine-tenths vodka and I've been known to hold my own with tequila, especially Cuervo Gold or better; the up it has works on me, hours before the bigger down.

The bartender set us up with a couple shots of Three Generations, and Erik showed me pictures of the things he made with his hands: miniature replicas of grand Tudor houses, fourteen thousand miniature bricks in one of them, and oak toothpicks in the floor for miniature dowels; jewelry boxes in the shape of airplanes and rabbits; a wooden bench with the sun rising, every color of wood across the back.

He told me a story about five thousand penguins who walked to the Antarctic Ocean single-file in an arrow-straight line, about a scientist who tried to make them break their line and walk around him, about how all five thousand of them, even the ones in the way back of the line, sat down in perfect order to wait the scientist out.

He told me about the monarch butterflies that returned again and again thirty-five hundred miles from Canada to Mexico to his girlfriend's family farm, the one for whom he made the jewelry boxes, the one who'd died of lung failure not even three years before.

He told me about *feng shui*, about how to build a house so the luck stays inside it, about his Asian mentor, also dead, who left him the dragon ring he wears on his one whole hand.

In North Dakota he and his granddaddy used to go down to the hardware store and buy dynamite, bring it back to the farm, and blow up the rocks.

"Drove my daddy crazy," he said. "Course that was a pretty short trip."

He held the forefinger of his right hand, one digit shorter than the others, in the air. "If there's one thing I've learned about power tools . . ." he said.

His glasses reflected the blue and gold of the bar lights.

"Medic," he shouted to the bartender. "We've got wounded down here."

He told me about the years he spent getting political prisoners out of China, bringing them to America, helping them get on their feet.

"One guy comes over, right?" he said. "And when I ask him what English words he knows he says, in Chinese, *just two phrases, but one or the other will work for anything an American says to me.*"

Erik motioned at the bartender to bring us shot number five.

"So I ask what the two phrases are and he says 'One is *You're shitting me*' "—he fingered his shot glass—" 'and the other is *How little we know.*' "

"I'm a sucker for a good storyteller," I told him, and I knew that if he asked me to, I'd sleep with him that night for sure.

In nine months Carter did three things that made me know it wouldn't be too hard to get over him. The first was in Baton Rouge, at a music festival when he leapt up on stage with a group of young musicians playing reggae, grabbed the tambourine off the percussionist's table, and started strutting around the stage like a chicken.

The second was in Illinois, when he asked me to take his picture in front of the sign for the town called Normal, and when he thought I had my head in the trunk digging for my cameras, I caught him practicing the look he wanted to have on his face, not once, not twice, but three times.

And the third, well, I'm not sure I can say the third thing out loud.

I ceded victory after fourteen shots, my head swimming, my sentences turning into oatmeal. Erik, who showed no sign of inebriation, bought a couple of beers for the road.

I had the presence of mind to load him in my pick-up though, the wherewithal to drive the fifteen miles down the dark county road to the ranch.

It was a moonless night and the Milky Way spread itself

across the night sky thick as Kayo syrup and I wished for my camera and a couple hours to play with it, and then I remembered I had a live one in the car. The great square of Pegasus rose over the Divide to the east. Behind it would be Andromeda, a whole galaxy hidden in the folds of her skirts.

That's when Eric told me about the antidepressants. "I probably should have told you at the bar," he said, "I haven't had an erection in almost two years."

I studied Queen Cassiopeia bright in the sky right above me. I thought *Maybe I'm carrying some weird ancient curse.*

"I'd like to touch you," he said, his eyes fixed on a broken porch board below him, "and I think you might like it too."

He put one hand on each of my breasts, the severed finger on his right hand meeting the tip of the nipple, and his eyes turned into a question.

"Yes," I said, and I took him to bed.

For the next four hours his hands never stopped moving. He touched me like a blind man who had just one night to learn what is *woman*, and I fell in and out of sleep like a sweet and perpetual dream. By the time the sun was hitting the top of the Divide outside my bedroom window I had a far greater understanding of all the pictures he'd shown me. I felt deep in my insides the perfect placement of each of those fourteen thousand tiny bricks.

At seven o'clock Erik got up and went to the kitchen and I threw my flannel nightshirt on and followed him. He opened the fridge and took out a cold beer. My stomach lurched a little when the malty smell reached me. I tried to keep the question out of my eyes but he answered it anyway.

"Fifteen years ago was when the shitwrecks started," he said. "First my little sister, then my father, then my building, then all the toys. One woman left me, another got sick, next was my mentor, then my best friend." He looked around the kitchen. "You got a liquor cabinet in here?"

I pointed to the cupboard next to the sink.

"I wanted to off myself about a million times but I knew it was more than my mother could handle, so I thought I'd do it slowly, one delicious fifth at a time." He poured himself a water glass of Cuervo Gold.

"My mother drank herself to death," I said. "It's not very pretty."

"You're very pretty," he said. He took my hand and led me back to the bedroom and started to touch me like it was some kind of religion again.

At noon he said, "Why don't you show me what's wrong with the plumbing."

I'd told him I'd been living all summer with only one operating sink and no indoor toilet, everything frozen and broken after so many years in disrepair.

We crawled into the rat space under the house.

"Well," I said, "when Carter was here he told me that this one's just for the outside spigots, and he said that this one over here is probably the main."

I crawled further into the rotten underbelly of the house, watching Erik bend his body over on itself like a snake.

218

"Carter thought the leak is just past where the main connects, out of sight and maybe buried, and I thought if that were true the ground would be wet here, but Carter . . ."

Erik held up his hand.

"Who is this Carter?" he said. "Is he a plumber?"

"No," I said, "he's in the movie business, which means he knows how to act like a plumber."

"Great," said Erik. "Let's see if we can't leave him out of this conversation then, huh?"

In the end, Carter broke up with me in the middle of the Weminuche Wilderness, on the second morning of a four-day backpacking trip. I said being with him for eight months and not having sex was like trying to tap dance with one leg tied up behind my back and that's when he ended it, that very morning, before we'd even gotten out of the tent.

We spent the next forty-eight hours walking or sitting in silence. Every so often he'd pull out a piece of paper and write something down. Back at the trailhead, while loading our cars, the list fell from his pocket and onto the ground long enough for me to see a few items: *1. Too broad through the shoulders; 2. Upper lip too thin; 3. Unappealing waist-to-hip ratio; 4. Permanent discoloration on shin.*

"This is only the end of Act One ," he said, kissing me on the cheek and stuffing the list back in his pocket. He got in his rented Lumina, blew me a kiss, and drove away.

After Erik fixed the plumbing, he rewired the garage, and after that he got the old tractor going, and after that he shored

219

up the side of the house that leaned the worst with cement blocks.

I made us quesadillas with fresh habañero peppers I'd gotten two weeks before on a shoot in Tucson.

"You ought to lift this house up and put a new foundation under it," he told me. "That oughta be the very first thing."

"You're bleeding," I said, watching a red rivulet move down the side of his beer can.

"Man hath no greater love than to shed blood on his boss lady's plumbing," he said.

"I can't afford a new foundation," I said.

"In that case," he said, looking out toward the river, "you ought to think about putting the whole thing on floats."

Erik took me for a drive in the burned-out Blazer his neighbor back in Kansas had given him.

"I think we should turn here," he said, all of a sudden, and he swung the Chevy around so fast I thought we'd both go flying out the jimmied passenger door.

The sign said Black Canyon with a handpainted arrow and the road was dirt and hadn't been traveled since the rain at the beginning of last week. I'd heard the land around Black Canyon was some of the wildest in the county, full of rocky cliff faces and windswept pinnacles, high plateaus still snow-covered often late into July.

We drove till the two-track ended in some watermelon snow a hundred yards from the canyon's north rim. I jumped out of the Blazer and ran to the edge.

The rock on top was smooth and golden but it got more

jagged and blacker the further it fell two thousand feet from where I stood. The canyon walls were streaked with striations, deep and darker even than the black river that gleamed in the bottom. It was a distance too vast not to want to fall into. The river rushed up the canyon to meet me. The trees on the ledges below me wouldn't maintain their size.

"I had a feeling about this," Erik whispered, and took a quick step backwards, but I stayed fixed right on the edge.

"Even somebody who'd never had a bad day would have to feel the pull here," I said.

I'd been scared all my life to say the word *suicide*, but I sat down on the edge and let my legs dangle into the void. I wanted to tease the edges of my own possibilities, wanted to feel the pressure of pushing off into nothingness from the smooth rock under my hands.

Erik sat against a boulder slightly back from the edge and away. He picked up my camera, took my picture with my hands on the rock and my head bent way over, pulled a hip flask out of his pocket, and took two long pulls.

I looked at the bottle, then back over the ledge. "I think you've got it all wrong," I said.

I looked hard at him then and again he snapped the shutter.

"If you had really given up," I said, "you couldn't touch me the way you do."

He set my camera on self-timer, tiptoed over to the edge of the canyon, and sat down next to me. The click of shutter was loud.

I got up from the ledge and brought him in close through the lens of my camera, brought the shutter down, then backed up a step and brought the shutter down again.

Then I imagined him jumping, imagined me driving his truck back to Hope without him, notifying the sheriff, and then telling Paul. I imagined the wake and the fireworks it would require, imagined the size of the thing they'd have to blow up to approximate the loss.

"I'm usually pretty good with heights," he said, standing, "but this one's more than I can handle." And I knew we were both safe in whatever kind of love we were in that day, a match made, as Paul Stone liked to say, in hell.

"Tell you what," Erik said. "Let's go back to that snowfield and I'll make you a snow angel, and then you'll get on top of me and smother me with these." He pulled the front of my Danskin down, cupped both breasts in one big hand.

The sun was low on the Divide and already the wind was getting colder.

I knelt above him while he lay on the crusty June snow in only a T-shirt and Levi's, waving his arms and legs like mad to make the angel, his head thrown back again and laughing, fog on his glasses, his ears bright red.

"You have to be freezing," I said.

"I'm Norwegian," he said and the tequila bottle next to him glinted in the sun.

"Penguins and boobies and rutabagas with wings," he said, "these are a few of my favorite things."

I balanced myself on his chest for a moment to get my bare knees out of the snow.

He said, "If I ever do anything that hurts you, you just smack me on the back of the head, okay?"

"Okay," I said.

"Good," he said. "It'll be our own secret sign."

It was well after dark when we left the Black Canyon, and halfway down the mountain we hit a bump and the headlights quit.

I stood on the side of the dirt road holding a flashlight and watched Erik rip into the wires under the hood of the Blazer. Something so powerful moved inside me when I saw his big hands wrapped around those skinny wires that I had to gulp air to keep holding the flashlight still. I remembered a yellowed notebook I found full of my grandmother's writing. On the first page all by itself the following: *God loves a man who knows how to use his hands.*

The next afternoon Paul came to the ranch towing his trailer full of Erik's cannons; a few carloads of town kids came along for the ride.

We shot can after can of Coors Light at the barn's metal eave and watched six fluorescent light bulbs tumble and roll across the gathering twilight. But the kids had come to see the bowling ball cannon, and if they were going to shoot it I wanted them to do it before it got all the way dark.

"It'll put a little damper on the evening if we kill one of the horses," I said to Paul, looking out across the pasture at the horses I was keeping to help finance the place.

"Yeah," Paul said, "but think of the story we'd all have to tell."

Erik dug a hole in the ground deep enough to hold half the cannon. He mixed together three types of black powder, each one a little more powerful, and poured it out of my Pyrex and into the bottom of the barrel.

"We could shoot it straight up," Erik said, grinning, "and then we'd find out which one of us thinks our God is the true God."

"Not today," Paul said, and Erik aimed the nose of the cannon across the pasture, up toward the Continental Divide. He made us all stand back as he swallowed the last of the day's first fifth of tequila, then he carefully lowered the bowling ball into the cannon's dark hole. He ran a couple of wires from the glow plugs in the base back to his truck battery, crouched behind the front tire and said, "Here we go."

But the cannon didn't go off. Not the second time he hooked it to the truck battery, nor again when he hooked it up to the 110 running straight out of the house. He tried again and again, but the only thing we heard was not a *boom* like a cannon, but a *ping* each time the big breaker switch went off inside.

Erik added more gunpowder and tried it again, and when that didn't work he threw in a whole gallon of Coleman fuel and a lit pack of matches. Then he came to the house to see if we had any leftover fireworks to throw in there too.

"Be careful." The words came out of my mouth before my hand could stop them.

I watched him stick first his hand right in front of the mouth of the smoking cannon, then his head, then his ear, then his face.

"There are some people here, Erik," Paul yelled to him, "who would rather not watch you blow yourself up."

He grinned at us and shotgunned another Budweiser. Then he got some rags out of the truck, ripped and twisted them into a long skinny fuse, soaked them in gasoline, lit one end and stuck the other into the cannon's mouth.

This time he didn't even run backwards. The cannon smoked and shuddered and rocked in its cradle. Again, it didn't go off.

He walked around the cannon for a minute, stopped and studied it hard. Then he lifted all hundred and twenty pounds of it onto his shoulder, still smoking, made a noise like a locomotive, and threw it across the yard.

"Jesus H. Christ," Paul said.

The cannon landed with a thud against a fence post. The bowling ball rolled out of it and the holes looked at us like a face.

"So it really is a death wish then," I said to Paul, "isn't it?"

"Absolutely," he said, and when he saw my face he said, "What in the world did you expect me to say?"

The kids got tired and went into the Crooked Creek for last call. Even Paul said he couldn't watch anymore and got in his truck and headed home. Erik kept walking and walking around the cannon, sipping on a new tequila bottle and talking to himself. I wrapped myself up in a blanket and swung in the porch hammock, glad at least that all the horses had made it through the night.

I woke up when I felt his hands on my shoulders.

"How'd you get such a soft touch?" I asked him.

"Exotic woods," he said. "Very expensive. You only get one chance to cut them right."

225

He bent down to kiss me and over his head I saw Scorpio's Stinger, and Cygnus the Swan flying straight down the Milky Way. On the eastern horizon, just up and rising was the Old Moon in the New Moon's arms. Erik took off his glasses and his face in the moonlight was the face of a boy, freckled, near-sighted, way too hopeful in that moment for what lay behind the eyes.

He lifted me from the hammock, carried me out to the middle of the yard, and set me down where there was nothing around us but sky, wide and deep as the ocean.

"Before I got my glasses," he said, "I thought the stars were cotton balls."

Then he put his hands back on my shoulders and kissed me again. He kissed me in that meadow like our lives depended on it, like it was some kind of world-class competition, and we were the defending champs. He kissed me till the stars above me turned to whirlybirds and Chinese dragons. He kissed me till I was almost too far gone to feel the pressure of him on my leg through his pants.

"I think we're having a little reawakening here," he said, his mouth still wrapped around mine.

"Oh my God," I said. "What should I do?"

He pulled a glow-in-the-dark condom out of his back pocket. It was a French tickler, had a little mountain range of thicker latex that glowed even deeper than the tip.

"Put it on me," he said, "then you can show me where Jupiter is."

The next morning I had to leave for two weeks to shoot the

Perseid meteor shower over the Pacific for the tourist council in Washington State. Erik said he might stay on at the ranch a few days before he went back to Kansas, replace the rotting porch boards, maybe even fix the fence.

He drove me to Alamosa. "You miss me now," I said, at the airport's only gate.

"I will," he said and the air went out of him in a rush like a tire.

"And you take care a little, will you . . ." I said. "Try not to . . . you know . . . detonate."

He shook his head yes, or maybe no, knowing neither answer mattered.

I kissed the top of his head, then his mouth. The ticket agent jiggled the doorknob to get my attention.

I said, "I'm crazy about you."

And he said, "Crazy, period."

The air was hot on the tarmac. I turned around once, twice, three times on the way to the airplane and he was still there and waving. I got in my seat, a window on his side I knew he couldn't see into, and he was still there. All through the checkout procedure and then through a ten-minute ground hold he didn't move from the window. And when the pilot cranked up the engine, and the little plane finally began to move away, he raised his hand slowly, half wave, half embarrassment, and stayed in the window till we lifted the wheels off runway A.

The phone rang at two a.m. in the middle of my first night in Washington and I came up from a dead sleep smiling.

"I've got poems in my head," he said, "and paintings." Laughter bubbled up and out of him like a waterfall.

"I'm drunk," he said.

I said, "It doesn't matter."

"This will scare you," he said, "and I don't want it to, but I haven't seriously considered killing myself in seventy-six hours and twenty-three minutes."

"It doesn't scare me," I said, only half lying.

"I've never walked away from any edge in a straight line before."

"No," I said.

"And there's no reason to believe I'll be able to now."

"No," I said.

"The last lady I loved is dead," he said. "The one before that ripped my guts out and left me in the nuthouse. You understand that these are fairly high stakes?"

"Yes," I said.

"I'm sure I'm not saying any of the right things," he said.

"You're doing fine," I told him.

"I'm not sure," he said, "but I think the thing I am might be peaceful."

"I can't tell you," I said. "I've never had any idea what that is."

I was just about back asleep when the phone rang again. It was Carter's best friend Allen to tell me Carter was in Montreal, only one step ahead of a film crew, but desperate even so to get a message to me. He wanted Allen to sing me "Daisy Jane" and "More Than a Feeling." He wanted me to know he was almost ready to begin Act Two.

228

I cut Allen off after only one verse and told him about Erik as easily as if he were a court reporter investigating a petty crime.

He said, "What do you want me to say to Carter about sex?"

I said, "Tell him I've discovered that it's very simple. That you have it, then you have it again, then you have it again; and then you get up and have breakfast."

Okay. Here's the third thing. One night, long after I'd stopped even hoping for anything, Carter got in bed with me and snuggled into my shoulder, facing me frontwards for the very first time. "Did you feel that?" he giggled. "My wee-wee touched your buns."

On the coast of Washington I spent my days in the darkroom and my nights in the sand dunes waiting for the stars to fall down.

I met a woman there named Gloria who grew gladiolas and garlic in her garden for money and was in love with a Polynesian man named Joey who she said drank too much beer.

We rode her horses out to a beach that was covered at low tide with every color of sea glass, stars of red and green and sky and indigo, winking up at us out of the sand.

She told me the story of how she and Joey got together. How they'd been high school sweethearts, had lost touch for twenty-five years, how she started suddenly dreaming about him, how in her dreams he was always sick or dying, in some kind of terrible trouble that she couldn't prevent.

229

Her husband had walked out on her after eighteen years of marriage. She was trying to manage the garlic farm on her own. But the dreams continued and she called a long-ago number that belonged to Joey's sister. She was more than a little surprised when it was Joey himself who picked up the phone.

The first thing he told her was that he was a junkie, that he'd spent most of his life in prison, the rest in Vietnam. She asked him if he looked the same and he said yes but his hair was white. All the guys in prison called him the snowy owl.

When she went to California they had less than twenty-four hours together to see what was between them. She was raising three daughters then, and was concerned for their safety. He said he'd come help her with the farm, said if she wanted he'd trade the drugs in for beer.

She spent two months in the deciding; unlike her, she said, not to know right away. She was driving home one night from work, thinking she'd go mad with indecision, when a huge white bird streaked across her windshield. She called Joey and told him to come the next day.

The tide was coming in, covering the glass and making the horses jumpy. I watched Gloria ease her big gelding around a log that blocked our path.

"The trouble with loving the crazy ones," she said, "is when you get tired, and need to rest, the normal guys just don't interest you anymore," and she patted her horse's neck harder than normal, and the tears came up in her eyes.

In the middle of those two endless days of walking out of the deep woods with Carter, when all the silence had become too much, I said, "Okay Carter. I'm a genie and I can grant you three wishes. What are they."

He stopped walking for a moment, stretched his back against his pack and said, "A house in the Caribbean, perfect eyesight till I die, and effortless ability on the twelve-string guitar."

"Good wishes," I said, and started walking again.

I heard him walking behind me, contemplating, I suppose, all he hadn't wished for, and why.

"Okay," he finally said, drawing a breath as big as an obligation. "I'm a genie, and you have three wishes."

I listened to the soles of my hiking boots hit the ground underneath me once, twice, and then three times.

"No, Carter," I said, "*I'm* the genie."

Erik didn't call again the whole two weeks I was in Washington, but on the day before I left I got a videotape in the mail of him and Paul performing the Power Tool Olympics: boxing drills and racing belt sanders, beer-chugging vacuum cleaners and high-diving circular saws.

When I flew back into Alamosa, he was waiting for me in the cage that extends from the waiting room out onto the runway. He was wearing a chauffeur's cap, dark glasses, a leather jacket, and a sock for a tie safety-pinned to his collar, carrying a sign with my name on it.

Back at the ranch Paul was waiting for us in a red-and-black shirt that said Alpine Bowling and a stainless-steel WWI helmet sitting square on his head.

As I got out of the car he lit the fuse and in less than ten seconds the cannon exploded, and we watched the ball recede like something out of Wile E. Coyote, heard the holes in it whistle like a spinner top gone mad. Then it disappeared into the white sky, out of sight, out of hearing.

"Listen," Erik whispered, "it's on its way back down."

And the whistling did come back, getting louder and louder, until I wanted to dive under Paul's truck in case reentry happened right above our heads. We saw the cloud of dust where the ball fell in the pasture.

"Forty-nine seconds," Paul said, smiling. "Even at only two hundred miles an hour, that's an impelled distance of almost eight thousand feet."

Erik winked at me over the cab of his pick-up. From across the pasture all six horses came thundering back towards the barn.

Erik headed across the field in the direction of the little dust cloud. His giant frame was hunched like always, but I thought I saw something lighter in his step. That's when I saw that my house was sitting true as a level against the side of the hill.

"Wait a minute," I yelled to Erik. "What have you guys been doing out here?" He grinned at me over his shoulder and kept walking to the place where the bowling ball fell.

"He's fourteen days into detox," Paul said. "Five beers a day, no hard stuff, a couple of shots on Sunday, he says, if he's been good."

"Can he do that?" I said. "Is that even possible?"

"I don't know," Paul said, "but there's not many people can shoot a bowling ball farther than a mile."

We watched Erik move in and out of the shadows the afternoon thunderclouds made on the meadow. A distant rumble turned both our heads westward, a different kind of cannon talking back, and I remembered sitting on the edge of the

232

Black Canyon, a chasm as dark as this meadow was light, and I wondered what would have happened if my mother had sat on the ledge where I did, and I understood that a death wish is a life wish as sure as love is the flip side of fear.

I showed Paul the pictures we took at Black Canyon.

"Gun powder and nitroglycerin," he said. "It's the same exact thing on your face as his."

"I'll go make us some lunch," I said, and started walking towards the ranch house.

"Uhh . . . don't mind the parakeets," Paul said. "The ones in the freezer. They've been traveling with Erik a real long time."

"Parakeets," I said.

"Their names are Perky and Stationary," Paul said. "It's kind of a long story."

Across the pasture Erik had found the ball and was jumping up and down and waving. Paul waved back and gave him the thumbs-up.

"Men are like puppies," Gloria had said when the last of the glass on the beach got covered. "You can't ever give them too much love."

One day soon I'm going to ask Erik to build me a darkroom. After that, a skylight over my bed. I've got a new foundation under my house and now that I'm not afraid we're falling into it, I'm starting to get attached to this view of the river.

When I ask Erik how we got so lucky he shrugs and says, "You're the genie." He says this ranch is the best place in the universe for a girl who wants to shoot at the stars.

The Kind of People You Trust with Your Life

THE GLIDER PILOTS COME up from Colorado Springs the third week in September each year to catch the aspen trees turning from green to gold. There are fifteen or twenty of them in all and they bring ten planes, and for a few days the skies above Hope, usually so empty, are filled with a flock of huge and silent silver birds.

In the late afternoon their long wings catch the sun one at a time as they make their big slow turn at the head of the valley, lining up with the airstrip to land. There's nothing but sunlight and cornflower-blue sky, trees every color of fire and the mountains with their early snow—and then the sudden gleam of silver, like a star come up a few hours too early. And I don't care who you are when you see it—how little you care about above-ground travel—something will leap in your insides at the sight of their thin wings reaching, and you'll want, at least for a moment, to know what it is to fly.

Hope's airstrip is smack dab in the middle of the valley, paved during the tail end of the mining years and long enough to set down a 727 if you know what you are doing. The glider pilots like Hope because the valley floor is at nine thousand feet, and they can be up among the peaks of all the surrounding thirteeners in no time, can get towed that high even, if there aren't any thermals to lift them into the cool thin air. They like tumbling their gliders over the valley's steep walls, like what the terrain demands of them, the tight turns and corners, the sweet acrobatics the mountains make out of the air.

The pilots offer rides to the locals who want them: fifty dollars for thirty minutes. The worst day in Hope, they say, is a fair sight better than the best day down in their big flat city out on the plains.

I like to do my flying in the middle of the night when I'm sound asleep and dreaming or on a 747 where, if one engine quits, you've got two more to get you home, but B.J. insisted that I try gliding.

It's a once-in-a-lifetime experience, she said, though she does it yearly, and the pilots are smart and kind, every one of them. The kind of people, she said, you felt good to trust with your life.

The stories were all around town about last year's accident, how the pilot went up empty just before the front came through, how he got himself caught in a thermal bigger than he could fly out of, how he got carried higher and higher—

235

above sixteen thousand feet—until the storm finally did come, seventy-five-mile-an-hour winds that blew the glider not only down but sideways, and eventually straight into the cliff face the maps call Bristol Head.

B.J. had gone up the day of last year's storm, was up the same time as the guy who died on Bristol, got caught, in fact, in the very same thermal. She was with a pilot called Gray, one of the old-timers who'd been trained at the Air Force Academy. Serious as a heart attack Gray was, steady as a rock.

They were in radio contact, B.J. said, with the grand gliding poobah on the ground, who had seen the other craft crash just moments before but had the good sense not to tell Gray and B.J. When the bottom fell out of the air mass that held them and it started raining sideways and the winds started pushing eighty knots and Gray tried to bring the thing down toward the runway, the poobah said, "This wind is ninety degrees to the airstrip, Gray. All I can do is wish you good luck."

"That's what he always says when he thinks we aren't gonna make it," Gray said to B.J. Then, "What do you say we prove the bastard wrong."

They had no choice but to hit the runway at a forty-five-degree angle; to turn the side of the glider to the wind would have been suicide. Gray let the thing bounce once at that angle and then turned the nose straight across the runway to face the wind. He gambled that they could fly in place long enough for the folks on the ground to get to them with tie-downs. Gray and the glider went home to Colorado Springs without a scratch. B.J. says she's been waiting all year for a chance to get up there and do it one more time.

236

No one in Hope was surprised when Erik started drinking again. They all waited for it like another bad winter, and when it came they did what anyone would have done: put an extra layer of Visqueen between themselves and the truth of it, went inside, and waited for things to warm up again.

I didn't blame them, knew I might have chosen that way myself, but I didn't have the option. Erik did all his drinking inside my house.

I focused on work and tried not to notice when he went from five beers a day to seven, and then thirteen and then more. After a couple of months of living with it I flew to Los Angeles to do a shoot of some cowboys in Compton who kept their horses boarded like dogs in junkyard lots, but perfectly cared for, their stalls immaculate, their feed bins filled with the best-quality hay.

I called home one night to see how things were going. Ellie the dog's bout with distemper had resurfaced in the form of occasional seizures. Erik had promised to watch her closely, and give her two kinds of medicine, both a preventive and a recuperative if a seizure occurred. It took less than a second of hearing his voice for me to realize he was hammered, maybe worse off than I'd ever known him to be.

When I was a child, I didn't know the word *alcoholic*. I only knew that my universe changed every day at five-thirty from something predictable into something twisted, something tilted on its axis. I didn't know how long Erik's binge had been going on or how long it would continue, but I did know that if we lost Ellie, I would want retribution for her—and it scared me what I thought about when I thought about what kind.

When I got home and tried to talk to him about it, Erik said, "It's like a dog who pisses on the carpet. You have to catch him in the act to make the punishment work."

"You're not a dog," I said, "and you should go back to Kansas and decide how much and how often you really want to drink."

It took him a week but he finally sobered up enough to get in his truck and drive for fifteen hours, and it took about that much time for the ranch to feel all empty again.

B.J. said it wasn't in my cards to make it work with an alcoholic and she sounded so sure of herself I let her do my explaining in town. She's been keeping a pretty close eye on me and I am grateful for it. Gliding, she says, will give me just the jumpstart I need.

I've invited her for breakfast on the morning we are supposed to go, and while waiting for her I'm drinking tea and reading *Psychology Today* and wondering whether going up in an airplane without an engine falls into the category of things I don't have to do anymore to prove I am macho, or things that would be *good* for me to do because it would give me an opportunity to freely show my fear.

"I'm scared," I say, trying out words that are rarely part of my vocabulary in the quiet of the empty kitchen. "I don't want to go," is the sentence I try out next.

B.J. comes in the door in a hot-pink flight suit three sizes too big for her, a clothespin holding it together; her high school

238

Buddy Holly glasses, broken at the temple, sit a little crooked on her face.

"Excited?" she says between bites of banana.

"Can't wait," are the words that come out of my mouth.

B.J. puts water on for my second cup of tea without even asking. "I don't really get what you're worried about," B.J. says. "You've done much scarier things than this."

And it's true, I have, but less and less frequently, and, as the years go by, with more and more care. What I haven't been able to do is take the final step backwards, to turn the *how*, if it's possible, back into an *if*.

"Listen to this," B.J. says, reading aloud from my most recent *Astronomy Magazine*. "It says that right now is the best time to view Algol, the demon star. Algol's light dims and gets steadily brighter in perfect three-day cycles. It's called an eclipsing binary, actually two stars, not one, that revolve endlessly around each other and temporarily obscure each other's light."

"Sort of like a bad relationship," I say.

"Or a good one," she says. "Each one gives the other a little time to rest."

"You're very pink and full of optimism this morning," I say.

"And you are . . ." she says.

"Scared," I say, and notice that the earth doesn't tremble. "Of going gliding, I mean."

"You're going to love it, Lucy," she says. "Everybody's scared the first time. Besides, this day couldn't be more different from that crazy day last year." She isn't quite concealing the disappointment in her voice. "Not a cloud in the sky this morning," she says, "not even a breath of wind."

239

"Surely even you must think that's a good thing," I say.

"Oh, I'm not hoping for a storm," she says, "but gliding's only half the experience. A few clouds help the pilots find the thermals. You have to catch a thermal if you're going to be able to soar."

"And soaring is something I want to do?" I say.

"If you want the full experience," she says.

But I'm not at all sure I do. Gliding sounds like more than enough excitement for my very first time airborne under God's own power. The full experience, whatever that is, might just have to wait till I am ready for it.

"You should eat some breakfast," B.J. says.

"Right," I say. "For the turbulence."

"That," she says, "and also because whenever you go up in a plane that has no engine, you can never be sure where and when you're gonna come down."

Our glider pilot, whose name is Bobby, has long hair under his camel jockey hat and a Fu Manchu mustache, looks sixteen years old, and is partially deaf. He says there hasn't been a bit of lift in the air all weekend, but they are hoping this afternoon will be better.

I tell Bobby I want to go first, want to go before there are any thermals, that a gentle tow up and a quick ride down is just what the doctor ordered for me.

I am strapped in, in front of Bobby. What there is between me and eternity is a Plexiglas window and a paper-thin aluminum nose.

"I'm scared," I say again to B.J. as she stands nearby snapping pictures with one of my cameras.

240

"Everything okay up there?" Bobby asks me.

"How would I know if it wasn't," I say, but he doesn't answer me and I realize it's because he hasn't been able to read my lips.

We each have a rudder control between our legs, each have a set of aileron controls on the floor.

"Don't touch that stick if you can help it," he says, "and try to keep your feet off those pedals."

I unlatch my shoulder harness and turn around to face him. "What will happen if I don't?" I ask, as loud as I can, and slowly.

"Nothing good," he says, leaning forward and strapping me back in my harness. "Trust me on this. But if anything happens to me, it's the simplest machine in the airways. You steer on the flat with this one"—the rudder does a suggestive circle between my thighs—"and the pedals work your flaps." They jump up and down under my hiking boots. "You know enough about how a plane flies to land this baby in the event of an emergency?"

"No way," I say, as loud as I can stand to.

"Good," Bobby says. "Then I guess we're out of here."

A boy, no more than nine or ten, is responsible for checking the connection between the towrope and the glider. A couple of men come out on the strip to run with us and hold the wings level while we get our speed.

The little yellow towplane starts its engine. Thumbs-ups are given all around and then we start to roll.

B.J. stands on the runway, waving with one hand and taking pictures with the other.

241

"We'll get off the ground first," Bobby says. "Full of gas he weighs five times more than we do."

The words are no more out of his mouth than our wheel is off the runway, the rope to the back of the towplane holding us down. Then the towplane is off too and flying straight up the river toward my ranch, and for a moment I think how great it will be to see it for the very first time from the air, and I even forget my fear. But then the towplane banks hard to the south over Moonshine Mesa and starts the first circle that will get us up high, and the fear comes back, a little like an infection, in the same part of my guts, but stronger than before.

I watch the yellow towplane hit pockets of air that make it bump up and down, watch the strain we put on him going into tight corners. Below us, and somewhere on the edges of my consciousness, aspen groves the size of entire counties back east are almost fluorescent: yellow and saffron and occasionally orange, some south-facing slopes still holding their green.

In the distance on all sides of me is the country I love more than any other: Half-moon Pass and the La Garita, Baldy Cinco and San Luis Peak. But I am too busy inventing a catastrophe a minute to notice, and then the yellow plane straightens out and heads for the air above town.

The town of Hope lays itself out below us like a pop-up greeting card. At the end of Main Street two fifteen-hundred-foot rocks rise, jagged and angry as the gates of hell on either side of the relatively tiny silver-bearing creek. The rocks look great in tourist photos; they work even better as a place to shoot fireworks from on the Fourth of July. As a place for one plane to pull another that doesn't have an engine . . . call me crazy, but I'd think again.

Bobby giggles, which I take simultaneously as a good and bad sign. He says, "He's gonna try to get us some lift off those walls."

We are headed, as near as I can tell, straight between the toothy rocks that guard town.

"I'm gonna see if we can catch this thermal," Bobby says, and pulls the crank that makes the rudder jump between my legs. The big metal hook clanks loud against the bottom of the aluminum glider and I realize we are free.

We clear the tips of the guardian rocks by what seems to me inches, and the towplane has turned south and away over Bachelor Mountain. Below us I can see the remains of the silver mines: the Amethyst, the Midwest, and my favorite, the Happy Thought.

The pedals below my feet come to life again, and Bobby turns the plane so hard in a loop it seems we are spinning around the stationary tip of one wing.

"Watch the altimeter," he says. "We're going up."

And we are climbing: 11.5, 11.6, 11.7.

"We're gaining almost three hundred feet per minute," Bobby says, "and we don't have an engine! That's faster than any other plane in the air except a jet."

12.4, 12.5, 12.6. The top of the fourteeners behind Silver City come into view: the jagged Handies Peak and the stately Wetterhorn, and Uncompahgre Peak, its bizarre angle and copper stains looking like a cone of rum raisin ice cream on a too-hot August day.

243

Now below us Hope looks even more like a miniature, a game to play on a lazy Sunday, something Erik might have made with his hands.

13.9, 14.3, 14.7. Isn't there some rule about oxygen over fourteen thousand feet?

"This is the best lift I've had all summer," Bobby says. "You must be my good luck charm."

The needle hovers for a moment right at fifteen thousand feet.

"There's an impenetrable cliff to the north of here," Bobby says suddenly. "I think we should see if we can make it."

My mind plays the sentence over and over, trying to tease out every possible meaning. Bobby takes the plane out of its upspin and turns it north toward Bristol Head.

"This is unbelievable!" he says, almost whispering now. "We're still going up."

The plane is moving faster and faster. "We're going ninety-five knots," he says. "And . . ."

"We don't have an engine." I say the words with him.

Bristol Head rises up out of the valley floor below us, its big flat alpine top some color between green and gold, tiger's-eye after hours in a tumbler, but I only see it out the corner of my eye.

Fear is rising to the boiling point inside me, heated white-hot from within until it is a pure thing, until there isn't room for anything else, even casual observation, even—and this is how I know how bad I have it—the desire to record it on film.

"On the other side of this flat rock," Bobby says, "is the sheerest cliff you've ever seen." But I already know that. It is

244

the cliff where last year's joyride ended. It is the cliff I look up at from my ranch every day.

The first thing to remember about the full experience, I think as we hurtle toward the edge of Bristol Head, is that it so often comes upon you whether you are ready or not.

Then we cross over the edge of the cliff and the bottom falls out of the rising air, and we start down the front of the cliff face with a vengeance.

You must surrender to it, was what Carlos Castaneda told me once, *or be lost.* I relax my death grip on the sides of the plane. *Take a breath,* I think, *take a picture.*

"Ready to do some maneuvers?" Bobby says.

"I think for right now this is good enough," I say, before I remember that with Bobby all the questions are rhetorical.

Then Bobby turns the plane upside down.

We barrel-roll down the cliff face of Bristol Head, turning all the way over like a raft in a river, only in the river I was always flipping backwards, ass over teakettle, and we are flipping forwards this time, head over heels.

The skin on my face sucks back against the g-force. The rock face, the valley, the fields of barely turned aspens spin in an illogical order. Then Bobby straightens her out for a moment and it feels like we are climbing again.

"How'd you like that?" Bobby shouts.

"That was amazing," I say, though I know that he can't hear me. Because all of a sudden I'm not scared anymore. I understand that what we've done is nothing like flipping in a river. There is no water to drown us, no rocks to hurt us, nothing all around us except sweet golden Colorado air. And it doesn't seem anymore as though we are flying in a plane without an engine; it seems more like we've been let in on some kind of secret, allowed to move through space on the back of a wonderful lunatic toy.

The smile on my face feels like it's straining muscles and it occurs to me that it might be the first one since last month when Erik started hitting it hard. Alcohol could do that to me, make me scared of everything, scared of the wrong things, scared of the things that could set me free.

"Bobby," I yell, "let's please do that again!"

I try to get my camera up to take a picture but the g-force won't let me.

We are right over the ranch now. I can see the familiar bend in the river, the wide green swath of Antelope Park. I can see Middle Creek, Ivy Creek, even the tiny Lime Creek as it tumbles across the meadow and past my ranch house on its way to the Rio Grande. I can even see the skylight Erik built me so I can look at the stars above my bed, and I know for all his kindness that he'll never have the full experience, that he's spent his whole life thinking that he's lucky to be gliding, when he and all the rest of us were really meant to soar.

"Ready?" Bobby says and I give him the thumbs-up over my shoulder.

This time it is wingovers, a gentler motion than the barrel roll, the movements of a corkscrew, one I can keep track of. I even manage to get my camera up to take a couple of ranch pictures upside down.

That's mine, I think, and know with the thinking that whatever good comes my way will come because I have found a place to say those words about. It's not owning the ranch so much as being responsible for it, knowing for the first time ever how to use the word *home*.

"You want to do a high-speed dive?" Bobby asks me.

"Yes," I shout, "I want to do everything!"

He puts the runway out the front window, and points the nose straight down.

B.J. is standing right where I left her. I imagine her eyes getting wider and wider as we dive, eighty, ninety, a hundred, a hundred twenty miles an hour out of the sky. I imagine the smile that will cross her face as we pull back up.

If you go to the bottom of a deep enough well, my first professor of astronomy told us, *even in broad daylight you can see the stars.*

I never believed him enough in those days to test the theory. Now I don't have to. Now there is a star in the sun-drenched sky and I am inside it. There are all kinds of theories I'll never have to test again.

When I was sixteen years old, my father took me aside and said, "Lucille, one of these days you are going to wake up and realize that you spend your whole life in the gutter with somebody else's foot on your neck."

I think what he said might have been true for Erik. I have fought my whole life to make it not true for me.

"We'll give you one more thing to tell your friends about," Bobby says, but whatever it is I know I've got plenty.

I'm in a plane with no engine, gliding over my very own home in the Rocky Mountains, spinning and whirling over fields the color of angels. We just did another high-speed dive into a barrel roll. Bobby says we haven't even gotten started yet.

The Whole Weight of Me

IT'S NOT EVER VERY easy to get from Hope to Province-town. That night it meant a six-hour drive to Albuquerque, a plane from Albuquerque to Denver, another from Denver to Chicago, another from Chicago to Boston, and a three-hour drive in a rent-a-wreck Chevy Cavalier convertible with a shot muffler out to the tip of the Cape.

It had been a long winter in Hope, spring colder than any-one could remember and slower to come. My night-sky series had made it into six galleries back east, stretching from Boston to D.C., and the photographs were getting noticed to the tune of I-might-be-able-to-pay-the-back-taxes-on-the-ranch-after-all.

On the 1st of July I was scheduled to teach a workshop at the

248

Fine Arts Center in Provincetown. A freak snowstorm blew through Hope the night I packed my bags.

When I got to Provincetown I went straight down to Commercial Street and took myself out to dinner: lobster and a half bottle of good California Chardonnay. I wanted to write that sentence just like that, natural, like taking myself out to a nice place to eat was something I did regularly, even though in thirty-five years of living mostly alone this was the very first time.

The restaurant had a nice hum about it, the sound of lovers and families on vacation. I read every item on the menu twice and then tried to fix a pleasant and self-possessed look on my face.

I liked the waitress, thought by the way she talked she might be a photographer too, and for a moment I hoped she'd recognize the name on my credit card, but she didn't.

Back out on Commercial Street it was getting dark and the carnival was in full swing: a seven-foot Hispanic man stunning in a backless black shift and stilettos, men in leather and latex and clothespins hanging out by the hundreds on the steps of the post office, and a Chrysler convertible full of cross-dressed debutantes, their wigs rustling in the fish-tinged air.

The gay men moved up and down the street in packs, the lesbian women in pairs, desire as tangible as patchouli in the air. Even the rare hetero couples, some of them looking like they hadn't touched in years, clung to each other, though whether out of fear or rekindled desire it was impossible to say.

The store was called Toys of Eros, and I had seen one like it when I lived in Oakland, though I'd never had the nerve to go inside. I looked at the shiny steel vibrators, the leather harnesses in which you could mount them, the covers of the instruction books in lesbian love. I wondered for a moment how I'd gotten into the store in the first place and blamed it on the Chardonnay.

"If you want me to demonstrate anything, just say," the counter girl said. She had jet-black hair and braces, a leather shirt, tight-fitting and laced up the front.

In a glass case near the back of the room was an assortment of Japanese dildos made of soft translucent plastic in muted colors and with some kind of animal attached at the base, curving first outward and then in. The kangaroo, the rabbit, the great brown bear, noses and ears turned inward, poised at the ready.

"Aren't they fine?" the girl said. "And you can control the speed of the animals independently of the rest."

"I'll take the rabbit," I said, like I was ordering dinner in a French restaurant, like I spent eighty-five dollars on an imported Japanese vibrator every day.

"I'll have to test it for you," she said. "We have a policy where we can't take anything back." The dildo turned in slow, then faster circles; the rabbit burrowed, shuddered in the air.

My credit card was hardly out of my hand before her smile broadened.

"Hey, I know you," she said. "I saw your photographs in Boston—you're teaching here this week. I tried to get off work to take your class."

"Thanks," I said.

"I love your pictures," she said, "and now I know what kind of vibrator you like." She laughed easily. "Just kidding," she said. "You enjoy this now."

There were twelve photographers in my class and they came from all up and down the Eastern Seaboard. One of them, a woman named Marilyn from Connecticut, looked enough like me to be my sister. They were smart and tough in that East Coast way that always surprised me. I dismissed them after an hour of introductions, thinking it was going to be a good week.

After class I saw my name on the bulletin board in red letters.

"Toys of Eros called. You forgot your batteries." Each letter of the message was two and a half inches high.

"What you need," Marilyn said over chocolate gelato with boysenberry sauce on the patio of Bubula's restaurant, "is a nice bond trader."

"I don't even know what that is," I said.

Marilyn's friend Dorothy had told her if she bought a blue packet of Dunhill cigarettes and walked around with them in a conspicuous fashion, it meant she was a lesbian looking for love. And because Marilyn was neither, was in fact a bond trader's wife with a big house and three children, she won my heart forever when she pulled the Dunhills out of her purse and sat them on the table between us.

"The truth is," I said, "there's not a man I've met lately who doesn't disqualify himself in the first five minutes. I'm thinking more and more about trying it with a woman. I'm thinking about going to China and adopting a baby girl."

"That's how my sister felt," Marilyn said, "before she met Roger. Before that she had every kind of bad thing you could name."

Just then, between all the leather and dyed spiky hair there emerged a heterosexual couple. She had long blond hair and a simple green velvet dress and carried a baby in a pack between her slim shoulders. He wore a rough silk suit and loafers, held her hand, and cooed to the baby. They stood out in Provincetown exactly as much, I thought, as the convertible full of debutantes would have stood out in Hope.

"They seem to have managed to put it all together," Marilyn said, laughing. "Don't tell me for a minute you wouldn't take that."

"Have you noticed," I said, "how many of these lesbian couples look like each other? I mean height and weight and clothes and even hair."

"They call it mirroring," she said. "Dorothy told me it's got to do with self-love and acceptance."

"I don't know," I said, "if that would work for me."

"It would tell you a lot about how you see yourself," she said.

"My mother used to say, 'Lucy, if a fat girl is what they see the first time they look at you, it doesn't matter what you say or do after that, you'll always be a fat girl in their eyes.'"

Marilyn looked up and down the length of my body, which was fit from the winter of cross-country skiing, my muscles taut, my limbs long and strong. "How did you look then?" is what she finally asked.

"Like every other skinny kid in a halter top and cutoffs," I said. "I have pictures to prove it, though there's never been a day of my life when I haven't felt as big as a barn."

"Me too," she said, and started to play with her ice cream. I looked at her body, which was sturdy and well proportioned, her skin tanned the color of rosewood.

252

"I never told that to anyone," I said.

"It's all the sex that people are having around here," she said. "It rubs off, makes you free." She tipped a Dunhill out of the pack and let it sit unlit between her fingers.

"My mother used to have me stand with my hand under the tap water," she said, "squeezing food through my fingers to give me the illusion of digestion."

"Every morning," I said, "even when I was five, my mother would say, 'Let's see if we can get all the way to dinner without eating anything at all.'"

"We had very complicated rules when we went out to dinner," Marilyn said, "which was always. No appetizers or dessert ever, and if you wanted extra credit you could order . . ."

"An appetizer instead of dinner," I said. "And no bread."

"I still don't do bread," she said, "but I think it's the only holdover."

"I always think," I said, "if I never spent another minute feeling bad about the shape of my body, what would I do with all that space in my brain?"

"Love somebody," she said, "raise children, all the real-life stuff people do if they ever get out of their heads."

"So then it might be a good thing to fall in love with a mirror," I said.

"Or," she said, "a man who can show you that your mother was wrong."

I thought about Carter Thompson, who said my wrists weren't slim enough, and Erik, whose interest in sex dried up when he did, and hadn't returned when he went back to the booze.

"There's a reason," Marilyn said, "that our mothers were like that, but we don't have to go there if it's going to freak you out."

"No, I know what you mean," I said, but I wasn't at all sure I did.

"Get clear on that and there will be good love out there waiting for you," Marilyn said. "I know it." She stuffed the Dunhills into her backpack and signaled for the check.

The far end of Commercial Street was blocked to traffic and a street band was playing. The musicians were from Africa, half white and half Zulu, and they had brought a Zulu dancer, a woman three times my size in what my mother would have called an unflattering costume, and when she danced, when she moved her body—half to the music it seemed and half to the rhythm inside her—even the stiffest among us had to dance in the street.

Up onstage the men and the large woman were doing the Zulu war dance, a movement old as Africa where the warriors appear to put one leg at a time up, over, and around the back of their heads.

"That would make an impression on all those enemy tribes," Marilyn said, and then she started to dance.

I started to dance too, slow at first, but then faster and faster as the song gathered force. I threw my arms and legs in the air in a way that let me forget—for a moment, and then more—to worry what I looked like, and I knew if I could keep dancing just that way forever, Marilyn would be right, and good love would come.

On Tuesday night I gave my techniques talk to the whole
Fine Arts community and it was after that that he approached.
It was raining outside the lecture hall and I had my hood up,
and I remember thinking I probably looked silly but it would
be sillier still to take the hood down in the rain.

"Are you Lucy O'Rourke?" he said. "My name is Marcus,
Marcus Larisa. I love your work. All that I've seen of it. I
wanted to be able to say that to your face."

"Are you the painter?" I said. Marilyn had told me that the
guy teaching the painting seminar was cute.

"No, no, I work at the New York Public Library, fundrais-
ing mostly, with a little time to write. I'm here for a couple of
weeks finishing a book on the history of the Cape."

He was getting rained on, hard now, but he didn't seem to
notice. His hair was black and made darker still by the rain-
water. A drop caught for a moment in his lashes and ran
straight to a tiny mole on his cheek.

"Listen," he said, "would you like to go out with me sometime?"

I raised my eyebrows under the hood.

"Tomorrow night," he said, "or Thursday?"

"What are you doing right now?" I said.

"Nothing," he said, though I could see that his friends were
waiting for him.

"Just a minute, then," I said, "I'll grab my keys. Do you need
a coat or something?"

"No," he said, "the rain's getting ready to stop."

We walked the length of Commercial Street until it ended
in a two-mile jetty—a breakwater, they call it—over a thou-

sand tons of rock brought in from somewhere and placed in a line as straight as a road more than a mile across the Province-town harbor and out to the lighthouses on Wood End and Long Point.

The rain had stopped and turned into a mist that whipped around in the night wind and made the lights from town look like globes at Christmas. I was still wearing the dress from my lecture, but I'd had the sense to change my heels for Tevas. Still, the rocks were slippery and I couldn't see where my feet were with my dress billowing around my ankles.

There are five stories I tell about myself when I want some-body to fall in love with me, either seriously or only for sport. They are stories from the road, mostly, adventure stories I've tried to tell with my camera, but for some reason they come out better in words. I was on the third one—about the time I spent two weeks in jail in Belize for taking night shots of the drug-runners landing their Sea Otters offshore in the break-ers—when Marcus asked me if it made me uncomfortable just to talk. Then he asked me why I wasn't married.

"I always pick the wrong man," I said. "I'm kind of famous for it. My friend Henry says I can turn anybody into the wrong man."

"I guess that makes you the wrong woman," he said.

"Sometimes," I said. "Sometimes they were just losers. But they've all given me photographs, they've all given me stories."

"That's all losers have to give, isn't it?" he said. "Stories."

"In graduate school they told us that's all there was," I said, "the image and the story you could tell with it."

"Graduate school," he said. "All those people talking around the edges, but nothing in the center."

"That's me," I said, "but I'm working on it."

"Me too," he said and he took my hand.

By the time we got a half mile out, the wind started howling and the waves were kicking up over the rocks and leaving puddles at our feet.

Everything I knew about coastal New England would fit in the pocket of my long and colorful dress, but I thought I remembered something about the tides changing big and quickly.

"Hey," I said, staying on one rock while Marcus jumped to another, "do you know what you're doing out here?"

"No," he said, "I assumed you did."

And he lifted me from my rock to his and kissed me and it was way too soon but I kissed him back.

"I think it could get scary," I said, "if the tide came in fast. We'll do it tomorrow," I said. "I won't wear a dress."

"You mean you want to see me tomorrow?" he said, and when he turned his head toward me his whole face was laughing.

"Yes," I said, though I hadn't thought there would be such a simple answer, and he squeezed my hand and we turned back toward the lights of Commercial Street, back to my room in the Fine Arts Center barn.

On the couch he pulled my feet into his lap and started rubbing them as naturally as if we'd been at it twenty years. He told me I looked tired and I told him that I wasn't, which was true but he took it as an invitation to kiss me again. I liked the way he kissed me, liked the taste of the sea salt on his mustache, liked to put my hands in all that thick black hair.

The first time his hands touched my breast I pushed him away.

"Okay," I said. "Now you tell me your story."

He sat back on the couch and looked straight into my eyes. "I have a beautiful son who is the center of my life. I was in a very bad marriage for a long time and one day I woke up and I knew it was over. I was staying in it for my boy, but I was eventually able to see that I could be a better father if I was a happier man. I have my own life now. I have good friends and the writing that I love. The last three years have been all about learning to live with authenticity, and I know it must be working, or I would never have had the nerve to ask you out."

"That's a good story," I said, and then, "If you want you can kiss me some more."

Maybe it was because of his dark eyes, and the last time a dark-eyed boy kissed me I was seventeen years old. Maybe it was being back on the East Coast of my childhood. Maybe it had something to do with feeling my own bare shoulders against the cheap corduroy couch. But I didn't let him take my shirt off that night, and I finally asked him to leave.

"It's because I really like you," I said, and meant it.

He said, "You really like me, but."

"I really like you, period," I said, "and so I want you to go home."

"Like the old days," he said, and by his smile I knew he believed me. "Like the lovers in 'Ode on a Grecian Urn.' "

"Exactly," I said, though I couldn't remember much about those lovers. "Tomorrow night," I said. "We'll make the end of the rocks."

———————

After class Marilyn and I went to get ice cream. Soft-serve vanilla, but in Provincetown they swirled their vanilla psychedelic: green and pink and yellow and blue.

"I think it's great," she said. "I'm just saying don't sleep with him."

"He's a good kisser," I said. "Afterwards he looks me right in the eyes." We walked out to the end of the dock where the fishermen unloaded their boats.

"Don't you have any interest in protecting yourself, Lucy?"

"You mean condoms?" I said.

"I mean your heart."

A hundred seagulls filled the air above us as the sun went down behind the village and the sky turned some color halfway between pink and blue.

"Everything good I've gotten in life I've gotten by plunging in," I said.

"Sure," she said, "and everything bad you've gotten in your life you've gotten by plunging in."

There was no arguing with that, so I stayed silent. I watched a fishing boat come to the dock right at the precise moment a station wagon pulled up to meet it. A dark-haired man waved and smiled, turned and cursed the engine. The woman in the car ran to grab the stern line and wrapped it fast around a cleat.

"What does he do?" Marilyn said, and I knew she meant in the world, and when I told her he was a historian, she pursed her lips like it was just as she suspected, like historians had just passed rock stars in the consolidated bank of broken hearts.

"Look, Lucy, if you don't sleep with him and he never calls you, you won't have lost anything." The fisherman raised himself up onto the dock using only his forearms and then bent to give the woman a long deep kiss.

If I don't sleep with him, I thought, I'll be the only person in Provincetown not having sex.

I said, "Marilyn, this is the nineties, and in the nineties there's an argument that says if I do sleep with him and he doesn't call me, I will have gained something."

"You know in your heart that's a lot of shit," she said.

"I know in my heart that you care about me," I said, and put my arm around her. "Marilyn, I'm thirty-five years old and I'm as nervous about tonight's date as I have ever been. Doesn't that count for something?"

"There's a reason you do this, Lucy," she said, "and you know in the deepest part of you that the news isn't good."

"You're right," I said, "but here I am again."

"You tell him for me," she said, "that if he goes back to New York and tells all his artsy friends he fucked Lucy O'Rourke, I'm coming for him. I know where that library is. Don't you think I won't."

"Why don't you tell him?" I said. "Why don't you come over and wait with me for him to pick me up?"

The knock on the door came at 8:04 exactly. Marilyn and I jumped together, but I got there first. He was wearing a white cotton shirt and olive linens. How many times in the last fifteen years of cowboys and carpenters, I thought, had I wished for a man who knew how to dress.

I excused myself to the bedroom to—now that I'd seen his outfit—decide what to wear.

When I was packing back in Hope I remember thinking, *it doesn't matter what I wear if everybody's gay*—and now I was paying for it. I had three things to choose from. None of them good.

If I wore the heavy cotton gardening shirt over a flowered skirt, I'd look somewhat thin but not at all sexy. If I wore the reversible rayon tunic I'd look like I'd made an effort, but also like I wanted to hide in a tent. If I wore the black dress with the side slits and cleavage, he'd see way too much of everything that's wrong with me.

"And what do you see when you think of the future?" I heard Marilyn say, and I tried to hurry up.

I had all three outfits on three times each, staring and turning and holding in my stomach, hating my hips and my waist and my belly, cursing my mother for making it so that I could still look in the mirror and have no earthly idea whether I looked good or not.

I settled on the gardening shirt, on the theory that confidence is sexier than cleavage, opened the door and stepped out.

The Martin House had wood floors and antique tablecloths and a dessert menu that included the prices of all the art on the walls. The choices were endless, squid-ink pasta and salmon carpaccio and black-caviar mashed potatoes. I turned the menu over and over again in my hand.

There was something about happiness that my body wasn't used to. I couldn't imagine, for instance, being happy and eating at the same time. I was having a hard time focusing on the menu, the words sitting there and seductive in their way but not quite making sense. And if ordering was so hard, I wondered, what would happen when the food came? If I got it in my mouth, would I be able to swallow it, would I remember the simple things like how to hold my knife and fork?

Marcus appeared to be having a similar problem and had sent the waitress away twice when I remembered the tiny blackboard that sat on our table.

"The specials," I said.

And he said, "Good idea."

I said, "I couldn't go to sleep last night."

"I'm sorry," he said. "It's because of my stumbling."

The waitress made a third pass but didn't land.

"I didn't sleep," I said, "because I was happy."

"Because you were happy," he said. "Why didn't you tell me? Why have you been holding back?"

"You mean all these months?" I said.

"What's happening here?" he said, and his shoes closed around mine under the table.

"Something," I said, without sound, but he heard.

Moving down the street that night was less like walking and more like floating, between the bands of leathered men and the babies and junkies, in front of bars full of tattooed women and men taking off their dresses. I saw a wooden sign that said Café Heaven and thought *from this day forward, I'm eating there.*

We walked out to the end of the fishing pier where three hours earlier I'd taken Marilyn's vow not to sleep with Marcus. At the cannery a generator clicked on and off and he sat me up on one of the pilings and kissed me. Then he told me every right reason he had for falling for me, then he told me about the parts of my body that he'd seen so far and liked.

Back on the brown corduroy we kissed ourselves into some kind of frenzy, but every time he went to take off my shirt I pulled it quickly back on. I hadn't for some reason imagined that scenario when I was choosing what to wear, how the waistband of the skirt would look against the whiteness of my middle. The lights were so bright there in the living room, and I was even more afraid of the bed.

"You aren't ready for us to make love," he said. "I know that." And it came as a shock to me to hear it from his mouth as the truth. "But I want to lie with you in the dark," he said, "and put my arms around you, and go to sleep and wake up with you and take you to Café Heaven for breakfast." He gave me a look that said he knew everything, and reached for the light switch and then took my hand.

The next day my class and I did such good work we stayed for two extra hours. At exactly seven-thirty that evening, Marcus once again knocked on my door.

We walked to the dunes that ring the end of the island, and lay on our backs. Three foxes played in the sand just below us, and though there was no moon we could see them in the starlight, could listen to the whispers their paws made on the sand.

I was wearing the less daring of last night's two rejected dresses. It was colorful and close and tea-length, sort of small around the ankles, not the best dress for walking the break-water, but before too long there we were.

The tide was rushing in through the rocks underneath us

and sounding for all the world like the Rio Grande in spring-
time outside my door, and I told Marcus about Hope and the
place my grandma left me, how with a good summer rain the
pasture got covered with lupine, how the aspen trees changed
in patterns as intricate and regular as the finest woolen weav-
ings, spread themselves like an Indian blanket over the hills
that rolled up toward the Divide.

I could imagine him coming to visit me there, putting sleigh
bells on the horses one cold Christmas morning, a fire in the
woodstove and the meadow silent as prayer.

If I listened hard to the water, I knew, it would tell me
everything. I had asked it again and again all these years for
forgiveness, and I thought that Marcus might be its answer, its
blessing, its gift.

"What are you thinking?" Marcus said.

"That I don't know how to be happy," I said. "Strong, and
excited, spontaneous, even brilliant, but this happiness thing is
like another girl's clothes."

"Look at that," he said, and pointed to the spaces between
the rocks just ahead, which seemed to glow with more than
the reflections from the lights of the town. As we approached,
it got brighter, this light from below, and we laid our bodies
across the rocks and hung our heads over to see what it was.

My first thought was God or maybe Carlos Castaneda. My
second was that a Provincetown eccentric had rigged up an
underwater light show, something secret and beautiful to
impress his best dates.

But when we got our faces down close to the water we saw
not light bulbs fixed into position, but very-fast-moving parti-

cles of light. There must have been a hundred thousand of them moving all at once through the spaces below us, diamond necklaces of lights, and the submerged rocks were treasure chests designed to catch jewels. There were contrails of light, mare's tails of it, as though we were looking into the sky instead of the water, and the earth was spinning so fast the Milky Way had gone out of control.

Marcus reached down and came up with a handful of watery light that he let fall across my bare arm. I scrambled down to the low edge of the breakwater, hiked up my dress, and put my feet into the bay. The lights ran across them and between my toes. I kicked up arcs of water higher than my head into the night. My dress was soaked now, and I pulled it off and made a shallow dive into the lighted water. When I opened my eyes under the surface, I felt like I was swimming in the stars.

Marcus sat on the edge watching me, with his shoes off and his good pants rolled up and his feet in the water.

"Come here," he said, after I'd made a couple of circles, and I swam close to him and tried to draw him to me but he lifted me up out of the water instead and stood me next to him. It was dark but not so dark that he couldn't see me. I closed my eyes tight, tried to will the shame away.

"You're beautiful," he said. "Look at you, Lucy, please open your eyes."

And I opened my eyes and looked down at my body and I saw how the luminescence had clung to me as I came out of the water, clung to my breasts and my thighs and my belly, how it dimmed in the air and then revived itself where Marcus's hands touched my skin.

We watched the lights twinkle and dim together, and then he scooped up more lights and let them run over me, some of them clinging, some of them washing away. He looked at all of me then—taking in, memorizing—so long I thought I couldn't bear it, but I did.

I was cold for a moment, the night air on my wet and still body, but then his fingers were on me snuffing out the lights one at a time like candles, and then they were inside me, and his mouth was on my neck, and his voice in my ear, another kind of caress, and I got so warm with his hands that it seemed like all the light had moved inside.

"I'll fall," said a voice that I knew to be mine, the self who knew the rocks were steep and sharp and how I'd never stand through that kind of pleasure, but the rest of me, wordless, thought *small price to pay.*

"It's okay," he said, "hold tight," and I closed my arms tighter around his neck and let him take the whole weight of me.

The next morning we were back on Commercial Street and he said, "The most amazing thing happened the other day at this AA meeting," and the way my insides froze I didn't know how I kept walking.

"There's a man I know from New York up for the weekend. He was scared to go alone, so I went along," he said, and I drew another breath.

Then we went to the Center for Marine Life and found out that the lights were microorganisms called bioluminescence. The volunteer said they required touch to illuminate, some kind of friction, and I flushed when she said it, but she didn't see.

The next stop was the jewelry store. A memento, he had said; I think he used the word "earrings" and I had admitted I'd like something to keep. But inside the music was loud and then there he was with a ring in his hand—silver on the edges, a band of gold in between—saying I think this is lovely, Lucy, what do you think?

I took the ring from him and held it in my hand, the weight of the silver, the delicacy of the gold. I made a noise of approval, a nod and a murmur. He took the ring back from me, counted his money, came up forty dollars short, turned his wallet upside down for the jeweler and said, "This is what I have."

I steadied myself on the windowsill and looked out. The front yard of the store was full of Barbie and Ken dolls in suggestive positions—there must have been a hundred. One Ken in a wedding dress stepped off a fun bus into the arms of another. Two Barbies in leather rode a funcycle to the Crossdressers' Ball. Another Ken sat happily waist-deep in a tub of I Can't Believe It's Not Butter, his arms and legs pointed up to the sky.

I turned back to Marcus and offered him my right hand and held my breath as he slid on the ring.

Later, in the dunes where Eugene O'Neill wrote his masterpiece, we watched the sun go down into the blue blue water of the bay.

"How beautiful is that?" he said, when his eye caught sight of the ring. Then he fell to his knees like he was about to start praying and pounded the sand with his fists.

"What," I said, when he had fallen onto his back, eyes closed, one long arm flung over his chest and his toes kicking sand into the wind.

"You're the teacher," he said, eyes still closed, "you figure it out."

"You love me," I said, because it was the only answer, and he rolled back to his knees and pulled me down to him.

"I love you," he said. Just as simple as that.

I ran up the stairs to Marilyn's dorm room on the last morning to try to catch her before she left for home. She was sitting up against her headboard reading an oversized book.

"I'm not leaving," she said. "I talked to the bond trader last night. He says I deserve another week of R and R. You should stay too if you can swing it." She patted the bed next to her for me to sit down.

"I'd like to," I said, "but I'm going to drive Marcus home to the North Bronx, and then I promised my father an overnight at his house."

"And then you're driving all the way back to Boston for your flight?"

"I'm a road warrior in the Cavalier," I said. I fingered the picture of the bond trader next to her bed. "He's cute," I said.

"Seems like a long way to go for a couple of men who might not have your best interest at heart," she said. She picked up the pillow and set it over her stomach.

"He told me he loved me."

"Your father?"

"Yeah, right," I said.

"Lucy," she said, "Marcus can't love you yet."

"I don't know," I said, pulling the pillow off her lap and hitting her over the head with it. "I'm feeling pretty lovable right about now." An image of the lights on my bare belly came back clear and fine. "Do you know anything about bioluminescence?"

"A little," she said, "but I haven't seen any in a very long time."

"We swam in it last night," I said. "I wish you could have been there."

"I'm very glad I was not."

"No, really Marilyn. I think you might have loved your body, seeing those lights on it. I think maybe I loved mine."

"Not me," she said. "Not in this life."

"I have something for you," I said, and went back out the screen door where I'd left the matted print leaning against the wall. It was a shot I'd taken of Marilyn at the street dance, her body swirling, slowed in its motion by the f-stop and the twilight, her eyes shut tight, the unlit Dunhill still between her fingers, a look on her face of deeply concentrated joy.

She took the print from my hand and I could see on her face that she knew she looked like a million dollars, and that she wanted to squeal or spin or do some other girl thing in response to it, but she just gave the photograph a long satisfied look and set it down on the bed.

"And I have something for you," she said, holding out the book she'd been reading. It was called *Paris Was a Woman*. "I have no idea if it's good or not," she said. "I got it because of the cover photo." On the front of the book two young women in 1940s clothes sat at a Paris sidewalk café deep in a conversation that seemed a great pleasure to them both. Marilyn said, "We should have been there together."

"Maybe we will be, one day," I said.

269

"No," she said. "We should have been there *then*." Then she saw the ring on my finger. "For Christ's sake, Lucy, I leave you alone for ten damn minutes and you go and get married on me."

"No, no," I said, "it just looks like . . . it's on the other hand. I mean it just . . . well, I don't really know what it is."

"Do me a favor and find out," she said, "like sometime later today."

"What if he's for real, Marilyn? What if I've paid my dues and learned my lessons and this is my reward?"

"Then he surely won't mind you asking what the ring's all about."

"What am I gonna do without you telling me how to handle myself?" I said.

"Same thing I'm gonna do without you telling me how to handle my camera. Anyway," she said, handing me the bond trader's business card with the home phone circled, "you know where to find me."

"It would still be good, you know, in Paris," I said.

"This week, Lucy, Provincetown *was* Paris," she said. "You call me and let me know how it goes with that man."

We were cruising down Highway 6 in far less traffic than I thought there would be on a Sunday afternoon. Marcus was holding the wildflowers he'd bloodied his hands to pick for me in his lap, and the top was down, the muffler louder than ever. I was brave with the noise and my hands on the wheel.

"I want to come see you in September," I said.

"That would be great," he said, in a voice that said clear as a bell that it wouldn't. And it was like someone had spliced together the wrong rolls of film from two different movies; it was that instantaneous how everything changed.

The traffic snarled near East Sandwich and the sound of the muffler beat loud in my head. My face in the rearview was not the same woman; even my finger looked pinched and ugly under the ring. And there in the seat beside me was not Marcus anymore but Gordon, Carter, Josh, Erik, and all the others who said *love me love me love me, but not quite that much.*

"I'm not like them," Marcus said, "but my life is a little like theirs at the moment. Let me tell you the story, Lucy, please."

It was an East Coast story, full of lawyers and therapists and a botched custody agreement, an ex-wife who snatched a little boy out of a car seat and left thirty-minute rants on the answering machine, and a new agreement on the verge of being signed, a world so remote from mine I didn't even understand until Marilyn told me on the phone the next day that what it all meant was that Marcus wasn't really divorced.

What I did understand immediately was that I had to be a secret—at least for a little while—and I had promised myself that I'd never be a secret at least thirty-nine steps ago.

The traffic started moving again. Marcus's voice was calm and full of reason: he hadn't expected to meet someone this soon, the lawyer had told him to give his wife her sweet time, he hadn't told me the whole story because it was all so hackneyed, the whole thing would be resolved in a matter of months. On and on to reason after reason, so many reasons that any reasonable person would have to see her way to understand.

It was taking immense concentration for me to work the gas and the brake pedals, to keep my hands from bouncing off the wheel. And all the repetitions in my life seemed suddenly like a traffic jam on an East Coast highway. It was the end of the twentieth century and you couldn't tell the difference between a Saturn and a Lexus or a Camaro anymore. I wanted to be able to take myself seriously. I wanted to be able to change my life.

"I need to see your face," I said, "to have this conversation. This is all a little meaningless when I can't see your face."

"Let's stop then," he said, "get something to eat."

The restaurant was called Al Fresco and all I knew when we walked through the door was that we were a long way from the Martin House.

"Would you like a view?" the waiter said without looking at us.

"Of what?" Marcus said, and we got one, right up against the window overlooking the strip mall.

I excused myself to go call my father.

"I seem to be running a little late," I said. "The traffic's been horrendous."

"Can you not see, Lucille," he said, "how you set these things up for yourself?" And my heart stopped again for a minute until I realized that he was only talking about the Sunday traffic.

It wasn't until I saw the waiter's face that I knew I was crying. I pointed at the menu: penne, pencil points my mother always called them, one of the two meals my family ever seemed happy to eat.

"Tell me what you need," Marcus said. It was an expression

that in suburban New York sounded pretty basic, but I knew as I was sitting there that I'd never heard it before.

"I think," I said, "I need to get through this one on my own."

He nodded. The food came. It seemed like only seconds later when the waiter came back and asked if there was anything wrong. We picked up our forks.

"I do need something from you," I said, eyes fixed on his uneaten ravioli. A wave of pain started in my chest and extended outward and I let it ripple through my calves and biceps and roll out of me through my fingers and toes. I took a deep breath and winced as another one hit me. No one had told me that it would be so physical, this cutting off of the old ways of being, this sudden possibility of letting go.

"I need you to leave me alone until it's over, and I don't mean just the divorce, I mean all of it. The middle-of-the-night phone calls, the suicide threats, the busting through the door at six a.m. for a bed check. I don't even want a postcard from you until it's over, until you've stopped believing it's all her fault."

Outside it was getting dark. A firefly came to the window, flirting, I thought, with the candle between us.

"You're a smart woman," he said, "way smarter than me," and I tried not to laugh out loud.

"I'm afraid," I said, "that isn't saying much right now. But I could be. Given a few more lessons and a little time to practice. I imagine we both could be."

"I swear, Lucy, if you wait for me through this, I'm yours forever," and he folded his napkin on top of his plate.

I didn't say *the last person who said that to me is dead four years*

273

from cancer. I didn't say *the birds who eat fruit have more time to sing*. I didn't say how tired I was of the Castaneda challenge, having to act with love all the time, when the biggest part of me was fear. I didn't say what Marilyn would have said: that a smart person wouldn't use the word *forever* during the first week.

I thought for a minute about all the good shots I had taken of Marcus in Provincetown, I thought about what a good story all of this would make. Then I thought of what Marcus had said about losers and their stories. Some of my best friends were losers, and we'd had some good stories between us. But I didn't want to be like them, not for my whole life.

"Okay, then," is what I did say, and again, "Okay."

I drove Marcus the last fifteen miles to his apartment. We sat in the Cavalier in front of his mailbox at the end of the lane. The crickets were manic and the night was damp and everything smelled of sweet tea.

"This is just the beginning," he said and kissed me. Then he turned away and walked back toward the house.

I sat for a long time getting dewed on before I started to shake. I tried to get the top up, but my fingers wouldn't work the latches. I turned the ignition on and started shaking even harder. Then I turned the car back off.

It was the old Lucy, I thought, who wanted to go running back there, the one who'd never trusted anybody, the one who knew that what all people had in common was that eventually they left. Or was it the old Lucy who would gun the engine and screech the tires and not even look in the rearview mirror because she knew if she did she'd see him talking on the phone to his ex-or-not-ex-wife.

274

The more important question, of course, was what the new Lucy would do, and even though I was pretty sure the old Lucy wouldn't be around much anymore, I was a little bit afraid the new Lucy hadn't yet shown up.

Back on the expressway, things were even more confusing. I hadn't paid attention to Marcus's instructions, and though I knew where I wanted to go, all the wrong bridges kept intervening: the Tappan Zee, the Throgs Neck, even the Triborough; they'd sneak up on me, and I'd have to take the last exit, circle back to the city again and again.

I came close to giving up, to pulling over at a gas station and calling Henry so he could say everything I knew he would, like didn't I remember our rule about married men, and what did I think the end result of a week-long fling in Province-town, of all places, would be anyway, and honestly, Lucy, don't you think by accident you'd just once do something right?

Henry had been my life preserver more times than I cared to admit, and because of that he needed me to be drowning. But I was stronger than the girl he pulled out of the river in Cataract Canyon. I could swim and float and tread water and even hold my breath for as long as it was required, maybe long enough for a divorce to get final, certainly long enough to get myself over the George Washington Bridge.

On my fourth and final turn back towards the city, I saw it rising out of the mist above me. The city was lighting the sky like daylight and the bridge was almost empty in that cool three a.m. The lights on either side ran past the corners of my eyes so fast I could pretend they were the luminescence, the radio played something jazzy and monotonous, and I knew

how the road went from there to my father's house, and I
didn't think I'd make any more wrong turns.

It was when I got on the other side of the bridge and saw the
signs that I began to understand my options—so many places
other than my father's house to go. *Philadelphia. Washington.
80 and West*. I considered the likelihood of the Cavalier making it all the way to Hope and decided it probably wouldn't.
Then I saw a sign pointing back to New England and the
Cape and made my decision right then.

I could be back in Provincetown in time to take Marilyn to
breakfast at the Café Heaven and we'd talk about the things
I'd been afraid to talk about before. We'd walk Commercial
Street, and shop strictly for unnecessary items: foot massage
lotion and antique shawls. We'd eat lobster for dinner and
drink Chardonnay the way I did that first night when I
bought the Japanese rabbit and believed myself open to anything. I'd take her out to the place where the lights danced in
the rocks and I'd figure out some way to get her to swim in
them. I wasn't sure what would happen after that, but I knew
whatever it was or wasn't would be okay, because the point
would be to laugh in that water together, to see those lights
touch our bodies like stars. And she would go home to her
bond trader. And I would go back to my ranch and see if
another round of seasons would make me any smarter, and
wait there by the river for the new Lucy to come home.

Epilogue

ELLIE THE DOG AND I still do the walk every day unless it's raining, down the driveway, out across the front of the property, up the Forest Service road to Spar Hill Pass and on up to the lookout. From here we can see all of Antelope Park and the Rio Grande running through it loopy as my grandmother's handwriting, twelve thousand acres of the neighboring Soward ranch, ringed all around by the Continental Divide.

Red Mountain is catching all the alpenglow we can stand this evening, and there are twenty head of elk lying in the road like belligerent dogs and Ellie gets to chasing them, but only so far. Bristol Head stands in its late-afternoon shadow, my ranch sitting below it like an afterthought dwarfed by everything, even that baby of a river only twenty miles old.

277

We stopped in the barn on our way up here today, and I found some photographs taken in the twenties in a box in the hayloft—a stern-looking woman, a stooped-over man, a passel of children being told to look serious, none of them managing, an unruly dog.

If you think of a photograph as a kind of a story, then you'll know that the woman prays late at night to be menopausal, that the man has just set this season's traps on the ridge, that the smallest boy worries about his own silence, that the oldest girl is writing letters to her sweetheart in Durango, that the father beats him senseless every night in his dreams.

It's all done the way Houdini did it, angles, lights, and mirrors. I've had a camera hanging around my neck since my fingers could make it focus. I'm afraid how it drives me toward the deep heart of the world, I'm afraid how it keeps me from it, how the stories come with each click of the shutter, how the camera keeps saying *what then* and *what then*. Stories are relentless things that won't take no for an answer. They tell themselves by what's not shown more often than by what is.

There's almost never fog this high in the Rocky Mountains, and when it does come it is gone so fast and so early in the morning it feels like a memory or a dream. What we have instead of fog is big storms and bright sunshine and air so clear you can't ever disappear in it no matter how far you walk. The land never disappears either; it is there day in and day out, the clouds painting shapes across it, the lakes and rivers throwing your own image back at you so clear that you can't ever fail to see.

It's September 21st, a day I love for the balance it carries with it, and B.J. and Paul Stone are coming for supper. B.J.'s bringing a raspberry pie and Paul's bringing some elk steaks. I'm making a salad from what's left of my garden, and the mashed potatoes with half-and-half and garlic that are getting a little famous around here.

There's a burst of Indian paintbrush growing at my feet, the blossoms the most delicate mixture of ruby and white, and I focus the lens downward and take a still life with hiking boots, liking the way the washed-out brown leather frames the flowers, which are supple and bright.

I had a teacher who told me I should strive to be invisible, that the camera was designed to be an instrument always sitting on a tripod, activated as if by a stray gust of wind. I knew he was lying, even as he said it, knew a photograph tells the story of two lives simultaneously, the one in front of the camera as well as the one behind. I knew the more complicated the relationship, the better the photograph. The world's greatest work is really all self-portraiture, the artist as subway, as mountain, as sky.

It's when I look up from the paintbrush that I see the little girl—maybe seven years old—walking up the hill toward me. She's wearing a red-and-white polka-dot dress and black shoes, white socks with lace around her ankles. She's carrying a suitcase that's small, and yet it seems too big for her to carry it alone. I follow the trail she's made in the tall grass back to Middle Creek Road and see a bicycle leaning on its kickstand, a big flowered basket attached to the front.

She's up the hill in no time, and she sits down on the grass and opens the suitcase, folds her arms across her chest like she's waiting to see what happens next. Ellie doesn't growl or even bark at the little girl, which is an all-time first in our year together. She pads right up to the girl with only a hint of caution, licks her hand twice, chooses the side away from the suitcase, makes three quick circles and lies down.

The little girl looks familiar, and since she's walked right in like she owns the place, I don't want to admit I've forgotten her name.

"Hi," I say, and she holds up one hand but doesn't say anything.

The suitcase, I can see, is full of 8x10 photographs as unfamiliar to me as the ones in my grandmother's barn. She sorts through them for a minute and then hands one to me. I can see that she's got a plan, so I sit down on the other side of Ellie. People have always said I'm good with kids but that might be another lie they've told about me, and there's something about this girl that's making me wish I was anywhere other than here.

In this first picture the little girl is pedaling her tricycle hard and fast down a busy street. A young, pretty woman is just out of focus behind her. She has just stepped out of a car, and is running down the street after the girl. A light rain is falling and the woman's trench coat is flapping out to either side. The cars that are starting to pile up behind her have their headlights and windshield wipers on. It is twilight.

The little girl finally speaks. "What my mother says," she explains, "is that I was on my way to get ice cream. What my father says is that I was on my way to see him at work."

Ellie has fallen asleep beside the little girl and starts to whimper, as she often does, in her dreams. The little girl rubs Ellie's back lightly till she's quiet, then reaches into the suitcase and pulls out another 8x10.

In this one she is being pushed along in a stroller. Two big dogs walk one on either side of her, German shepherd mixes, one mostly light, the other mostly dark. The camera is in tight; the woman who is pushing the stroller is cut off at the waist. The little girl, who appears about five years younger than she does today, looks straight ahead, unsmiling. She's got one hand on each dog, clutching the fur in a kind of a death grip that the dogs, for some reason, have decided to allow.

"That's Salt and Pepper," the little girl says. "Neighborhood dogs who tried to protect me. Sometimes after we went inside they would sit at the bottom of the driveway for hours, until my father came home and threw rocks at them to make them go away."

The next several pictures are blurry and almost too dark to make out, which means either somebody's made a mistake with the aperture, or they've been taken inside at night with no flash and very little available light. There is a woman with her head down on her arms on the kitchen table, her fingers wrapped around a highball glass. There is a big man, face-down on a bed too small for him, his knuckles dragging on the floor. There is a small figure curled into the round of a clothes dryer.

"That's where I hid," the little girl says, "before I got too big."

I'm still trying to place this girl and what I'd like to do most of all is cheer things up a little, so I tell her how I've always taken pictures, that it's my favorite way to tell a story. I talk about how I always try to balance light and darkness a little better than in the ones she's just shown me. How a picture can't work without plenty of both.

She looks at me with her eyebrows raised, and then something like disappointment crosses her face.

"There's only one story," she says, and goes back to shuffling through the pile.

Thunder rumbles in some far-off place and Ellie wakes up enough to curl herself even tighter against the little girl's leg, her whole body shaking now the way it always does in a storm.

In the next photograph the little girl's head is turned, to watch a springer spaniel puppy who has also turned to try to put himself between the little girl and her father, who has just entered the room and is reaching down as though he intends to pick her up. The puppy's black-and-white-splotched ears are pinned back to his head and he is growling the way puppies do when they aren't really sure what they are doing. The little girl's face is in the process of falling, her laugh catching in her throat, her eyes widening. The father is turned toward the girl, and mostly away from the camera, but even at this oblique angle I can see the anger in his body.

"They got rid of the puppy after two days," the little girl says. "They said they had to because it kept knocking me down."

I look toward the driveway, hoping B.J. might show up early and help me deal with the little girl. I try to change the subject again by telling her about some pictures I saw recently, the latest shots from the Hubble Space Telescope, pictures that show hundreds of thousands of galaxies in a part of space where scientists had always thought there weren't any galaxies at all.

In the shots I remember best, one of the new galaxies is blowing right through another one. Before-and-after pictures: first a perfect spiral and then a torn raggedy doughnut. When I saw them I thought about my credit card bills, my mortgage, all the little things I worried about from day to day.

"So like we could just be sitting here," I say to her, "eating a sandwich, and all of a sudden some other galaxy could come blasting through."

The little girl chews on her finger in silent understanding, as though this possibility is something she has known about her whole short life.

"There is only one story," she says, like it's something she's just thought of, like she hasn't just said it a minute before.

In the next picture the little girl has opened the passenger door of a moving car. The camera has caught the moment right between the time she has pushed herself off from the running board and right before she has hit the pavement. Behind her in the photo, her mother, again out of focus, has just become aware of what she is doing, her mouth just beginning to make the O shape of a scream, her knee bent in her leg's movement from the gas to the brake.

"What they said," the little girl says, "is that I was trying to be like Mr. Magoo."

In the last photo the little girl shows me, she is lying under a huge cement urn, screaming in pain.

"What they said," the little girl says, "is that I thought it was full of water and fish."

I look hard at the little girl and she gives me the tiniest of smiles.

In every picture she's shown me she has big dark circles under her eyes.

I look again toward my driveway, but there's still no sign of anyone. "You know," I say, "I don't know how long it took you to get here or anything, but is there any way we could do this another time? I'm having some friends for dinner. Or maybe you'd like to come eat with us."

The little girl sighs. "I thought it would be best to start slowly," she says, "but if you're in a hurry we can cut to the chase."

While I'm wondering what kind of seven-year-old uses an expression like *cut to the chase,* she hands me the next 8x10.

In this one the little girl is falling backwards. Her father, whose back is to the camera, has his hands tight on either side of her small collarbones and is pushing her down the back stairs. She is trying to keep her balance, trying not to fall onto the new white gravel that her mother has laid only a few weeks ago. She is tripping backwards over the logs that hold the gravel in place. She is looking away from her father, toward the purple tulips.

And I have to close my eyes then because I don't want to think about how the tulips are her favorite color and how there are more of those than any this year and how her mother said it meant that she would be lucky, that this would be her lucky year, and how she thinks about those tulips as she finally gives up at the bottom, to him and to gravity, as her head hits the ground. She is still thinking of those tulips when he throws her against the woodpile, their bright yellow centers

284

that remind her of a smile. She keeps thinking about them the whole time, how they close up every night, *so nothing can hurt them* was what her mother had said. She is still thinking about them after he leaves her and she crawls into the clothes dryer because it *is* just her size and she thinks *maybe the lucky part hasn't started just yet.*

When I open my eyes the little girl is smiling again, but it's all kindness now, hardly a trace of fear.

"Wow," I say.

"Yeah," she says.

And I say, "Come here and sit on my lap."

The wind has picked up, making the grass wave like something out of God's own vision of Paradise, and I know what I'm supposed to do next but I can't quite bring myself to do it.

"You know where I was going that day on my tricycle?" she says, looking up at me, her hair whipping in strands around her mouth. "You know where I've been going every day of my life?"

I shake my head but she knows that I know we both know the answer.

"I'm not very good," I say, "at taking care of things."

"You'll get better," she says, and she makes a sound that's almost a laugh. "You're my only chance."

Ellie's wagging her tail and looking at me out of the corner of one eye, making sure I'm clear on her opinion of what I should do.

"There's more pictures," the little girl says.

"We've got time," I say back, and when I do, her whole body loosens its grip on itself.

"We'll get you some blue jeans," I say. "First thing, and some shoes that make sense."

The little girl rolls on her back and kicks her heels in the air. "I knew you'd be like this," she says, "once you got used to the idea."

She closes up the suitcase, stands up, and brushes off the back of her dress. "I guess I'll leave these with you," she says, "for safekeeping."

She's pushing her luck with that word *safe* and she knows it.

"I'll see you soon," she says, and starts running down the hill. Then she changes her mind and lays herself down, polka dots and all, and rolls all the way to the bottom, where she gets up and starts walking through the grass that's so tall it almost swallows her up.

Ellie hasn't stopped wagging her tail for the last ten minutes. *See?* is what she's saying and I'm right there hearing it.

All those years thinking the truth would kill me and what I feel like doing instead is having a roll down the hill.

I look in the other direction and B.J.'s in the driveway now, holding a big batch of yellow sunflowers, and Paul is pulling in right behind her, no doubt hauling some new invention in the back of his truck that he plans to try out. Someone else gets out of B.J.'s car and I see that it's Bobby, the glider pilot, and I can hardly believe it's that time of year already but then I look around me at the color in the hills.

They are greeting each other and talking, my friends, a bouquet of bright colors in their fuzzy outdoor clothes, and I'm remembering the dead of winter, buried here under five feet of fresh powder, how white everything was for weeks on end,

286

the mountains, the river, even the sky, as though it had all been frozen crystalline, and then, when spring came, how it got a little warmer each day and the color came back to the world like paint-by-numbers, the blue water rising to the surface of the river, the black paintbrush ridges of the mountain tops, tufts of brown sage shooting up through the thinning snow drifts, and the cornflower blue of a late-April sky.

For a long time I was swallowed like that, by something cold and colorless, but autumn is here and soon the color will be peaking; I can feel it in the air like the late-summer rains.

Ellie, who has been watching each car pull up the driveway, puts her pet-me paw up on my thigh and when I reach down she makes a little singing noise all by herself and takes a few steps in the direction of our guests and then lowers herself like a wild dog and turns to look back at me.

"In a minute," I say, as she catches sight of a butterfly and chases it into the pine trees that scatter themselves on the top of the hill.

I look back at the house again and allow myself a moment of wishing that Marcus were here and could join us for dinner. But the slow change in the seasons has taught me some patience, how to spend the days in living when I would once have spent them waiting, how to love the snow every day till it changes to rain.

"Okay, I'm ready," I say to Ellie and take one more look around me, south to the Divide and everywhere else to the river, back up toward the grave of the woman who knew a lot more than I thought she did when she chose me to come and tend this heaven.

There have been those in my life who believe I am meant to wind up alone here: my father, Henry, it's what my grandmother says every night to me speaking from the grave. It's easy to believe being alone is the strong thing, but the river taught me long ago that it's a stronger thing still to make yourself fragile. To say I love you, I dare you, I want you with me.

A dog. A friend. A little girl I'd almost forgotten. She was right when she said there was only one story, and here I'd been trying to tell it all along. As B.J.'s fond of saying, the sky's the limit after that.

The elk are bugling from the hills right behind me and the afternoon sun is washing the ranch buildings a color so rich I know I can't get it with my camera.

There's never been a better time to step into the picture.

I pick up the suitcase, whistle once for Ellie, and start down the hill at a run.